"Call Me Jeremiah, Charlotte. We're Supposed to Be Lovers, You Know."

"Yes, but we aren't. You know it. And I know it."

"Ah, but Jean-Claude doesn't, and we must keep up appearances. Where's he gone off to anyway?"

"Upstairs, to bring down a bed."

. . . Then he moved, his hand coming up to rest against her neck as his thumb gently caressed the curve of her jaw. His fingers touched the back of her head, and pulled her face toward his.

Charlotte's gaze was riveted to his mouth. A little voice in the back of her mind kept telling her that this really wasn't happening, that it was all a dream, but the erotic spell she was under refused to let her believe it . . . And when his face was so close that it was nothing but a blur, she silenced her misgivings and felt the brief, tingling touch of his mustache before his mouth closed over hers . . .

Dear Reader,

We, the editors of Tapestry Romances, are committed to bringing you two outstanding original romantic historical novels each and every month.

From Kentucky in the 1850s to the court of Louis XIII, from the deck of a pirate ship within sight of Gibraltar to a mining camp high in the Sierra Nevadas, our heroines experience life and love, romance and adventure.

Our aim is to give you the kind of historical romances that you want to read. We would enjoy hearing your thoughts about this book and all future Tapestry Romances. Please write to us at the address below.

The Editors
Tapestry Romances
POCKET BOOKS
1230 Avenue of the Americas
Box TAP
New York, N.Y. 10020

Fox Hunt

Carol Jerina

A TAPESTRY BOOK

PUBLISHED BY POCKET BOOKS NEW YORK

Books by Carol Jerina

Fox Hunt
Gallagher's Lady
Lady Raine

Published by TAPESTRY BOOKS

This novel is a work of historical fiction. Names, characters, places
and incidents relating to non-historical figures are either the product
of the author's imagination or are used fictitiously. Any resemblance
of such non-historical incidents, places or figures to actual events or
locales or persons, living or dead, is entirely coincidental.

An *Original* publication of TAPESTRY BOOKS

A Tapestry Book, published by
POCKET BOOKS, a division of Simon & Schuster, Inc.
1230 Avenue of the Americas, New York, N.Y. 10020

ISBN: 0-671-54640-6

First Tapestry Books printing June, 1985

10 9 8 7 6 5 4 3 2 1

To Debbie Traylor and Judy Croll,
whose unflagging support
has been of enormous help

Fox Hunt

Chapter One

PARIS AT DUSK HAD TO BE THE MOST BEAUTIFUL sight Charlotte had ever seen. A soft purple haze seemed to envelope the ancient city where kings had dwelled and mobs had run rampant less than a hundred years before. The ensuing darkness managed to shroud much of the grim ugliness that most large cities possessed, while silhouetting the many great monuments in an eerily beautiful light.

From the window of her hired cab, Charlotte watched as other horse-drawn carriages passed by on the wide Champs Élysées. A turn of her head took her gaze to the nearby sidewalk, where gas lamps spaced intermittently along the famed boulevard were being illuminated by lamplighters with long, pole-like wicks. In the shadows, she spied a pair of lovers entwined in a

1

passionate embrace, and a twinge of something like envy mixed with regret tugged at her heart. Recognizing it, she quickly dispelled it with an impatient sigh.

Maybe Paris *was* a city for lovers, she thought, but she wasn't going to let that fact depress her. She had reached the spinsterish age of twenty-seven only one month ago, and she knew that there would never be one special man to fill her life. Oh, she occasionally felt lonely, like tonight, but she had learned a long time ago that she could be content with what fate had dealt her.

Not being a great beauty like her two older sisters, she *was* resourceful and intelligent. And some had even told her that she possessed a dry, unusual wit. More important than all of that, though, she had an income of her own, and she didn't have to rely on a member of the male gender to support her. How many married women her age could boast of that? Back home in Texas and Louisiana, there were few!

The cab in which Charlotte was riding turned off the wide Champs Élysées and entered a quiet cobblestone street. In a matter of moments it stopped before the entrance of her modest hotel. She descended from the cab, making sure that her long lilac skirt did not trail down into the muddy puddles of water or the piles of freshly dropped horse manure that littered the street. She paid the driver, and the man bobbed his head wearily before setting his horses into motion again.

Two elderly gentlemen smiled at Charlotte as she entered the hotel, and she returned their greeting with demure politeness. At the reception desk, where she retrieved her room key, she asked the young clerk in flawless French if any messages had been left for her.

"Non, mademoiselle," he responded with a negative shake of his head. "However, I was told to inform you that your letter was delivered to the Sorbonne earlier today, just as you requested."

"Merci," Charlotte replied, realizing that since her cousin Jean-Claude was otherwise occupied for the evening, she was going to have to dine alone . . . again. "Oh, one more thing, *monsieur.*"

"Oui, mademoiselle?"

"Would you direct the kitchen to send up a tray to my room? I do not wish to dine in the salon tonight."

"But of course. Will there be anything else?"

"Non, that is all." And with a smile she turned and started toward the stairs.

Drat it! After having spent a thoroughly delightful day seeing the sights of Paris, she didn't feel like being cooped up in her room for the rest of the evening. But with Jean-Claude unavailable, she really didn't have much choice.

As she ascended the stairs, she realized that she shouldn't blame her young cousin for his lack of attentiveness. After all, they had only met three days ago when she'd first arrived in Paris. She couldn't really expect him to ignore his plans and obligations and cater to her, his American cousin. But it would have been nice to chat with him over dinner—to chat with him about their similar backgrounds.

Their grandmothers were sisters who had been born and raised in Paris until time, new husbands, and great distances had separated them. Charlotte's grandmother had married and moved to America shortly after Napoleon was deposed, while Jean-Claude's grandmother had moved to Provence with her husband. The sisters had continued to correspond over the years, keeping each other up to date on all the goings-on in their lives. And when her grandmother had died a few years ago, Charlotte had eagerly taken up the correspondence with her Great-Aunt Marie. After a carefully phrased hint here and there in her letters, she had finally received the invitation from Great-Aunt Marie that she had been waiting for—to come and visit her in France.

At the top of the stairs, Charlotte turned down the corridor and walked toward her door. She knew that if it weren't for the modest legacy *Grandmaman* had left her she would never have been able to afford this trip or the few clothes she had purchased before leaving home. Her teacher's salary just barely covered her daily living expenses back in Baton Rouge. But she was here now, in Paris, and every penny she'd scrimped and saved so far had been well worth it.

After she had let herself into her room and closed the door, Charlotte's thoughts jumped to the days ahead. She would be able to see a bit more of this ancient city—the museums, the great monuments, the stately gardens—before journeying down to Provence, where she would at last meet her great-aunt. Then, with many fond memories to look back on, she could return to her dull, unexciting, very predictable life as an old-maid schoolteacher. Well, *teacher* anyway, she amended with a smile.

A twist of the lamp knob illuminated her small room with its worn carpet and slightly shabby furniture. Though not in the most exclusive hotel in Paris—for she certainly couldn't have afforded that—her room was clean and comfortable nonetheless. She crossed to the window and opened it, then stood for a long while gazing out into the beautiful, warm summer night. Stars twinkled overhead, and in the distance she could make out the imposing structure of the Eiffel Tower, just recently opened for the Exposition.

Expelling a sigh, she turned and made her way to the dressing alcove that was separated from the main part of her room by a tall folding screen. She undid her *pelisse* and removed her hat, wanting to make herself more comfortable before her dinner arrived. As her fingers busily unfastened the row of tiny buttons down the front of her lilac dress, her gaze encountered a brief reflection of herself in the small mirror hanging above the wash stand. She quickly turned her back to it, not liking what she saw, and finished removing her clothes.

After twenty-seven years, she knew only too well what she looked like—an Atwater to the very core. Her two sisters were petite and auburn-haired like their mother, while she, unfortunately, was tall and dark like their father. Though her features were decidedly more feminine, she still possessed his long nose and wide, full mouth. Only her face—which was oval, with a gently pointed chin—was shaped like her mother's.

She had pulled on her wrapper and was tying the sash when she heard a noise in the next room. It wasn't a startling sound, but it did give her cause to wonder if the breeze from the window she'd opened had overturned the lamp. Heavens, she didn't want to start a fire!

Deciding to set her mind at rest, she stepped around the folding screen and froze, icy fear instantly flooding her veins. Standing in her room was the most frightening thing she'd ever seen.

It was a man, tall and lean, and dressed completely in black, from the tips of his shoes to the executioner's mask bound about his head. Only his sandy-blond-mustached mouth and clean-shaven jaw were exposed to her terror-stricken gaze.

"Oh shit!" she heard him mutter. "Wrong room!"

Charlotte opened her mouth to scream "Rape!" but her voice cracked, and it was not the loud proclamation she had wanted.

In the blink of an eye the intruder lunged for her. He clamped a large hand over her mouth, shattering any further chance she might have had to cry for help. "No!" he declared in perfect, unaccented English. "No, I'm not here to rape you. Honest to God, I'm not!"

Charlotte had the presence of mind to think, *he's American,* but she did not let that fact deter her from fighting him with all the strength she possessed. She twisted and wriggled in his arms, wanting only to extricate herself from his steely possession. The large hand on her mouth muffled her protesting screams as he turned her around to face him. It was then that she got a good, clear look at his sapphire-blue eyes, partially revealed behind the black mask's slits. Narrowing her own, she redoubled her efforts.

"You shouldn't be here!" the intruder proclaimed nervously. "This room is supposed to be unoccupied!"

Charlotte made a hysterical response to this, but it sounded garbled and incoherent against his palm.

"Look, lady," he began cautiously. "If I take my hand away, will you promise to be quiet?"

Be quiet for a rapist? Was he mad?

At the brisk negative movement of her head, the intruder's full mouth twisted into a grimace. "Damn it, you don't leave me much choice then."

His moist hand fell aside, and Charlotte knew that her chance to call for help had come. She opened her mouth to scream, but her words were stifled instantly by the masculine lips that covered hers, and anger immediately overtook her fear. How dare he take such liberties with her!

She tried to free her mouth but found that she was unable to move her head. His large hand was clamped against the back of her neck, holding her firmly in place as he continued to kiss her. Charlotte became so preoccupied with the feel of his lips that she failed to detect the movement of his other hand, that was sliding into his trousers pocket. His lips, so soft and teasing, caused an unwelcome lethargy to invade her legs and almost destroyed her power of reasoning. But then she suddenly remembered —she still had on her shoes!

Ceasing her struggles for a moment, Charlotte allowed a moan to form deep in her throat. It sounded like the soft purr of a woman on the verge of succumbing to passion. But it wasn't. It was the moan of pure self-satisfaction. Her attacker wasn't to know that, though. And soon he, too, moaned and began to deepen their kiss, his tongue sliding past the barrier of her teeth, his hand loosening its constricting hold on her neck.

Charlotte felt him relax and lifted her foot slowly so that he wouldn't notice what she was doing. Then she drew it back, paused a moment, and kicked him as hard as she could.

"Yeeouch!" He jumped away from her, grabbed his injured leg, and began to hop about the room like an ungainly stork.

"You–you animal!" she snarled, reaching out blindly for something, *anything* with which to protect herself. Her hand encountered the handle of her umbrella, and she hauled it in front of her, holding it like a knight wielding a broadsword. Stalking him, her gray eyes narrowed into menacing slits. "You rapist!"

"No! I told you before, I'm no rapist!" Still hopping around, the intruder's good foot hit the leg of a chair. He lost his balance and fell to the floor with a thud. Suddenly finding himself at her mercy, he cried, "For the love of God, lady, don't hit me with that!"

"Why shouldn't I?" she challenged. "You come

into my room, take liberties with me. . . . Why shouldn't I beat the bloody daylights out of you?"

"Because I didn't know you were going to be here, that's why!"

"Oh my Lord!" In the back of her mind, Charlotte suddenly recalled the rash of burglaries that had taken place since the Exposition began. "You're a jewel thief! Why—why that's almost as deplorable as a rapist!"

"I'm not a jewel thief or a rapist."

"Then what are you?"

He didn't answer her immediately. He just lay there on the floor, gazing up at her apprehensively through the slits in his mask.

Charlotte allowed a sardonic smile to twist her lips, then moved to hover over him, the tip of her umbrella poised above that most vulnerable of places on a man. "Take off that stupid mask and tell me who you are!"

"No," he negated with a shake of his head. "I can't do that. It's better if you don't see my face."

Her weapon's lethal tip prodded his masculinity. "If you don't, I'll—"

"All right, all right!" His hand left the floor, where it had been supporting his weight, and slowly untied the large silk triangle about his head. He whisked it aside, not seeming to notice or care that it landed on the floor near the end of the bed.

Charlotte glared down at him, wanting to remember every single detail, from his wide forehead below the unruly mop of blond hair to his slender, aristocratic nose. He looked more like a schoolboy than any would-be rapist she'd ever imagined. But the tiny lines etched around his blue eyes belied this fact. He was well past boyhood, she surmised. Probably in his late twenties or early thirties.

"Seen enough yet?" the intruder queried cautiously. "I'd like to get up from here if—"

"You stay right where you are! You're not going anywhere until I get some answers."

"Really, it would be better for the both of us if—" But he broke off and gasped as her umbrella dug deeper into his groin. "What do you want to know?"

"Your name, for one thing."

"Fox," he confessed. "Jeremiah Fox."

"No, I mean your *real* name."

"That *is* my real name."

The look Charlotte shot him mirrored her disbelief. "All right, Mr. Jeremiah Fox, just what are you doing here?"

"I–I'm working."

"Working? For the hotel?"

"No, I . . . work for someone else," he admitted hesitantly.

"Who?"

"Look, I don't really see what difference it makes *who* I work—"

A quick twist of the umbrella's tip caught a portion of the tender skin beneath his trousers and pinched it. *"Who* do you work for?"

"I'm an agent for the United States Treasury." The confession was made in one quick breath, and when Charlotte finally, slowly removed her weapon, he breathed a sigh of relief.

"An agent?" she asked, one of her brows arching. "For the United States Treasury? Really,

Mr. Fox—if that's your real name—I'm not quite as gullible as you seem to think I am. I know for a fact that the Treasury Department has no jurisdiction outside the continental boundaries of the United States. And even if they did, why would they send you here to Paris?"

"If you'll let me get off this damn floor, I'll tell you."

"There's no need to be vulgar." With a disdainful tilt of her chin, she retreated a step so he could sit up. In truth, she wasn't the least bit offended by his use of profanity—she'd heard much worse back home in Texas! But she *was* a lady, and she must not let him forget it.

"May I get up . . . *please?*" The curling of his mustached upper lip made his polite inquiry sound insincere.

"Sit on the end of the bed," she directed. "Then start explaining yourself." As she moved further away from him, the toe of her shoe encountered the small glass flask that he'd dropped when she kicked him. She looked down at it, then held her wrapper and petticoats aside to bend over and pick it up. "What is this?"

"Well, it's—No! Don't open it! It's chloroform. It'll put you to sleep!"

"I *know* what chloroform does, Mr. Fox." Holding out the flask of colorless liquid, her gaze beheld both it and him. "You were going to use this on me, weren't you?"

"Yes," he admitted with some embarrassment.

"Why?"

"Well, like I told you before, you weren't supposed to be here."

11

"So you were going to dispose of me with this before you got on with your . . . your agenting?"

"Something like that," he nodded.

One part of Charlotte told her that he just might be telling the truth about being an agent. After all, what man his age could look so sheepish if he wasn't? Yet another part of her refused to let her believe it, and she demanded, "Start from the beginning, Mr. Fox. If you *are* the agent you say you are, then what are you doing here?"

Jeremiah hobbled over to the end of her bed and sat down. His large hand reached down and rubbed his throbbing shin, his eyes watching her closely. "Have you ever heard of counterfeiters, Miss . . . er, Miss—?"

"Atwater," Charlotte supplied, and she gracefully dropped onto the chair that had tripped him. "Yes, I know what counterfeiters are. Why?"

"There's a ring of them here in France."

"Oh?" She planted the tip of her umbrella into the carpet and rested both hands atop its handle. "And just what do they have to do with you?"

"My superiors back in Washington sent me here to find out just who they are and what they're up to."

"And you naturally assumed that I was one of them. Well, you're dead wrong about that! I'm a schoolteacher, not some criminal."

"It's not *you* I'm after. Hell, I didn't even know you were going to be here in this damn room. The fact is, I–I thought I was entering the room next door. I'm after *him!*"

"Monsieur Boland?" Charlotte stiffened as a

look of utter bewilderment crossed her face. "*He's* a counterfeiter?"

"One of them, yes."

"But he's such a *nice* little old man." And kind and polite, she thought. He had been most solicitous of her the day she checked into the hotel. They had met in the hall, and he had spoken to her for a few minutes before wandering off.

"Nice has nothing to do with it," Jeremiah scoffed. "He's a master artisan, a lithographist who can copy anything put before him. I've seen his work; I know!"

"But a counterfeiter!" Charlotte shook her head in disbelief. "My word, it must be a monumental undertaking, copying our coins."

"It's not our coins they're counterfeiting, Miss Atwater. That would be much too time-consuming and expensive. They're copying our greenbacks."

"My word!" she gasped again.

"Do you have any idea what a flood of fake currency could do to our economy? Why, the American people have very little faith in the paper dollar as it is. Counterfeit money would destroy it completely."

At that moment there was a sharp knock at the door, and Jeremiah flinched. "Who's that?" he whispered.

"It must be room service with my supper," she informed him, rising to her feet.

"You've got to get rid of them. I can't be seen in here!"

Charlotte silently agreed. If he were seen with her, her reputation would most certainly be sullied. "Well then, take my advice and leave."

13

"There isn't time," Jeremiah countered, jumping to his feet.

"Oh, for heaven's sake!" she groaned. "Then if you won't go away, hide yourself until they've gone."

"Where?"

She looked about the room but soon realized that his lanky frame would not fit beneath the bed, which was the largest piece of furniture in the room. Then, spying the folding screen, she pointed to it. "Hide over there in my dressing room. They won't be able to see you in there."

Jeremiah limped toward the alcove and disappeared behind the screen. Charlotte approached the door, depositing the flask of chloroform into her wrapper pocket. When she was certain that he couldn't be seen from the doorway, she checked her wrapper, rearranging it so that her creamy chest was covered, then opened the door.

Out in the hallway stood, not the waiter from the kitchen as she'd expected, but a tall, slender, grinning youth with dark, slicked-down hair and a top hat held in the crook of his arm.

"Jean-Claude!"

"Cousin Charlotte!" He leaned toward her, planted a kiss on her cheek, then casually brushed past her into the room. "I got your message and had to hurry over. I have just spent the most delightful day."

"Jean-Claude, you can't come in here!"

"I must tell you how exciting it was," he went on, ignoring her protest. "My friend Philippe and I went sailing high above the countryside in his balloon. It was fantastic! I felt like a bird—a wingless bird, suspended above the earth. Marvelous, it was simply marvelous! I must talk Philippe into taking you with us the next time he goes up."

"Jean-Claude, you don't understand. You have to go!" she stressed, closing the door behind her.

"But, *cherie,* I have only just arrived!" His gray eyes, so like hers, scanned her wrapper-clad form. "Ah! You are worried about appearances, *n'est-ce pas?* But you should not be. You are in Paris now, not in your provincial America. No one will question my being with you while you are so delightfully *en déshabillé.* We are cousins, *non?*"

"Well, yes, we are, but that's got nothing to do with it! You still have to go!"

"Charlotte, you worry too much." A slow, sensuous grin deepened the grooves in his boyish cheeks as he began to close the distance between them. "Such a surprise you were, *cherie.* When *Grandmere* told me to meet your train, I must confess I was a little annoyed by the prospect of having to greet what I thought would be my dowdy little colonial cousin. But you are not dowdy at all. You are quite beautiful." His arms wrapped around her before she could step out of his reach.

"Stop it, Jean-Claude!" Even though it was nice to hear, and quite a boon to her ego, she could not let his flattery overwhelm her good sense. Trying to pull herself out of his embrace, she repeated, "We are cousins, remember?"

"But very distant cousins, *cherie.* It is our grandmothers who were sisters."

Realizing what a failure *that* ploy had been,

15

she tried another. "All right then, I'm *older* than you!"

"Older?" He chuckled. "What are one or two years, *cherie*? In an affair such as ours will be, it is the heart that matters, not the age."

Affair! Oh Lord! Charlotte groaned inwardly. *Ten years without a man in my life, and then I get two of them in one night!*

"Jean-Claude, there is more than just a couple of years separating us," she argued, twisting her head in time to avoid his questing mouth. "I'm seven years older than you."

"But that makes it even more exciting!" he purred against her slender throat. "I have always had a certain fondness for older women."

"Not this older woman!" And again she turned her face as his mouth sought hers.

In the alcove, Jeremiah suppressed a groan when he heard the young Frenchman's amorous declaration and Miss Atwater's feeble protest. She had kicked the hell out of *him* without a qualm; why couldn't she do the same to Jean-Claude? Then he almost swore out loud when he heard a second knock sound at the door. For a dowdy little schoolmarm, she sure was getting a lot of attention.

"Let me go, Jean-Claude," he heard Miss Atwater demand. "I have to see who that is."

"But of course, *cherie*."

Jeremiah heard the loud kiss that followed this breathy vow and realized he would have to find some other place to hide. By the sounds of it, Jean-Claude was going to be here for a while.

Looking behind him, Jeremiah spied the huge armoir, its door opened invitingly. With the

16

voices in the other room masking his movements, he slipped inside the large piece of furniture and pulled a cloud of Charlotte's petticoats and dresses around him. Not wanting to suffocate amid all the feminine frippery, he wisely left the door ajar just a fraction.

In the next room, the waiter wheeled in a cart laden with Charlotte's supper. With an elaborate sweep of his arm, the man uncovered the cart, exposing a small tureen of soup, a plate of crusty bread, a bowl of creamy butter, and a pot of tea to Charlotte's disinterested gaze. Then he continued to stand there, even after she'd thanked him, staring at her blankly.

He was waiting for a gratuity, she realized. "Just a moment," she muttered, and headed for her purse.

Jean-Claude knew that *he* should be tipping the waiter but decided to let his cousin have the honor. He had other plans for his money. Shifting his weight from one foot to the other, he felt something wrap around his shoe. He looked down and saw to his surprise a black scarf lying on the floor. A frown pulled his brows together as he bent over and scooped it up. Then, with his back to Charlotte and the waiter, he stretched open the large triangle and grinned broadly at the two eye-slits. *This cannot be Charlotte's,* he thought with amusement. *It has to belong to someone else. But who?*

Charlotte managed to usher the now satisfied waiter out the door. She was about to close it again when the little old man next door suddenly stepped out into the hall and gave her a gracious smile.

17

"*Bonsoir*, Mademoiselle Atwater."

"*Bonsoir*, Monsieur Boland." As he slowly approached her, Charlotte wondered how this sweet, gentle old thing could possibly be a criminal. Surely Mr. Fox was lying. Small, white-haired, and with a neat goatee covering his pink chin, Monsieur Boland looked more like some timid bank clerk than a hardened felon.

"Did you see the Eiffel Tower today?" Boland inquired, stopping in front of her.

"Yes, I did. It was quite fascinating." She started to say more but noticed that Boland's gaze had slid past her. She looked behind her and saw that his attention now rested on Jean-Claude, who was standing in the center of the room with his hands clasped behind his back. "Oh! This is my cousin, Jean-Claude Beauvais. He is a student at the Sorbonne. Jean-Claude, my neighbor, Monsieur Boland."

Jean-Claude stepped forward to shake the old man's outstretched hand. When he did, Charlotte felt a cold shaft of fear shoot up her spine. Clutched in her cousin's fist was the black mask that Mr. Fox had been wearing!

The young Frenchman ignored her slightly horrified look and maneuvered the silk into his left hand before completing the gesture he had initiated. Ending the handshake, he stepped back and let his gaze dart furtively about the room, seeking some sign of the presence of the mask's owner.

"Are you going to be taking your lovely cousin about Paris tomorrow to show her the sights?" Boland inquired.

"Alas, I cannot," Jean-Claude confessed,

bringing his visual search to an end. "I have an anatomy lecture to attend."

"Anatomy, eh? You are studying medicine?"

"*Oui*," Jean-Claude nodded.

Monsieur Boland smiled as if he approved. But the smile quickly faded. "Then you will be all alone on your outing, *mademoiselle*. You must not do that! A girl your age is not safe all alone in Paris."

"I agree," came Charlotte's sardonic reply. And then another shaft of fear shot through her when, out of the corner of her eye, she spied Jean-Claude moving closer and closer to the alcove . . . and Mr. Fox!

"You must allow me to escort you to the museum tomorrow," the old man offered.

"Museum?" Her voice broke as she tried to suppress her rising hysteria. Jean-Claude had stepped behind the folding screen. "Oh, *yes*, the museum! Why, thank you, I would be honored."

"*Non, non, mademoiselle*, it is I who will be honored."

Jean-Claude paid little attention to what his cousin was saying to her elderly neighbor. His eyes were riveted on the opened armoir door. *Aha!* he thought proudly. *This is where he is hiding. And I will wager that he is Charlotte's lover!*

He extended his arm and widened the crack with one finger. Spying the thatch of blond hair and the pair of startled blue eyes behind the ruffles of a fancy petticoat, he grinned and winked knowingly before kissing the tips of his fingers. By dangling the scarf in front of the blue eyes, he silently signaled that he approved wholeheartedly of this delightful deception. Then, with a flourish, he stuffed the scarf into his pants pocket and turned away.

Jeremiah had been holding his breath, fearing what the young man would do, but he released it in a long sigh when Jean-Claude departed without revealing his presence. Thank God, Boland still didn't know he was here!

But then the reality of what had just transpired registered, and Jeremiah stiffened. The little twit had thought that *he* and Miss Atwater were—

Well, why not? he thought after the improbable notion had rolled around in his head and taken root. *Maybe it's not such an unbelievable ruse after all.*

"Until tomorrow then," Monsieur Boland was saying when Jean-Claude joined them again.

"Yes, until tomorrow." Charlotte managed to appear gracious as the little old man kissed her hand and shuffled off down the corridor. She closed the door and leaned against it, her breath coming in short, labored gasps. What an ordeal! Then her head jerked around, and she saw the impish smile that played about her cousin's mouth and knew in an instant that he had discovered Mr. Fox.

"*Cherie*, you should have told me that you had another," the young man chided indulgently. "I would never have tried to come between you."

"Another?" she croaked. "Jean-Claude, you don't understand. I—"

"Oh, he understands all right." Jeremiah stepped out from behind the screen and was beside Charlotte in two lazy strides, winding his arm about her waist as if it were the most natural thing for him to do. "It's out in the open now. Your cousin seems to be a man of the world. We shouldn't have to keep our little secret from him, darling."

Darling! She glared up at him, her eyes wide with astonishment. Wanting only to wipe the silly smirk off his face, she forced herself to match his insincerity. "If that's what you wish ... *dearest*. But we certainly wouldn't want your *wife* or your *twelve children* to be hurt by our little affair, now would we?"

"Twelve children?" The look on Jean-Claude's face could only be described as shocked. *Mon Dieu*, he thought. *These Americans are certainly prolific, and not provincial at all!* "Mon ami, I will never breathe a word. My lips are sealed!"

"I knew we could rely on you," Jeremiah remarked, his hand tightening about Charlotte's waist. Beneath the hem of her petticoats, Charlotte's foot found his instep, and she stepped hard on it. A strange sound formed in the back of his throat as he felt her weight. "Your cousin has such a ... *way* about her," he grunted, quickly shifting her onto his hip so that she was now off his foot. "I just couldn't resist her charms."

"Oh, I understand, *mon ami*. Truly I do!" Seeing the way his cousin and her handsome lover were looking at each other, as if they couldn't wait to be alone to release their passions, Jean-Claude quickly said, "Oh, I must go now. I have stayed much too long as it is." He turned and started for the door, but when his hand touched the knob a thought occurred to him, and he looked back.

Charlotte and Jeremiah had moved in the interim. To Jean-Claude it appeared as though they were about to embrace, unable to contain their urges any longer. In reality, though, they were on the verge of strangling each other.

"*Monsieur?*" Jean-Claude blushed and crooked a finger at Jeremiah. "*Un moment, s'il vous plaît?*"

More than willing to extricate himself from the unpredictable hoyden beside him, Jeremiah stepped away from Charlotte and approached the young Frenchman.

"The black mask, *monsieur,*" Jean-Claude whispered. "What do you do with it?"

This elicited a choking gasp from Charlotte, but Jeremiah ignored it, resting one hand on Jean-Claude's shoulder as he opened the door with the other. "I'll have to tell you all about it some other time. I'm sure you understand."

"Ah, *oui. Oui!*" And with a wink and a wicked little grin, Jean-Claude stepped through the door and was gone.

Chapter Two

"TWELVE KIDS!" JEREMIAH BARKED. "WHAT IN hell possessed you to say that?"

"Well, I *am* supposed to be your mistress, aren't I?" she countered with saccharine sweetness. "I had to make it sound convincing, otherwise Jean-Claude might have challenged you to a duel." She began to stalk about the room, fluffing a pillow here, kicking a chair leg there.

"But twelve kids! I'm not that old!"

"You're not?" Her pacing ceased, one of her finely shaped brows raising skeptically.

"No, I'm not! How many thirty-five-year-old men do you know with twelve kids?"

"Here in France there are probably a lot of them. They begin their amorous encounters very young, from what I understand."

Recalling Jean-Claude's rather uncousinlike

23

attitude toward her, Jeremiah was inclined to agree. The boy had more brains in his crotch than he had in his head—as his old grandfather would have said. With a rueful shake of his head, Jeremiah limped over to the chair and sat down, wanting to take his weight off his injured toes.

"Why did you have to stand on them so hard?" he complained.

"You're lucky you still have a foot to stand on. Telling Jean-Claude that I was your mistress, that—that was thoroughly despicable!"

"Well, you started it!"

"No, *you* did, by coming here in the first place. And just for your information, Mr. Fox, I don't believe one word of what you said about Monsieur Boland. If he's a counterfeiter, I'm the Queen of England."

"Don't expect to get a bow from me," he jeered, and got to his feet again.

"Oh, why don't you just go away?"

"I'll be more than happy to, ma'am."

"And I hope I never have to set eyes on you again."

Heading for the window, he remarked, "Well, Paris is a big city. We ought to be able to avoid each other if we try."

"Just where do you think you're going?" she demanded, jamming her hands onto her hips indignantly.

"Away. Like you told me."

"Not through the window, you idiot!"

"It's the way I came in. It's the way I'll go out." He swung one long leg over the sill, looked back at her, and tapped a finger against his mouth. "Want to come give your old lover a kiss goodbye?"

Her upper lip curled in disgust. "I'd rather take poison!"

"So much for true love," he quipped, and with a sketchy salute he disappeared into the darkness.

Outside, Jeremiah made his way cautiously along the narrow ledge and found himself thanking Miss Atwater for having been present in the room that should have been empty. If she hadn't been there, he wouldn't have overheard her brief conversation with Boland, informing him that the old man would be out of his room for a while so that he could search it. And that bit he'd heard about Boland taking Miss Atwater to the museum tomorrow was a stroke of good luck, too. Of course, with her tagging along, he just might have a problem on his hands should she spot him. But he was almost certain he'd be able to handle her. It was Boland he was unsure about.

The toes of his injured foot throbbed dully, as did his bruised shin. He pushed open the window to Boland's room and hopped over the sill. As he had expected, the room was dark, but he quickly rectified this by lighting the lamp and brightening the surroundings, which were quite similar to Miss Atwater's room. He spent the next few minutes thoroughly going through Boland's bureau drawers, where the old man had neatly placed his folded undergarments; the armoir, where Boland's shabby suits were hung; and the worn leather valises that rested in one corner of the dressing alcove.

His search unfortunately proved fruitless. There hadn't been one thing in the room to indicate where Boland would be making the counterfeit engraving plates—no note, no map, no train ticket, nothing!

With a disappointed groan, Jeremiah knew that he could do only one thing now. He would have to continue following the old man with the hopes that something vital would happen soon. A lot depended on his finding the plates . . . not the least of which was the economy of the United States.

He extinguished the lamp and exited through the window. Cautiously making his way down the outside of the hotel from the second floor to the pavement, he blessed the fact that this side street was badly illuminated. He'd have had a devil of a time explaining his actions to the local *gendarmes* if one had spotted him either entering or leaving in such an unorthodox way. And if he'd been arrested. . . .

He didn't even want to think about that. No one back in Washington, save Lafayette Roman, even knew he was on this blasted mission. Not even the American consulate here in Paris. Roman had arranged it that way because he hadn't wanted any rumors to start on this side of the Atlantic and spread back to the States. A panic would have surely set in. So, as it was, only one other person—beside Miss Atwater, of course, and she didn't count—knew of his reasons for being here.

By keeping well hidden in the shadows, Jeremiah made his way to his own hotel unobserved.

The narrow, dark alleyways between the buildings were his thoroughfare. Three streets and one block later, he spied the rear service entrance to his hotel.

He crept stealthily into the building to find himself near the noisy kitchen. Dinner was just now being prepared; Frenchmen, like all Europeans, ate much later in the day than Americans did. He heard voices and quickly mounted the rear staircase, not wanting to be seen by any of the waiters, who were still busy arranging tables in the dining salon nearby.

Two flights of stairs and one long corridor took Jeremiah to his suite. He darted inside and leaned against the doorjamb, breathing heavily. *I'm getting too old for this line of work*, he told himself. *As soon as I get back home, I'll tell Roman that I want a nice, safe desk job from now on.*

A lot of good that would do him, he thought, pushing his lanky frame away from the door. Roman had a nasty habit of turning a deaf ear to anything he didn't want to hear.

Jeremiah's black clothes were quickly removed and exchanged for a proper, more dignified evening suit that befitted a man of his supposed social rank. Ruffles graced the front of his white silk shirt, and a diamond stick-pin anchored his black silk cravat into place. His errant blond hair was slicked down on either side of a center part, as the current fashion dictated, and his mustache was neatly combed.

When he was last pleased with his overall appearance, he shrugged into his elegant black

27

evening coat and gazed at his reflection in the tall cheval mirror. *Not bad for a Virginia farm boy,* he thought smugly. *Not bad at all!*

The dining salon was just beginning to bustle when he entered minutes later. Groups of people —families, by the looks of them—were sitting around the larger tables, discussing the events of the day. At the smaller tables, couples conversed furtively across small floral centerpieces.

"Monsieur Steadman?" Jeremiah turned and saw that the *maitre d'* had addressed him. "Follow me, please. Your wife is already at your table."

He strolled behind the formally dressed Frenchman, weaving his way between the already occupied tables, and soon saw the petite blonde seated in a secluded corner.

"Sorry I'm late, darling." He dropped a kiss on the blonde's soft, sweetly scented cheek and took his place across from her.

"You're not too late," she responded, returning his smile.

"Would you care to see our wine list, *monsieur?*" the *maitre d'* queried.

Jeremiah said that he would, and the *maitre d'* produced a burgundy-vellum-bound list with a flourish, then snapped his fingers for the wine steward who was busy at another table. "He will be with you in a moment, *monsieur.*"

"Oh, there's no hurry," Jeremiah assured the man. "Is there, darling?"

"No, of course not," agreed the blonde.

When the *maitre d'* wandered away, her smile wavered. "How was your day?"

"More eventful than we thought it would be."
He leaned forward and gathered her left hand in
his, his long forefinger and square-nailed thumb
playing with her wide gold wedding band. "You
know that night clerk I bribed? Hugo?"

"Yes."

"I've got a good mind to castrate the little son
of a bitch."

"Oh *really?*" Gold-tipped lashes blinked rapidly over blue, concern-filled eyes. "What did he
do?"

"He damn near got me killed, that's what he
did!" It was only a slight exaggeration. Jeremiah
could still feel the point of Miss Atwater's
blasted umbrella digging into his groin, and his
foot and leg hurt like hell, too! "But I'm all
right," he tacked on the moment he felt her
stiffen.

"Jeremiah, what happened?"

"Now, don't get upset. It's just that the room
wasn't empty like Hugo said it would be."

"Oh no! Boland wasn't—"

"No, Boland wasn't there," he assured her.
"But I . . . I entered the wrong room, and the
woman who was in it was a little startled by my
appearance."

"Was she part of Boland's group?"

"No, I'm sure she's not. You know as well as I
do that bunch would never take the risk of
staying at the same hotel. It would look much
too suspicious at this stage of the game if they
did. They won't get together until they're ready
to print the money."

"Then who was she?"

"Oh, some spinster schoolteacher from America." A dry chuckle rumbled deep in his chest. "She thought I was a rapist."

"A *what*?" The blonde relaxed at this and allowed an amused grin to brighten her lovely features. "Jeremiah, whatever did you do to give her that impression?"

"Well, certainly not that!"

His explanation was interrupted with the arrival of the wine steward, and he spent the next few minutes deciding which vintage of wine would suit both him and the meal they would be having.

"She was about as surprised to see me as I was to see her," he continued when the wine steward had departed. "For a while I thought I would end up in the Bastille tonight."

"Darling, the Bastille hasn't existed for over a hundred years," came the blonde's indulgent reply.

"Oh, you know what I'm getting at, Judith."

"Yes, I'm afraid I do. So tell me, what happened?"

"Well, I did the only thing I *could* do under the circumstances—I told her the truth."

Judith slumped back in her chair with an audible groan, a look of disappointment crossing her face. "That was a very foolish thing to do, Jeremiah."

"I didn't have much choice." He could have said more but didn't. The last thing he wanted to do was elaborate on the position he'd been in. Being a woman, Judith would probably think it highly amusing. Instead, he said, "But for what it's worth, I don't think she believed me."

"How can you be sure, though?"

"Well, I can't. But she has met Boland, and she believes him to be merely a nice old man."

"Oh Lord. I do hope you're right." She sat forward, her spine once again returning to its ramrod straightness. "You've worked too hard on this to have it all end so soon. Albert—"

"Shh! I know, dear. I know." He gave her hand a gentle, reassuring squeeze. "But if he'd been in my place, you know he would have done what I did."

A nostalgic look softened Judith's eyes. "I had a letter from him today."

"You did? How is he?"

"Oh, you know Albert. He tries to put up a convincing front, but we both know he hates being confined to that damn wheelchair. He was so active, so vital before Boland's henchmen got hold of him."

"Yes, but at least they didn't succeed in killing him. We have to be thankful for that."

"Do we?" she countered quietly. "We aren't in his shoes, Jeremiah. Maybe it would have been better if they *had*—"

"Don't even think that!" Jeremiah's voice possessed a stern edge, and Judith dropped her gaze from his, blushing.

"I don't. Not really. But I'm sure *he* does."

Jeremiah knew then that he had to change the subject. "Did Albert happen to say how the children were?"

Judith's expression changed to one of pride. "Oh yes! It seems little Albert is mastering the art of harassing his younger sister. But Elizabeth is learning to fight back. Albert said that Nana found the two of them in the garden a few days ago, playing Red Indians. Little Albert had Elizabeth tied to a pear tree and was dancing around her, whooping and hollering something awful. Well, needless to say, Nana was outraged. She untied Elizabeth, but my darling little daughter then jumped on her big brother and tried to pull him bald-headed."

"Sounds kind of familiar, doesn't it?" Jeremiah chuckled.

"You never tied *me* to a tree."

"I never thought of it, to tell you the truth."

Their meals arrived shortly after the wine had been opened and poured, and they settled down to a pleasant discussion of childhood memories. It was something they almost never had the chance to do these days. But the topic soon reverted back to Jeremiah's encounter with the spinster, Miss Atwater, and he found himself telling Judith about the amorous French cousin, Jean-Claude.

"It sounds like a three-ring circus," Judith observed dryly.

"It was worse than that," Jeremiah replied. "I thought my days were numbered when he discovered me in that armoire."

"And you honestly lied about Miss Atwater being your mistress?"

"I had to! Fortunately, the boy believed it."

"Well, you did say he was French, darling."

"Miss Atwater wasn't too pleased about it. In fact, she tried to dig my grave a little deeper."

"How did she do that?"

Jeremiah felt the heat rush to his face and

knew that he was blushing. "Well, she, er, came up with a lie of her own. She said that I had a wife . . . and twelve children."

The giggle that sputtered forth from Judith forced her to cover her mouth with her napkin. As her shoulders vibrated with mirth, Jeremiah thought it the most delightful sound he'd heard in months. Soon her laughter became infectious, and he too began to chuckle.

"You wouldn't have thought it funny if you'd been there in my shoes," he professed at last, sobering.

"Oh, I don't know," Judith giggled. "I think I just might enjoy meeting your Miss Atwater. She sounds like a very unusual lady, Jeremiah."

"She's that, all right," he agreed. Now that he could look back on what had happened from a safe distance, he had to admit that there *was* something about Miss Atwater, something he couldn't quite pinpoint. When he had been holding her in his arms, kissing her as he tried to get that damn vial of chloroform out of his pocket, he'd felt a flicker of desire within him. That was strange, too, because there hadn't been a whole lot about Miss Atwater that resembled the fashionable beauties he was usually attracted to.

She fit her spinster description to a T. Her dark hair had been slicked back into a tight coil, accentuating her slightly angular features while enhancing the fiery intelligence in her dark gray eyes. And when his arms had been wrapped about her corseted body, he'd sensed instinctively that she possessed a lusciousness that a lot of other women lacked.

"Jeremiah?" Judith called to him softly.

He glanced up at her and blushed, surprised by the waywardness of his thoughts.

"She's impressed you, hasn't she?"

"Of course not!" he scoffed.

"Oh yes she has," Judith insisted patiently. "I saw that look in your eye just now. I know."

"You're talking nonsense, Judith."

"Maybe," she murmured, smiling. "Maybe not. It's just a shame you couldn't have met her under more ordinary circumstances."

"Judith!" There was a warning note in his voice.

"All right. I won't say any more," she relented with a coy little tilt of her head, but the smile still remained about her mouth.

Chapter Three

CHARLOTTE STOOD IN THE CAVERNOUS ROOM, completely awed by the opulence of her surroundings. Pink-veined marble pillars supported an ornately painted ceiling high overhead, while valuable paintings and statues lined the baroque molded walls. The heels of her high-buttoned shoes tapped softly on the polished marble floors as she followed Monsieur Boland further into the hall. No one back home would ever believe that a place like this could really exist outside the pages of a fairy-tale book.

"Impressive, is it not?" Monsieur Boland asked.

"Yes," she answered quietly, not wanting her voice to echo off the walls.

"One can understand, when touring great houses like this, why the French rebelled against their monarch."

There was an underlying tension in Boland's words, and it caused Charlotte to slice him a questioning look, but he was too absorbed in his own thoughts to notice.

"People who are starving to death," he continued, "don't have much respect or admiration for those who are allowed to squander fortunes on this decadent sort of lifestyle. It's obscene even to think they should."

Alarmed by his vehemence, Charlotte sensed that lurking beneath his kindly-little-old-man exterior was a very volatile soul. It gave her cause to wonder if perhaps Mr. Fox might have been telling her the truth about him after all.

Mr. Fox! The very thought of the man caused her to stiffen with indignation. Of course he hadn't been telling her the truth. Men like him couldn't tell the truth if their lives depended on it. He'd only told her that outlandish tale to protect his precious neck!

Feeling Monsieur Boland's hand tighten gently about her arm, Charlotte brushed aside the thought of her nocturnal intruder and allowed the old gentleman to escort her across the great room. They stopped before a row of shelves where a display of tiny, miniature portraits were arranged. She gazed at them, entranced by their minutely detailed beauty.

"Excuse me for a moment, *mademoiselle*." Monsieur Boland requested politely. "I see an acquaintance of mine to whom I wish to speak."

"Oh, by all means. Do go ahead."

"You will not wander off? I would hate to think of you getting lost in a place this size."

"You don't have to worry about that. I intend to stay right here and look at these beautiful treasures."

With a smile, Monsieur Boland turned and walked away. Charlotte saw him cross to a woman who stood beside one of the pillars. *She* was an acquaintance of Monsieur Boland's? How very odd! Richly gowned in deep burgundy silk, the dark-haired woman had a feral, somewhat dangerous look about her black, slanted eyes. Magyar eyes, Charlotte decided, seeing the way they seemed to bore straight through her.

With as much nonchalance as she could muster, Charlotte turned around and looked back at the display she was standing before. But just as her attention became absorbed in the beauty of the miniatures, she heard the woman's heavily accented voice rise sharply.

"In Cannes, no later than next week!"

Charlotte had to restrain herself from whirling around and glaring at the couple. If she did, they would certainly know that she had overheard their last exchange.

Monsieur Boland made some reply to the woman's outburst, but Charlotte didn't hear it because he kept his voice low and hushed. The woman, however, was not as cautious. Just as loudly as before, she said something about Marseilles and Nice being highly unsuitable and out of the question.

A frown marred Charlotte's forehead as she wondered what on earth the two of them were arguing about, if they were arguing at all. The conversation seemed rather one-sided to her.

It's none of your business, she warned herself. *Leave well enough alone. Eavesdropping will only get you into trouble, and you can't afford that right now.* So, with a resolute shake of her head, she started off in a direction that took her further away from the conversing pair.

With one part of her mind still thinking about Monsieur Boland and his strange acquaintance, she glided behind a pillar, intending to get a closer look at an interesting painting that hung on the wall there. In doing so, she accidentally bumped into another museum patron.

"Oh, *pardonnez-moi!*" she apologized to the very broad-shouldered back.

The man's blond head slowly turned. Charlotte got a good look at his face and felt her mouth drop open in surprise, her eyes widening considerably.

"Don't!" he whispered, clamping a hand over her mouth. "For God's sake, don't say a word!"

Charlotte growled and slapped his hand away. "You are forever trying to shut me up, and I don't like it! Just what the devil are you doing here, anyway?" she demanded.

"I could ask you the same thing," Jeremiah countered, his gaze flitting past her and settling on Boland and his voluptuous cohort.

"I'm here to see the exhibit. But you. . . ." She released a groan as the knowledge of his presence registered. "Don't tell me. You're *agenting,* aren't you?"

"Who's that woman he's with?" Jeremiah asked.

"How should I know?"

"Did he mention her name?"

"No, he just said she was an acquaintance." Then, furious with herself for having revealed that much, Charlotte groaned impatiently and stomped her foot. "What business is it of yours? He's got every right to speak to whomever he wishes!"

"Damn it, Charlotte, I need to know!"

"Miss Atwater to you, Mr. Fox!"

Jeremiah ignored her high-handed sneer. His gaze swept past Boland and encountered one of the museum guards, who stood across the room staring back at him suspiciously. He knew he had to do something, and quickly, to alleviate the guard's curiosity. Then he noticed a painting, hanging just behind the guard, of two lovers entwined in a passionate embrace. Without stopping to consider the consequences of his actions, he pulled Charlotte into his arms and clamped his mouth over hers. Maybe the guard would believe that they were a couple in love, who had just quarreled and were now making up. Lord, he certainly hoped so!

Needless to say, Charlotte was outraged. Mr. Fox was taking liberties with her again, and she didn't like it! As she struggled, an incoherent moan of sheer fury gurgled in her throat. She twisted and turned, and her hands pushed ineffectually against his broad chest. But the muscular arms that held her refused to loosen their hold, and she knew she would have to accept the situation until she could reprimand him later.

The idea of kicking him as she had done last night never occurred to her. Why should she, when his soft lips, playing so gently, so tenderly over hers, seemed to assure her that she was in no immediate danger? After all, what could he possibly do to her here in the middle of a crowded museum?

Small, and almost unnoticeable at first, a tingle took life within her veins. Her heart began to beat more quickly, and as the tingle accelerated a strange roaring sound rushed past her ears. Unable to stop herself, Charlotte melted against Jeremiah's long, muscular body.

This wasn't really happening, she thought dazedly. Not to her. Not here. Not now! She was much too mature to succumb to this sort of lustful adolescent behavior. Yet the heady sensation of his kiss, the play of his hands over her slender back, and the throbbing in her loins when she brushed against his rock-hard thighs seemed to belie her maturity and undermine her power of rational thought.

Her arms, trapped between their bodies, managed to gain their freedom. They slowly lifted until they were wrapped about his neck. Her fingers, gloved in pale gray kid to match her dress, splayed widely and wove through the thick mane of hair that brushed his nape. Her lips grew hungry for a more intimate taste of him and slowly parted. At the first gentle touch of his tongue on the tip of hers, she moaned and pulled him closer.

Even more surprised by Charlotte's reaction, Jeremiah was at a loss to explain the magnetic pull that drew him to her. Too easily, he found himself thrilled by her softness, excited by her sweet kiss, and astounded by her sensuality. He yielded to her seductiveness, forgetting his reason for having come to the museum.

Dear Lord, he wanted her!

It was this knowledge that caused Jeremiah to grasp for the last vestiges of his self-control. He wrenched his thoughts back to the present and loosened his hold on her, gently leaning her against the pillar they'd been standing near so that she wouldn't sink down to the floor in a spineless heap. A jolt of sheer desire surged through him when he pulled his head back and saw her passion-closed eyes and the lush, inviting ripeness of her parted lips.

What in heaven's name had happened to him? In the blink of an eye she had managed to bombard his sensibilities and overwhelm all his powers of reasoning. And what a disaster that would have been at a precarious time like this. Well, he couldn't let it happen again—that much was certain!

Charlotte realized that she was no longer being kissed and slowly closed her lips. The coldness of the marble pillar she leaned against penetrated through the thin layers of her voile dress where warm, strong hands had touched and caressed her before. Her lids fluttered open, and she beheld the lovely, gilt-framed painting hanging on the wall before her. She blinked in confusion, wondering what was amiss. Then she knew. The elusive Mr. Fox had vanished into thin air!

Damn him! she swore silently. *Damn his miserable hide!* Stiff with angry indignation, she wondered how she had ever let such a thing happen. And here of all places!

Her lips narrowed into a thin line. Her eyes became cold, gray slits of fury. Her bosom heaved with each deeply indrawn breath she took. Clenching her fists, she turned and stalked away from the pillar. So Paris was a big city, was it? Well, obviously it wasn't big enough for her to avoid meeting *him* again. And, heaven help her, this encounter had been just as infuriating as the first!

Charlotte's anger remained with her as she and Monsieur Boland continued their tour of the museum. She was so angry that she never thought to inquire about his acquaintance or what the woman had wanted. It took all the control she could muster just to respond politely to the old man's remarks. In the back of her mind was the memory of Mr. Fox and his very bad habit of appearing in the wrong place at the wrong time.

More than once, she caught herself searching for the infuriating Mr. Fox in the passing crowds as they went about Paris. Every tall man with blond hair captured her attention, until she realized that he wasn't who she thought he was. More than anything, she wanted to come face to face with Mr. Fox again, and the bigger the crowd the better. For she intended to embarrass him as thoroughly as he had embarrassed her!

The day dragged on, and dusk settled over the city without her encountering Mr. Fox again. In a brooding, uneasy silence, she journeyed back to her hotel with Monsieur Boland.

"You must be tired, my child," the old man observed.

"What?" Shooting him a confused look, his words managed to register in her preoccupied thoughts. "Oh, yes. Yes, I am, just a little. It's been a very long day." In more ways than one, she added silently.

"Well, you must be sure to have a nice, quiet supper and then go to bed."

"That won't be possible, I'm afraid."

"Oh?"

"No. You see, my cousin, Jean-Claude, is taking me out to dinner." He'd sent her a note that morning. *Surely your handsome lover will allow you one evening without him*, it had said. *If he is not otherwise occupied with his wife and twelve children, that is.*

"Such a nice boy," Monsieur Boland remarked. "You are very fortunate to have family here in Paris."

"Yes," Charlotte responded evenly.

"You said you were American, though, did you not?"

"Yes, I am, but my grandmother was French."

"Ah, that is your connection."

She nodded. "My grandmother's sister lives in Provence. I have plans to visit her there in a few days."

"How nice. You should have a very pleasant time there. The countryside is quite lovely this time of year."

A niggling imp of curiosity forced her to ask, "Are you going to be here in Paris much longer, *monsieur*?"

"No." His smile faded. "I regret to say that I, too, shall be leaving soon. Business, you understand."

"Just what is your line of work? I don't believe you've ever said." Inwardly, she prayed that his answer would be bank clerk or librarian or some other innocent occupation that would falsify Mr. Fox's tale.

"I deal in . . . mmm, unusual lithographs," he admitted with some reluctance.

"Oh, then our trip to the museum today must have been a great treat for you, since you are an artist. The paintings and statues there were certainly beautiful."

"Yes," came his wooden reply.

Charlotte wanted to press the issue further, but she was unable to do so. Their carriage pulled to a stop before the hotel, and Monsieur Boland did not hesitate in getting out and turning to assist her.

"Aren't you coming in too?" she queried when she saw him about to reenter the enclosed cab.

"No, I am expected elsewhere shortly. My acquaintance at the museum invited me to have dinner with her. You run along and have a pleasant evening with your young cousin."

But Charlotte's evening with Jean-Claude proved to be everything *but* pleasant.

It began amiably enough—dinner for two aboard a privately owned *bateau mouche,* floating down the Seine. Charlotte was instantly aware of the trouble and expense her cousin had gone to on her behalf. A large table, placed on the small deck of the boat, had been set with fine china, crystal, and silver on a snowy damask cloth. From the *bateau*'s wheelhouse nearby, she could smell the tantalizing aroma of French cuisine. One peek inside told her that the little woman who stood at the stove was working her heart out to get their food ready.

"To what do I owe all of this?" she asked Jean-Claude cautiously.

"*Cherie!* You deserve it, of course. A beautiful woman such as you should have only the finest that France has to offer."

"I thought we settled this matter last night," she patiently reminded him.

"But Charlotte, I merely wish to entertain you, not woo you from your lover."

However, something in the tone of his voice told her that he wasn't telling the complete truth.

Guiding her to one of the wooden chairs at the table, Jean-Claude continued, "I know that I am a poor substitute for the man you love, *cherie*, but you must understand, he *is* a married man and he *does* have an obligation to his wife."

"Yes, his wife," she agreed with a slight sneer.

"*Cherie*, you must not let the fact that you are his mistress upset you so."

One look at the warmth in his dark gray eyes told her that he'd heard the sneer in her voice and had mistaken it for jealousy.

"*Non, non!*" he resumed. "You are the light in his otherwise dull life. You glow with an inner beauty that his wife probably lacks. You are warm and comforting, where she is undoubtedly cold and unfeeling."

"Well, with twelve children, I doubt that she has much time to be warm and comforting."

"*Mon Dieu*, twelve!" he repeated with typical Gallic exaggeration, settling himself in the chair across from her. "I still cannot believe that, *cherie*. Though, I must say, he certainly *looked* virile enough."

"Jean-Claude, if it's all the same to you, I'd like to change the subject." She was regretting ever having told him such an outrageous lie. It was bad enough having him think of her as a married man's mistress, much less having him believe her to be the *petite amie* of one with twelve children! "We have this lovely evening together alone. Let's try and enjoy it, shall we?"

In the flickering candlelight, his gray eyes took on a glimmer of undisguised pleasure. He quickly covered her hand with his and brought her fingertips close to his mouth. "Ah, *cherie!* I was hoping you would say that."

Charlotte realized, too late, what a mistake she had made when he started nibbling her fingers. "Jean-Claude—"

"I want to give you an evening that you will long remember," he proclaimed huskily. "I want you to look back on this night, and this quiet, intimate moment we are sharing now, and think of me when next you are in his arms. Think only of me, *cherie!*"

"*Jean-Claude!*"

"I promise that this will be the most memorable night of your life, *mon coeur!*"

With a none-too-subtle jerk, she freed her hand from his and placed it in her lap, wiping her wet fingers with her napkin. "Why don't you"—*jump in the river and cool off*, she wanted to say but didn't—"pour the wine?"

"*Oui!* It will help warm our blood, *n'est-ce pas?*"

Little boy, she thought to herself, *yours is hot enough already!* "Just where are we going?"

"My friend Philippe houses his balloon not far from here. I thought we would see it by moonlight."

"Oh, that's right, your friend with the balloon!" she nodded. Allowing her gaze to drift upward, she noticed the not quite full medallion that was suspended among the twinkling stars in the deep purple heaven. "Does he fly it at night?"

"Sometimes," Jean-Claude nodded. "But we shall not need any craft tonight, *mon amour*. We will soar above the earth on our own. I have longed, since the first moment I met you, to show you how enjoyable and passionate a Frenchman can be."

Oh Lord, we're back to that again! "But I thought you understood, Jean-Claude. I'm not available."

"I do, *cherie*. I do! But the evening is still very young, and I may yet change your mind. That *Americain*, he is not for you."

"And you are?"

"*Oui!* I have not the wife nor the twelve children as he does. There is only me. And I know that I can give you far more than he ever could."

"I'm not so sure about that," she murmured, suddenly recalling Mr. Fox's gentle kiss.

"Let me entice you, Charlotte. Let me show you the kind of pleasure that we can derive from our love."

Growing tired of this amorous vein of conversation, she patiently suggested, "Why don't we just eat?"

"Ah *non*, we must not forget the food!" He issued an almost diabolical-sounding chuckle. "We do not want to grow weak when we will need all of our strength later on."

Having left its mooring place some time ago, the *bateau* floated lazily down the Seine as Charlotte and Jean-Claude dined on succulent breast of chicken in white wine sauce, tiny peas with mushrooms, and delectable creamed potatoes. They were passing by historical landmarks on both sides of the river, illuminated by the dim street lamps below and the silvery moon above. The great gothic cathedral of Notre Dame, looking proud and majestic by night, caught her eye as she bit into a crusty slice of bread.

"Paris is such a beautiful city," she commented dreamily some time later. The effect of the wine she had consumed was finally making itself known. She felt mellow, contented, and just a wee bit tipsy.

"A city for lovers," Jean-Claude purred, reaching across the table and capturing her hand.

"Now, Jean-Claude," she began to protest.

"*Non non, cherie!* Do not talk. You will spoil this wonderful thing that is happening between us."

"But nothing *is* happening."

"It could."

"No, it could not!"

She tried to wrench her hand away from his, but he refused to release it. Instead, he maneuvered his chair closer to hers and draped an arm about her back, pulling her against him.

"He is married, *cherie*. You must know by now that there can never be any future for you with him."

"Oh hell!" Wearily, she decided that now was the time to tell him the truth. Maybe if she did he would leave her alone.

"You see? You are finally admitting it too! Let me take you away from him. We can have such a future together, *cherie*. A future that will outlast any other known to man. Together we can—"

"Help!" came a faint cry behind them.

"What was that?" Charlotte jerked her head around in the direction of the sound just as Jean-Claude's questing lips grazed the edge of her jaw.

"It was nothing, *cherie*. Ignore it."

His lips were nuzzling the curve of her neck when the voice called out "Help!" again, closer this time. Charlotte pushed herself away from Jean-Claude and abruptly got to her feet, moving to the railing. Peering out over the murky waters, she caught sight of a head and a pair of floundering arms.

"Oh my Lord!" she cried. "Jean-Claude, somebody's drowning!"

Cursing his rotten misfortune under his breath, Jean-Claude slowly got to his feet. He found a coiled length of rope attached to the *bateau*'s wheelhouse and joined Charlotte at the railing. With a wide sweep of his arm, he flung one end of the line out over the water and almost immediately felt a tug at the other end. Then he began pulling the rope back in, hand over hand.

Helpless, unable to do anything but worry, Charlotte stood there as the person in the river drew closer. The moment she saw his head bob up alongside the *bateau*, she leaned over and grabbed his upraised arm. With all the strength she possessed, she pulled him over the railing and let him fall, face down, onto the deck. His shirt was bloody and torn, and his hair, covered with sewage from the river, was plastered to his scalp.

Grimacing at the sight, she knelt down beside the man and used the damask napkin she'd been clutching to wipe off his face. She shuddered as his body convulsed with each violent cough, and the dirty water that he had swallowed came spewing out of his mouth. What a hideous sight, she thought, and she sat back on her heels when he began to turn over.

But her sympathy for the nearly drowned man changed the moment she got a look at his face. Her eyes widened, her jaw dropped open, and all she could say was, "Oh no, not you again!"

Chapter Four

"DARLING!" JEREMIAH'S VOICE WAS A RASPY whisper from all the coughing he'd done. Through his water-spiked lashes, he gazed up at Miss Atwater, who appeared thoroughly disgusted by his presence. Then he noticed her young cousin standing behind her. "You saved me!"

"*Mon Dieu!*" Jean-Claude exclaimed. "It is your—"

"My lover," Charlotte groaned.

"We must help him, *cherie!*" Jean-Claude hurriedly bent down to assist Jeremiah to his feet.

Charlotte stood back out of the way, her disbelieving gaze following her cousin's movements. Only a moment ago he'd been trying to steal her away from Mr. Fox, and now he had nothing but polite concern for the man. His behavior didn't make much sense to her, but then he was a man, so what else should she expect?

When Jeremiah was on his feet, Jean-Claude led him toward the wheelhouse. *"Mon ami,* you are shivering. I know that it is now summer, but the river is still quite cold. We must get rid of your chill immediately. Yvette!" He called to the woman inside the structure. "A blanket, *vite, vite!"*

Not knowing what else to do, Charlotte followed them. But as she stepped inside the bright, warm wheelhouse, she saw the cut on the back of Mr. Fox's head and the blood that was seeping from it, and gasped, "What happened?"

"I was attacked." With a groan, Jeremiah sank down onto the bench near the stove and looked at Charlotte to see her lip curl in disgust. "By my wife's lover," he added deliberately.

"Mon Dieu!" Jean-Claude retorted. In the process of finding a bottle of brandy and a snifter in which to pour it, he missed the disdainful expression that appeared on his cousin's face. "Your wife, too, has a lover?"

"So it would seem," replied Jeremiah, rather overdramatically. "I didn't know a thing about it until tonight. And Lord, he's such an ugly bastard! I don't know what she sees in him." His gaze never once left Charlotte, even when she turned her head to roll her eyes in disgust. *Just you wait, Miss High and Mighty Atwater,* he thought. *This ought to wipe that look off your face!* "He's tall, dark-haired, and he's got very strange, slanted eyes. I saw them meet in the *museum* just this morning."

As he'd anticipated, Charlotte's head jerked back around, her shock instantly readable in her expression.

Boland's acquaintance, the Magyar-eyed woman, was the one who had attacked him! Deciding to play along with his ruse for the moment, she asked, "And your wife—what was she doing while her lover was beating you to a pulp?"

Jeremiah instantly caught on to her ploy and responded, "Nothing. Not a damn thing. She just stood there on the quai and watched him."

It saddened Charlotte to think that Monsieur Boland was not the kind, considerate man she'd first thought him to be. But how could he be if he'd allowed his acquaintance to attack Mr. Fox without offering to defend him? "Then you were right, and I was wrong," she admitted on a heavy, disappointed sigh.

Jean-Claude, having put the disjointed bits and pieces of their exchange together, came up with his own inaccurate conclusions. "You *suspected* that your wife had a lover?"

Jeremiah nodded and huddled deeper into the blanket that the Frenchwoman, Yvette, had wrapped around him. He took the glass of brandy from Jean-Claude and swallowed it in one gulp. "I knew something had been bothering her," he remarked, and held the glass out for Jean-Claude to refill. "She's been behaving quite oddly of late. Little things, you know, that only a husband would notice. And she hasn't been paying much attention to the children, either. Poor little mites."

"You must take them away from her!" Jean-

Claude declared vehemently. "A woman who would let such a thing as this happen to her husband should not be allowed to keep children."

"That's a point worth considering," Jeremiah agreed.

"Well, you can think about the children later," Charlotte retorted impatiently, wanting to get off the subject of his nonexistent wife and twelve children. "Right now we need to get you into some dry clothes. You'll catch your death in these wet things. How's your head?"

"It hurts." Jeremiah winced when he felt her fingers gently touch his sore scalp. "Take it easy, will you?"

"Don't be such a baby. I barely touched you. Ugh!" she grimaced. "This is awful looking. Jean-Claude, maybe we should try and clean it before an infection sets in."

"*Oui*, my thoughts exactly." Jean-Claude had already found a clean cloth on the edge of Yvette's work table and was approaching Jeremiah.

Charlotte took the cloth from him, as well as the bottle of brandy. She poured a liberal amount of the amber-colored liquid onto the cloth, poised it beside Jeremiah's head, and warned, "This might burn a little bit."

"Yeeouch!" Jeremiah jumped across the bench as the alcohol's sting penetrated his cut. "God damn it, that burns more than a little bit!"

"Oh, shut up and sit still!" Charlotte snapped, and dabbed the cloth against his head again.

"We should be at Philippe's shortly," Jean-

Claude informed them with a slight shudder. True, he was a medical student, but he could not stand to see anyone in pain. Not even his cousin's lover, who did not deserve her in the first place.

"I think it would be better if we just went back to Paris," Charlotte advised.

"No!" Jeremiah slapped her hand away as it came near his head again. "We cannot go back to my hotel. They'll know I'm alive if I do."

"This is ridiculous!" Charlotte moved away from him and shook her head. "If you're so scared of them, why don't you just go to the police?"

Not wanting to involve himself in what sounded to be the beginning of a lover's squabble, Jean-Claude quietly sauntered away to inform the captain of their change in plans.

As soon as he had disappeared, Charlotte leaned close to Jeremiah and whispered, "Did they really try to kill you?"

"What do you think?" he countered. "They didn't hit me over the head and shove me into the river just for the hell of it! Of course they tried to kill me!"

"But why? You were only following them."

"Yeah, and they knew it! I guess I wasn't as inconspicuous as I thought. Just before that woman hit me over the head, she let me know that she and her . . . associates, as she called them, had known about me all along. While I was trailing them, they were trailing me!" Then suddenly Jeremiah remembered Judith, and he groaned, "Oh dear Lord! I've got to send word back to my hotel before they go there and find . . ." He broke off, his thoughts racing toward the disastrous conclusion that he couldn't voice aloud.

"Find whom?" Charlotte asked, a frown of confusion marring her brow.

"It's too long a story to go into now," he replied vaguely. "Do you think your cousin would help me if I asked him?"

"Jean-Claude? Why ask him when I'll help you?"

"No, not you!" Oddly enough, it sickened him to think of Charlotte being in any kind of danger. "Chances are they spotted you when you helped me out of the river."

"But how could they? It was too dark for anyone to have seen us from shore. And anyway, we're so far down the river now, they've probably lost us."

Jean-Claude stepped back inside the wheelhouse then and cut short the response Jeremiah was about to make. "We will be at Philippe's in a matter of moments," he said. "Can you walk, *mon ami*?"

"They didn't break my leg, Jean-Claude," drawled Jeremiah. "Of course I can walk." And to prove his point, he stood up. But his spinning head caused him to weave unsteadily, and Charlotte was forced to wrap her arm about his waist to support him.

"How far away is Philippe's house from the river?" she asked her cousin as they made their way slowly outside.

"Not far," he responded.

"But it's not directly on the river, is it?"

"Do not worry your pretty head, *cherie*. It is close by."

"The French couple," Jeremiah began, putting most of his weight on Jean-Claude instead of Charlotte. "Will they say anything?"

"Non, mon ami, I will see to it that they do not."

At that moment the *bateau* came to a thudding halt as it bumped against the riverbank. Jean-Claude helped Charlotte lead Jeremiah up the boarding ramp and onto dry land. Then he returned to the *bateau* to warn Georges, the captain, and his wife, Yvette.

"Say a word of this to no one," he instructed them as he handed the woman a fistful of coins. "It is most imperative that you do not."

"You will not be returning to Paris with us, *monsieur*?" Georges inquired, eyeing the money that his wife was counting.

"Non. I will find transportation elsewhere. And it would be wise if you did not return to Paris tonight either!"

"Monsieur," Yvette glanced up at him. *"Merci!"*

Jean-Claude nodded somewhat distractedly, then hurried up onto the riverbank where he'd left Charlotte and her injured lover. He was beginning to like this sort of intrigue, hiding from unknown persons as he helped his friends escape to safety. It was probably not unlike what his great-grandfather had experienced during the Revolution, when he had helped British spies enter and exit the country.

"How far away from Paris are we?" Jeremiah asked as they headed off through a nearby grove of trees.

"Only a few miles or so. This was Philippe's uncle's farm before the old man died. Philippe has kept it, to our good fortune, because he wanted a place near the city. You see, the noise and confusion there bother him at times. And, too, he has room here to store his balloon. That is Philippe's greatest passion."

As they cleared the trees, Charlotte noticed a small, stone farmhouse not far away. "He isn't here now, is he?"

"Non, we were here only yesterday, remember? He will not be able to come again for another week. He, too, is a student, you know."

"But you're sure the house is empty," she stressed.

"Oui! There is a caretaker who lives with his family at the other end of the farm, but they will not see us. And when I return to Paris tomorrow, I will tell Philippe that I brought my *petite amie* out here for a midnight rendezvous. He will understand."

"Oh, I'm sure he will," Charlotte agreed dryly.

Jeremiah stumbled once, nearly falling to the ground as they made their way toward the darkened building. He was beginning to feel dizzier than he had been earlier, and the night air was chilling him to the bone.

Jean-Claude had to fumble with the latch on the door for a moment before it finally gave way and opened. Once inside, though, he hurried about, lighting the lamp and starting a fire in the smoke-blackened stone fireplace.

"Bring him over here, *cherie*," he directed to Charlotte over his shoulder. "He needs to be by the fire."

"Can you make it?" She looked at Jeremiah with much concern, seeing the way he slumped against the door.

He managed a weak nod, then pushed away from the door and stumbled over to where Jean-Claude had pulled a chair before the now roaring fire. The heat felt good . . . very good! But it did nothing to dispel the annoying chill that he still felt.

"How many rooms are there here in the house?" Charlotte asked her cousin as she searched through the cupboards for something to eat. It wasn't that she was hungry, but Jeremiah might be. A nice hot cup of tea laced with sugar would do well to ward off his chill.

"Two rooms upstairs and two more down," Jean-Claude remarked, producing a half-full bottle of wine from one of the cabinets. "We will have to light a fire in one of the bedrooms, though, if we want it to be warm enough for him."

Charlotte looked back over her shoulder at Jeremiah and said, "Maybe it would be better if we made him a bed down here in the kitchen. This stone floor will hold the heat a lot better than a mattress. And anyway, I don't think he's in any condition to climb a flight of stairs."

"You will not mind sleeping on the floor with him?"

"What dif—" Charlotte began, but broke off as the gravity of his question finally registered. As far as Jean-Claude was concerned, she was Mr.

Fox's mistress. To request other sleeping arrangements would be the same as denying it. And if she did that, Jean-Claude would probably start playing up to her again. "No, I won't mind at all," she ended on a rather dry note.

"Then I shall go up now and bring down a bed."

Jean-Claude departed, and Charlotte decided to heat up some of the wine he had found. She added some spices and a lot of sugar to it, then took the steaming cup over to Jeremiah, who was still shivering before the fire.

"Here, drink this." She held the cup out for him, and he frowned into its murky depths.

"What is it?"

"Well, it isn't poison," she chided. "Go on, drink it!"

Jeremiah took a tentative sip; then, finding the taste to his liking, he gulped it down completely. When it appeared as though Charlotte might move away, he felt a compulsion to keep her near. "Charlotte?" came his raspy purr. "Why are you doing all of this for me?"

"I don't know," she replied, and lowered her gaze. Kneeling down on the floor beside his chair, she felt suddenly hot inside and knew it had nothing to do with the heat from the fire.

"You know, you had every right to shove me back into the river. You didn't have to go to all this trouble."

"Mr. Fox, I—"

"Jeremiah," he corrected quietly. "Call me Jeremiah, Charlotte. We are supposed to be lovers, you know."

"Yes, but we aren't. You know it. And I know it."

"Ah, but Jean-Claude doesn't, and we must keep up appearances. Where's he gone off to anyway?"

"Upstairs, to bring down a bed. Well, at least a mattress."

In the brief moment of silence that followed, Jeremiah noted the play of firelight on Charlotte's face. With her hair coming loose from its tightly drawn-back coil, she had a softer, more feminine look about her. Her profile wasn't as unbecoming and harsh as he'd first thought. In fact, she was almost beautiful.

"I'm sorry I interrupted your evening." His apology caused her to turn and face him. Only one side of her face was illuminated, and he could see the way her lovely gray eyes had darkened to deep, fathomless pools.

"I'm not," she remarked, and felt the heat inside her grow hotter. "I was having the devil's own time convincing my cousin that I was not going to begin an affair with him. But I guess he isn't the type of young man who can take a simple no for an answer."

"He wasn't thinking with his head, Charlotte." *Just as I'm not,* he thought, lifting one hand to touch the side of her face. Her cheek was soft and velvety beneath his fingertips. "There's something about you. Don't ask me what it is, but there is something."

Hearing his huskily spoken words, she felt herself slowly lean toward him as the blaze within her went out of control. Her lips parted.

Her gaze, fastened to his well-shaped mouth, saw his mustached lips part as his head came toward hers.

But the tense, electric moment was shattered as Jean-Claude fell into the kitchen—literally! The mattress and bedding he was carrying landed squarely on top of him.

Charlotte was hard pressed not to laugh out loud at her cousin's comical entrance, but she silently thanked him for his badly timed intrusion. If he hadn't come in just now . . . well, there was no doubt in her mind what she and Mr. Fox would be doing. No, not Mr. Fox any longer, she amended thoughtfully. *Jeremiah.*

She moved toward Jean-Claude to help him with his heavy burden. "We'll need to push that table out of the way if we want to lay this in front of the fire."

Jeremiah's shivering returned as he watched the two of them push and shove the heavy piece of furniture to one side of the room. His wet clothes had dried considerably from the fire's heat, but his inner chill persisted.

"Where are you going to sleep?" Charlotte asked her cousin as they spread the sheets and blankets on top of the mattress.

"Upstairs," he responded. "One of the bedrooms has a very good view of both the road coming into the farm and the river."

"You don't suppose those people will try to—"

"No," came Jeremiah's hoarse declaration. "If they do anything at all tonight, they'll go back to my hotel and wait for me." As before, a vision of Judith flashed through his mind. However, this time he recalled something she had said to him earlier in the day, something about going out to dinner with friends. He hoped, for her sake, that she had done just that.

"Your wife's lover sounds quite diabolical," Jean-Claude observed, rising to his feet. "Even a bit demented."

Charlotte shot Jeremiah a look that clearly mirrored her thoughts. He frowned up at her, telling her without words to be quiet. They both knew that Jean-Claude was better off not knowing the truth of their dilemma.

"Here," she said to Jeremiah. "Let's get you out of those wet clothes and into bed."

"I will leave you then." Jean-Claude moved toward the door, but the hand Charlotte stretched out to him delayed his departure.

"Thank you," she murmured earnestly.

"There is no need to thank me, *cherie*. You have brought more than a little excitement into my otherwise dull life." He kissed her lips fleetingly, then winked back at Jeremiah. "Sleep well, *mon ami*."

Jeremiah stripped down to his drawers and slid between the sheets so that Charlotte could tuck the covers in around him. Then, turning his back to the fire, he watched her unashamedly as she stepped into a darkened corner of the kitchen.

"What are you doing?" he asked her softly.

"I'm getting out of my clothes."

"Mind if I watch?"

"Yes, I mind very much." But the huskiness of her voice belied her statement, and she didn't bother to turn her back to him as she slowly removed her bodice and stepped out of her skirt and petticoats. The electrical tension they had experienced earlier had returned and was much stronger than before, but Charlotte was incapable of dispelling it.

When Jeremiah saw her strip away her whaleboned corset, he felt a molten heat course through his veins and settle in his loins. It began to throb there as he watched her lift her arms above her head to pull the pins from her hair. Like dark, heavy silk, it fell over her shoulders and down her back, her upraised arms pulling her full breasts higher and higher until one pale globe nearly spilled out the top of her ruffle-edged camisole. And as she moved back into the firelight, he could see the thrusting outline of her nipples through the sheer cotton.

She sat down on their makeshift bed, pausing briefly to unbuckle her shoes and peel off her stockings. Then she slid between the sheets beside him.

"You're getting warm now?" she asked, turning onto her side to face him.

"That's an understatement," he chuckled.

"Mr. Fox . . . Jeremiah, you're in no condition at the moment to be thinking what you're thinking."

"Let me be the judge of that, Charlotte." Then he moved, his hand coming up to rest against her neck as his thumb gently caressed the curve of her jaw. His fingers flexed, touching the back of her head, and he pulled her face toward his.

Charlotte's gaze was riveted on his mouth. A little voice in the back of her mind kept telling her that this really wasn't happening, that it was all a dream, but the erotic spell she was under refused to let her believe it. This was real, all right! And when his face was so close that it was nothing more than a blur, she silenced her little voice and felt the brief, tingling touch of his mustache before his mouth closed over hers.

She tasted like sweet wine. Her mouth was so soft, so warm that Jeremiah could not stop the moan that formed in his throat. His tongue slowly snaked out and penetrated her parted lips but stopped at the barrier of her teeth. Then he heard her faint sigh before the barrier opened and allowed him to enter.

The scant few inches that separated them vanished as their bodies came together. The brush of his coarse chest hair against her was an exciting stimulant to her cambric-covered breasts, and she moved against it. His hand descended from her head to one weighty orb, and she felt her arousal increase even more.

Cupping her firm flesh in his palm, Jeremiah deepened their kiss. As his fingers went beneath the fabric of her camisole, they found the sleeping bud of her nipple and gently closed over it, eliciting a groan of pure sensuality from Charlotte. In one light movement, he uncovered the crest to feel its texture more intimately, and it hardened instantly beneath his touch.

She gasped for air when his mouth left hers. Her head fell back weakly onto the pillow, and there it began to move from side to side as his warm lips trailed a path down the column of her throat. Her spine arched as his kisses ignited small fires within her, and when his mouth closed over her nipple she inhaled sharply, holding her breath as time became suspended in space.

Her hands moved up to clasp his head. She held him lovingly as he teased and suckled her throbbing crest. As her leg bent, her knee found the hard staff that protruded between his thighs. He thrust his hips forward, and she rubbed against it enticingly as an ache began to pulsate in her loins.

"Charlotte?" came his hoarse, breathy voice.

"Don't stop," she begged him. "Please, it feels so . . . so wonderful."

"I want you," he confessed, and brought his head up to rest on the pillow next to hers. He gazed deeply into her passion-drowsed face.

"I know," she whispered.

"But can you . . . I mean, are you—?"

"No, I'm not a virgin, Jeremiah."

Rather than being shocked by this admission, he felt a wave of enjoyable relief wash over him. "Well, thank God for that!"

"What?" Charlotte came out of her sensual daze and pulled back from him when he started to kiss her again.

"I said, thank God—"

"I know what you said. I want to know what you meant by it."

"Charlotte, I wasn't insulting you."

"Then what were you doing?"

"I was trying to make love to you," he retorted, and moved away from her. "I thought that was what you wanted."

"I did, but now I'm not so sure."

"What's the matter? You said you weren't a

virgin. You know what's supposed to happen next."

"I know I do!" she snapped. "But you don't have to remind me of it. I'm not some strumpet, you know."

"I never said you were!"

"And just for your information, Mr. Fox, I haven't been with a long line of men, either! There was only one, and that was over ten years ago."

"There's no need to get mad."

"I'm not mad!"

"Then why are you yelling?"

"I'm not yelling! I just don't want you to think that I'm easy."

He mumbled something beneath his breath—something that sounded like "I know that!"—and folded one arm beneath his head to stare off into space.

A long stretch of silence ensued before he finally turned to look back at her. "Do you want to talk about it?"

"About what?"

"The other man. Does he still mean something to you?"

"Heavens, no! He didn't mean anything to me ten years ago."

"He didn't?"

"No, he didn't," Charlotte sighed, and knew she would have to explain her sordid past to Jeremiah now. "I was a very dowdy, very frumpy little girl at the time."

"Just how old were you?"

"Seventeen. You see, both of my older sisters were beautiful—they still are—and I was always the ugly duckling of the bunch. They were both engaged to be married, and they kept going on and on about how wonderful it was, being kissed and held by their fiances. Well, one day I decided to find out for myself just what all of the excitement was about."

Her pause increased Jeremiah's curiosity. "So? What happened?"

"Well, there was this man," she continued reluctantly. "Oh, he wasn't a total stranger or anything like that. He'd been to our house on a number of occasions to discuss business with Papa. I knew he sort of fancied me, because he would always give me these looks when he thought Papa wasn't watching him. Well, I let him get me alone one day, away from the house, and one thing led to another, and . . . well, you can probably guess what happened after that."

"Yes, I can imagine," he murmured, thinking how inconceivable it seemed. "And you've never let another man near you since then?"

"Well, where I come from, men don't want soiled goods. Oh, they can carouse around all they please, but their womenfolk have to be pristine pure. I've had one or two proposals from fairly decent boys," she admitted, "but I've always wanted something more out of life than what they could offer." She paused for a moment before continuing. "I went to live with my grandmother in Baton Rouge after it happened, and when I got my teaching certificate I began teaching French to a bunch of silly little rich girls."

"Your mother and father never knew that you'd—"

"No! It would have broken their hearts, and Papa would have killed Melvin."

"Melvin? That was the man who—"

"Yes." Jeremiah's chest began to vibrate with mirth, and Charlotte had to smile. "Believe me, he matched his name."

"Well, tell me," he chuckled. "Was Melvin any good?"

"I don't have many fond memories of the moment, if that's what you're asking. It all happened so fast, I couldn't see what all the excitement was about. I mean, having some sweaty hulk atop you, grunting and groaning, is not my idea of an enjoyable interlude."

"I suppose I should take exception to that remark, but I won't," Jeremiah replied, turning on his side to face her, the smile still pulling at his lips. "The time will come when you'll find out just what it *is* all about, Charlotte, and I intend to be there."

She gazed into his eyes, her playfulness returning. "You don't sweat and grunt, do you?"

"Yes, but in a much nicer way. And I won't be in a rush, either. I'll take my time and show you just how wonderful making love with me can be." *If Boland and his bunch don't get to me first, that is.*

Charlotte saw his expression change and knew what he was thinking. "Jeremiah, maybe we shouldn't be talking about—"

"Shh. Of course we should." He pulled her close to him, nestling her head beneath his chin. "Don't even think that we won't. We're in this thing together now, sweetheart."

"In what?"

When he didn't answer immediately, she asked again, "What are we in together, Jeremiah?"

He expelled a long sigh before saying, "I can't let you go back to Paris, Charlotte. Boland and his bunch probably know all about you by now, and it wouldn't be safe for you there."

"But I have to go back," she insisted. "All of my things are there."

"We can get *things* as we need them. No, you'll be better off with me."

"And where will that be?" she asked.

"I don't know," he admitted frankly. "I honestly don't know."

Chapter Five

THE CROWING OF THE ROOSTER HERALDED THE rising sun and startled Charlotte out of her deep, slightly erotic dream. She opened her eyes to see a mat of golden fur on the muscular chest beneath her cheek and suddenly realized where, and with whom, she was. A twist of her head took her gaze to the window, where the first faint rays of dawn were filtering in through the dusty panes of glass.

She nestled her head back in the hollow of Jeremiah's shoulder and tried to go back to sleep, but other sounds kept that from happening. Hearing the floorboards creak softly in the ceiling above her head, she knew Jean-Claude was now awake too. The rooster crowed once more, and with a shake of her head she decided to get up. As much as she wanted to remain here in the warm circle of Jeremiah's embrace, she knew she couldn't. There were too many things to do.

Slowly moving away from Jeremiah so as not to waken him, she smiled at the innocent look on his face. Although he'd told her he was over thirty, he looked much younger. If it weren't for the mustache brushing his upper lip and the heavy growth of stubble on his cheeks, she would think he was a lad in his late teens. But no mere lad could have aroused her as he'd done last night, nor could a lad have held his passions in check. They had slept all night, entwined in each other's arms, without once having to answer that most passionate of nature's calls.

It was the need to answer another call that caused her to don her dress and slip out of the house. When she reentered the kitchen a few minutes later, she found Jean-Claude quietly moving about as he searched through the cupboards for something to eat.

"There are probably fresh eggs out in the henhouse," she whispered. "Why don't you go find some, and I'll fix you an omelet."

"Do not bother, *cherie*. It would make too much noise," he negated with a shake of his head and opened the nearby larder. "Monsieur Fox needs his rest. I will just have some of this bread and then be on my way."

"You're going back to Paris?"

"I must, Charlotte. But with any luck, I will get there before I am too late for my morning lecture."

"Oh, that's right. I had forgotten you were still going to school."

Jean-Claude felt a stab of annoyance at her offhanded remark but decided to let it pass without comment. "Did he sleep all right?"

"Mmm-hmm." Charlotte nodded, looking back at Jeremiah. "Once he got rid of that horrible chill, he slept like a log."

"Like a what?"

"Oh, that's just a saying that we Americans have."

Jean-Claude cocked his head to one side, reluctantly accepting her explanation.

"Do you have any idea when you'll be able to come back?"

"*Non, cherie,* I do not. Probably not for a few days, though, at the earliest. But I will stop by the caretaker's cottage and inform him of your presence here. Philippe introduced us when we were here before, so the man knows me."

"Yes, please do that. I would hate for someone to think we're trespassing and come after us with a shotgun."

Having bitten off a large chunk of the stale bread, Jean-Claude could not respond for a moment. He chewed his bite and nodded his head in agreement. After he'd swallowed and had washed down the lump in his throat with a sip of wine, he asked, "When will you be coming back to Paris?"

"The way things look now, Jean-Claude, maybe never. I'll probably be going on to Provence, and your grandmother's, from here." Then she remembered all of her possessions that were still back in her hotel room. "Is there any way you could arrange for my things to be sent on ahead to Tante Marie's?"

"*Oui*. As it happens, I know one of the chambermaids at your hotel. She will be more than happy to do this one little favor for me in return for . . . mmm, shall we say, suitable compensation?"

Charlotte smiled, accurately interpreting her cousin's unspoken words. "Just promise me you'll do it without bringing too much attention to yourself. I don't want you getting into trouble because of us."

"Do not worry, *cherie*. Already I had made a plan to elude your lover's pursuers. They will never suspect that I am in league with you."

She led him to the door after he had finished his meager breakfast. Kissing him goodbye on his stubble-roughened cheek, she prayed that he was right. Her years of teaching in a girls' school had not prepared her to handle a situation as grave as this one was. *Grave!* Goodness, what a bad choice of words, she thought. But what a very appropriate one!

Jean-Claude was more than halfway down the narrow dirt lane and was slowly disappearing into the early morning mist before Charlotte turned and reentered the kitchen. Jeremiah was still sleeping peacefully before the now cold hearth, and she wondered what she could do to occupy her time until he awakened. Well, one thing was certain, she couldn't just stand around and watch him sleep. But she could finish dressing and find something for them to eat for breakfast. Glancing over at the pile of Jeremiah's discarded clothes, which were rumpled and covered with river-water stains, she knew she would have to find something for him to wear as well.

Her gaze shifted upward when she remembered the bedrooms upstairs. Maybe Philippe had some extra clothes in the house that would fit Jeremiah. She scooped up her shoes and stockings and headed for the door, deciding to find out for herself.

Adjacent to the kitchen was a warmly furnished dining room. Beyond that was an equally inviting parlor where a flight of stairs took her to the second floor. The first bedroom she peered into looked as if a cyclone had hit it—a cyclone named Jean-Claude, she thought with a smile. The bedding had been stripped away, leaving only the carved headboard and the rusty-looking springs that had supported the mattress. But in the corner of the room stood an armoire, and she now went toward it.

Colorful gowns of every description caught her eye as she swung open the door. Smiling, she wondered to whom they belonged. Philippe? Surely not. Probably one of his lady friends. She touched the clothes and wondered if something here would fit her as well.

Jean-Claude whistled under his breath as he entered the small village. People were beginning to bustle about the narrow, unpaved streets, and shopkeepers were setting out the arrays of goods that they would be selling on this market day. Geese honked raucously as a young boy led them with a long staff down the side of the street, while on the other side a farmer's wife called to the boy to be careful where his charges paused. After all, geese did have a way of biting unsuspecting victims.

His growling stomach told Jean-Claude that he would have to get something more substantial to eat before he made his way back to Paris. The meager slice of bread that he had eaten at Philippe's would not last him an hour, much less sustain him throughout the remainder of the day.

Across the street from where Jean-Claude now stood was a *boulangerie*. He could smell the yeasty aromas that were emanating from its opened door. Intending to make his way over to the shop and purchase a *croissant* or muffin, he stepped out into the street just as a dusty carriage entered the village. He wouldn't have paid much attention to it if the passenger inside had not decided at that moment to show his face in the carriage's window.

Jean-Claude had stopped to let the carriage pass, but as it rattled by him he found that he was incapable of moving one step further. The face he'd seen so briefly in the window caused something to register in his memory. The man was dark-skinned, with cold, dark, slanted eyes.

What was it Monsieur Fox had said? "I don't see what she sees in him. He's such an ugly bastard." Well, the man Jean-Claude had just seen had certainly been ugly. But that still did not mean that he was the same man who had attacked Monsieur Fox last night in Paris. After all, France did have an awful lot of ugly people.

He decided to find out for himself just who the man in the carriage was, and sprinted off in its wake. He raced around the corner but stopped dead in his tracks when he saw the carriage parked just a few feet away from him in front of the village's telegraph office. The man inside the carriage was getting out, the top of his head towering over the small conveyance, even as he bent over to say something to the unseen person inside.

One of the villagers, a merchant by the looks of his clothes, came around the corner of the telegraph office at that moment, and the tall man turned to him. *"Pardonnez-moi, monsieur.* Could you tell me if you have seen a stranger in the village this morning?"

"A stranger?" the villager queried with a bewildered frown.

"Oui. He would be about so high." The dark-skinned man held his hand out even with his head, which stood six feet, three inches from the ground. "And he has pale blond hair and dark blue eyes."

"Non, monsieur," the villager shrugged. "There is no one here who matches that description."

"He was traveling with a lady," the stranger added, as if this would make the villager remember something.

"Oh?" The villager arched an eyebrow at this.

"Yes, but I don't know what she looks like," the stranger admitted with a frown.

Jean-Claude breathed a sigh of relief on hearing this. At least his cousin was safe, even though it would seem that Monsieur Fox was not. He started to turn and walk away, but he stopped when he heard the dark-skinned stranger say to the villager, "I would appreciate it if you would ask around for this man. He goes by the name of Steadman. His, er, wife is with me, and it is most imperative that she find him."

His wife! Jean-Claude whirled around, knowing a sudden urge to get a look at this woman who had deserted her husband and all but abandoned her twelve children for the sake of her lover. Sauntering casually past the carriage, he let his gaze dart inside and noticed the beautiful, petite blonde who was sitting there. She appeared to be quite haggard, as if she had spent the better part of the night worrying about someone. But whom? he wondered. Her husband, who should be dead by now but wasn't? Or her lover, who had unsuccessfully tried to kill her mate?

It was this thought that spurred Jean-Claude into action. He knew he could not stay around the carriage, or the village, any longer. The strangers might notice him if he did. And he would not want them to begin asking *him* questions. No, he couldn't stay here. He had to go back to Philippe's and warn Charlotte and Monsieur Fox that they were in grave danger of being discovered.

Jeremiah reached out for the body that had kept him warm throughout the night. When all he could find was an empty space, he opened his eyes and blinked in confusion. Where in heaven's name had Charlotte gone to?

He sat upright on the floor and felt a dull throbbing in the back of his head. His fingers

combed through the matted hair at his nape and
encountered the noticeable lump that was there.
With a grimace, he knew that Boland's accomplice had come damn close to taking off his head
with that piece of wood she'd been wielding. He
just thanked the Almighty that she hadn't succeeded.

Getting slowly to his feet, Jeremiah looked
around the room for his clothes. They would
probably be a mess, but he had to wear something. When he could find no sign of them or
Charlotte, he felt his irritation begin to mount.
Surely she hadn't left him here alone, and
naked!

A sound from outside the house drew him to
the kitchen door. He opened it and peered outside, relieved to see Charlotte. With a soft chuckle, he leaned against the doorjamb, finding
pleasure in just watching her.

Charlotte was garbed in a colorful skirt that
was far too short for her considerable height,
and Jeremiah noted the trim ankles that were
exposed below the ruffled hem of her skirt. The
peasant blouse that she wore hugged her full
breasts, leaving her shoulders and arms bare.
Her hair, shining like highly polished mahogany
in the morning sunlight, cascaded in waves and
curls down to the middle of her back. To him she
looked like a lusty French farm girl with her
skirts pulled up to cradle the weighty bounty
that she carried within her apron.

Fat brown hens picked and scratched in the
dirt as Charlotte wove her way between them.
She paused for a moment beneath a blooming

fruit tree and reached up to touch one of the beautiful, pale pink blossoms that covered a lower limb.

If only I were a painter, Jeremiah thought, feeling a surge of heat course through his veins. *I would capture her as she is at this moment on canvas.* But he wasn't a painter. In fact, he couldn't even draw.

"Good morning!" he called out to her.

Charlotte's head jerked around, and he watched as the smile on her face widened. *"Bonjour!"*

"What have you got there in your skirt?" he asked as she started to move toward him.

"Our breakfast." She stopped in front of him and opened her colorful skirt wide enough for him to peer down into its pocketlike depths.

There his gaze encountered the multitude of brown-speckled eggs she'd gathered. Then, slowly, his eyes ascended upward, over her full breasts and wide expanse of creamy chest. "Looks good!"

"I thought so." She smiled and brushed past him into the kitchen. "Unfortunately, we don't have any bacon or butter, so fried eggs are out of the question. But would boiled eggs do for your breakfast?"

He assured her that they would and watched as she started a fire in the blackened stove. "Where's Jean-Claude?"

"Oh, he left for Paris about an hour ago," she explained, dropping the eggs one by one into a pan filled with water. She placed the pan on the stove and added, "He's really kind of nice, you know, when he isn't behaving so outrageously."

"He's a Frenchman, Charlotte. They're all decent, when they aren't trying to seduce a woman."

"Yes, I know."

"Where did you find those clothes?"

"Upstairs in one of the bedrooms. Oh, I found some things for you to wear, too. They might not fit very well, but they'll do until we can get your things cleaned."

"Did you happen to find a razor upstairs as well?" His fingers scratched at the overnight growth of stubble on his chin.

"No, I didn't think to look for one."

"Well, don't worry about it. I'll survive. Where are those clothes you found for me?"

"I laid them out on the end of the bed. There's an armoire full of things if you don't like what I picked out for you."

Leaving her bustling about in the warm room, he ventured out into the house. And when he returned some time later, he was dressed in the clothes she'd chosen. Dark trousers hugged his lean flanks, while a white, full-sleeved shirt bloused loosely over his muscular shoulders and arms.

As Charlotte found plates and bowls in the cupboard for them, Jeremiah busied himself by removing the mattress and bedding from the kitchen floor.

"How do you feel this morning?" she asked, placing the plates and the bowl of steaming eggs on the table.

"Much better than I did last night," he admitted. "Of course, I've got a nasty lump on my head."

"You do?" Frowning, she started toward him. "Let me have a look at it."

Jeremiah rested a hip against the edge of the table to lessen the difference in their height. She stood between his parted legs and began to examine the wound on his skull. His face was nestled against her full bosom, his nose halfway buried in her cleavage, and he felt his senses inflame as he inhaled her heady scent. His hands reached out instinctively and came to rest on her rounded hips.

It took Charlotte a moment to realize what he was doing, but she did nothing to fight him off. She couldn't. She was held in breathless anticipation of what he would do next.

Sliding his hands up her ribs, Jeremiah moved his face closer to her fragrant skin. With her weighty breasts cupped in his palms, he nudged them upward, nearly freeing them from the blouse so that his parted lips could nibble her flesh more effectively.

"Jeremiah," she sighed softly. "What are you doing?"

"Having breakfast," came his amused reply.

Charlotte pulled away and looked down at him, her hands leaving his shoulders to mold his face. "I'm not on the menu, Mr. Fox."

"You ought to be," he grinned boyishly. "You certainly look good enough to eat."

Her head cocked to a saucy angle. "You aren't by any chance part French, are you?"

"Nope. I'm just a man. While you," he declared, his gaze dropping to the swell of her bosom, "you are definitely all woman."

The kitchen door crashed open at that moment, and Jean-Claude came rushing in, gasping for air. By the looks of him, he'd been running very hard for quite a while. Charlotte hurried over to him, and he willingly allowed himself to lean on her.

"What's happened?" Jeremiah demanded.

"They're . . . looking for you," the young Frenchman gasped. "In the village . . . not far from here."

"How did they—" Charlotte began, but Jeremiah interrupted.

"Who was it? What did they look like?"

"Tall . . . slanted eyes . . . just like you said."

"Damn it!" Jeremiah swore savagely. "We've got to get away from here." The kitchen became a small, confining cage as he suddenly began to pace back and forth.

"But how are we going to leave?" Charlotte asked. "If they're watching the roads—"

"The river," Jeremiah countered. "How else?"

"No boat." Both Charlotte and Jeremiah turned to stare at Jean-Claude. "You do not have a boat," he repeated.

"Then we'll use horses," Jeremiah countered. "You do have horses here, don't you?"

Jean-Claude shook his head slowly from side to side. "Your only way out," he panted, "is Philippe's balloon."

"What?" Charlotte and Jeremiah demanded in unison.

The young Frenchman pulled away from Charlotte and stumbled toward the door. "Follow me. I know how to inflate it."

"What's this about a balloon?" Jeremiah barked to Charlotte as they raced out of the kitchen and across the yard.

"His friend Philippe flies a balloon," she explained. "They were up in it just a day or two ago."

Chickens rushed out of the barn, loudly squawking their annoyance, as Jean-Claude flung open the doors. Entering the darkened interior, Jeremiah could barely make out the large wicker basket that rested in the center of the dirt-packed floor.

"Help me with this," Jean-Claude ordered, pulling at an enormous bundle of multicolored silk that rested near a bale of hay.

Following the young man's lead, Jeremiah helped him pull the cumbersome bundle out into the yard and stretch it out before firmly anchoring the huge wicker basket to it at one end. But the longer they spent inflating the monstrous contraption, the more certain Jeremiah was that he would be discovered. It was madness, sheer insanity, to think that he and Charlotte could leave the farm undetected in this thing.

The red, white, and blue striped balloon slowly filled out, growing and expanding until it could no longer remain on the ground. Like an enormous awakening giant, it rose high into the air as the silk fabric grew rounder in shape.

While Jean-Claude and Jeremiah were busy tending to the balloon outside, Charlotte had returned to the kitchen and was gathering up all of their belongings. She found a small hamper and tossed as much food as she could find into it, knowing that she could leave no trace of their presence behind. Never once as she went about her chore did it occur to her to question whether Jean-Claude's presumption was accurate or not.

But it did occur to Jeremiah. As soon as Charlotte had disappeared into the house, he paused to ask Jean-Claude, "Are you sure those people were looking for me?"

"*Oui!* They described you."

"That's still no guarantee that they were Boland's men."

"Boland?" Jean-Claude frowned. Then his expression cleared. "Ah, the old man at Charlotte's hotel! No, he was not there. But your wife was . . . *Monsieur Steadman.*"

At the mention of the name, an all-consuming dread flooded Jeremiah's soul, causing his heart to sink to the level of his feet. Dear God, Boland's henchmen *did* have Judith.

He started to insist that Jean-Claude tell him everything he had learned, but he was unable to do so. Charlotte came rushing out of the back door at that moment with their basket of food and their clothes, cutting off any inquiry Jeremiah might have made.

"You must remember that this will make the balloon go higher," explained Jean-Claude, pulling on one of the ropes that increased the kerosene flame. "And this one opens the hole in the top to release the gases, making you descend." His hand touched the other rope but did not pull it.

Jeremiah looked at the two lines suspended above the basket, his mind taking in only half of what Jean-Claude was telling him. He could not

stop thinking about Judith or his fear that
Boland had captured her.

"Are you ready?" Charlotte asked, tossing
their supplies into the basket.

"No," Jeremiah responded uncertainly, "but
let's go anyway."

Jean-Claude wrapped an arm about Charlotte's waist and assisted her into the basket.
Once inside, she found herself standing among
squatty, half-filled burlap bags. She bent over to
toss some of them out, so that she and Jeremiah
would have more room, but discovered to her
amazement that they were quite heavy.

"*Non!* Do not toss those out!" Jean-Claude
barked. "They are filled with sand to weigh
down the gondola, *cherie*. You are not to toss
them out until just before you are ready to
ascend. And when you land you must remember
to place rocks in the bottom of the gondola. If
you do not, the balloon will go flying off without
you!" He quickly turned his attention to Jeremiah and added, "Now, you must tie me up before
you leave."

"Tie you up?" Jeremiah asked, confusion
wrinkling his brow.

"*Oui.* If the man who is looking for you should
come here, he must be made to think that you
have overpowered me and stolen the balloon."

Jean-Claude had already turned and was
heading inside the barn. Having no other choice,
Jeremiah followed.

Charlotte watched the two of them disappear
into the barn. A scant second later, she heard
the ominous sound of knuckles cracking against
bone. When Jeremiah reappeared, flexing the

fingers on his right hand, he sprinted toward the gondola and hopped in beside Charlotte. Then both began tossing out the bags of sand.

"What was that noise I heard?" she asked as the balloon began slowly to leave the earth.

"What noise?" Jeremiah asked, his attention fixed on the kerosene flames just above his head.

"Right after you and Jean-Claude went into the barn, I heard something."

"Oh that." Jeremiah shook his head. "I knocked him out."

"You what?"

"Well, there wasn't a rope handy to tie him up with, so I hit him." He glanced at Charlotte, noting her stunned expression, and added, "I did have to make it look convincing, didn't I?"

Chapter Six

CHARLOTTE PEERED OVER THE EDGE OF THE high-sided gondola and down at the beauty of the land below her. In the distance she could see the faint outline of Paris. They had passed over it just minutes ago, and already it was disappearing into the hazy morning light.

"This is marvelous!" she proclaimed, thoroughly captivated by the elation of flying. She could understand now the fascination Jean-Claude had found in the sport. "You can see everything for miles! There are rivers below us that look like little crooked blue ribbons, and the villages look like tiny dolls' houses set in patches of brown and green. Oh Jeremiah, it's the most fantastic thing I've ever seen!"

"Shut up, will you? I don't want to hear about it!"

She turned and looked down at where he sat

huddled on the floor of the gondola. He was wrapped in one of her petticoats and the skirt she'd been wearing the night before. "You're behaving quite ridiculously, you know."

"No I'm not. I just don't want to hang out over the side like you are to see what everything looks like."

"I wasn't hanging out over the side," she argued. With the top of the basket coming to the center of her chest, how could she? "You really should come take a look. There's nothing at all to be afraid of."

The hell there wasn't, he thought, and huddled deeper into her petticoats. "Look, if you don't move away, you're going to fall out."

Charlotte shook her head impatiently and emitted a sigh. "I'm surprised at you, Jeremiah. Really I am!"

In truth, he was a little surprised himself. He'd spent the better part of his youth climbing trees and jumping off the roof of his barn back in Virginia, but those heights had been minuscule compared to this! Only now, at the age of thirty-five, did he realize he was afraid of heights.

"I wonder how much longer we're going to have to stay up in this thing?" he grumbled after a lengthy pause.

"We've only been up for an hour or so," she remarked. "You should have seen Paris when we passed over it."

Passed over Paris! Jeremiah shuddered at the thought and knew that if there was such a thing as reincarnation, he'd more than likely been a mole in his previous life, while Charlotte had obviously been a bird.

Charlotte, witnessing Jeremiah's reaction, clicked her tongue and turned to stare down at the scenery again. It was so quiet up here that there was hardly any sound at all. Only the wind, whistling through the tiny holes in the basket and humming past the taut ropes that attached the gondola to the balloon, broke the blissful serenity. The sky about them was the shade of azure blue, accented intermittently with a fleecy white cloud or two. But to the south—at least Charlotte assumed it was the south—a darkening mass was forming on the horizon.

"It looks like there might be rain up ahead," she murmured almost to herself.

"That does it!" Jeremiah suddenly threw aside the petticoats. "We're going down now!"

As he got unsteadily to his knees, the gondola began to sway with his movement. Fearing for his safety, he grabbed the first solid thing that his hands encountered—Charlotte, as it happened.

"I don't think this is really the time or the place for a seduction, Jeremiah," she professed with forced patience, her gaze dropping to the hands that were grasping her.

"My God, woman!" he croaked. "I'm not trying to seduce you!"

"Then would you mind removing your hands from my breasts? You're about to pull off my blouse."

"*Do* something, for God's sake!" he cried, falling back to the floor. His skin had paled considerably, and his teeth were chattering. "Pull that rope and get us down from here!"

"But we haven't been up long enough," she argued, adjusting her white blouse back over her nearly exposed bosom. "In a few more minutes we can—"

"No! Not in a few minutes. I said now, and I meant now!"

"Jeremiah!" She turned to look down at him, her patience with him slowly coming to an end.

"If you don't pull that damn rope, Charlotte, I will!"

She looked at him for a moment, then smiled. "Go ahead. There it is." She gestured to the end of the descent rope, dangling near her head. "Go ahead and pull it."

Once again, Jeremiah tried to stand. And once again, the gondola swayed sickeningly beneath him. His already pale skin took on a grayish tinge as he looked up at her pleadingly. "Charlotte, pull the rope."

"You are without a doubt the biggest baby I have ever met," she snapped, disgusted with his cowardice. But her hand lifted to the end of the rope. "All right, blast you, we'll go down!" And with an angry jerk, she pulled the line as hard as she could.

In a matter of seconds, all fifty feet of the rope fell to the floor between them. Charlotte looked down at it. Jeremiah looked at it. Then, in unison, their faces turned upward, and they saw the great hole that now gaped in the top of the balloon.

"Why the hell did you do that?" he yelled, his stomach churning as he began to feel their rapid descent.

"You told me to pull the rope, didn't you?"

"I didn't mean for you to pull it all the way out! Dear God, we're going to crash now!"

The gases that had kept them afloat were escaping through the hole. The balloon, once fat and full, was beginning to shrink in size.

Charlotte wasn't frightened—not at first. But the farther they fell, the greater her anxiety became, until she was almost as hysterical as Jeremiah. "I don't want to die like this!" she whimpered, her body crumpling to the floor as her hands clung to the sides of the gondola.

"Just shut up!" Jeremiah barked, getting to his feet. "You'd better start praying that we get out of this alive, lady, because if we don't, I just may kill you!"

It seemed to Charlotte that an eternity passed within a matter of moments. Her ears were popping as the gondola fell further and further and the balloon grew thinner and thinner.

Through his panic, an idea suddenly came to Jeremiah. He bent over and ordered, "Start throwing out some of this stuff."

"What for?"

"It's weighing us down. If we can empty out the gondola, we might be able to stay afloat a little longer."

"But you *wanted* to go down," she argued.

"Not this fast, I didn't! Now help me!"

Their hamper of untouched stale bread and boiled eggs was the first item to be tossed overboard. It was soon followed by their bundles of clothing and the few remaining sandbags that had been tied to the inside of the gondola. When there was nothing left to toss out, Jeremiah cautiously peered over the side and spied a grove of trees ahead of them. Then he looked back at Charlotte.

Misinterpreting the expression on his face, her eyes grew wide with fear. "No! You're not going to throw *me* out!"

If the truth were known, Jeremiah hadn't even thought about such a thing . . . not until she had mentioned it. But she didn't have to know that. "You're the cause of this," he grated. "Why shouldn't I?"

"Because I pulled you out of that river and—and then I got you away from those counterfeiters, didn't I? Doesn't that count for something?"

Another look over the side assured him that they were going to hit the trees in a matter of minutes. If they were lucky, the limbs might cushion their fall. But if they weren't . . . if they skimmed over the treetops and hit the clearing beyond. . . . "Get ready to jump!" he ordered suddenly.

"No!" she shrieked. "Jeremiah, it'll be murder!"

He ignored her hysterical protest and moved toward her. Gathering her up in his arms, he told himself that he was doing this for her own good . . . and his! They had a much better chance surviving a ten-foot fall than they did a hard crash.

He was wrestling with her, trying to ignore her screams, when the gondola struck the first tree. The sudden impact caused him to lose his footing, and they both fell to the floor in an ungainly heap. Before either of them had a chance to adjust to what had just happened, the second, shorter tree caught the bottom of the basket and turned it over, dumping them out into space.

Loud thunder rumbled across the sky. But Jeremiah, just coming out of his dazed stupor, was more aware of the dry, cackling laughter that was coming from nearby than he was of the threat of rain. Opening his eyes, he frowned in confusion at his surroundings. A faded tartan plaid shawl was suspended above him instead of the blue sky or green tree limbs he'd expected.

Tartan plaid? he wondered. Had he died and gone to the Scottish section of heaven?

Hearing the cackling laughter once again, he slowly lifted his head off the lumpy mass that had been his pillow. He would have sat upright, but a sharp pain in his side caused him to lower his head back again, and he grabbed for his aching ribs.

"Charlotte!" he cried out, and heard his voice bounce off the walls about him. "Charlotte!"

The door at the end of the tiny room opened a scant second later, and Jeremiah winced as the bright sunlight flooded the darkened interior. Through his narrowed lids, he noticed Charlotte's familiar outline in the doorway.

"Oh good, you're awake," she announced, coming inside and closing the door behind her. "I was beginning to wonder if you'd ever come to."

"Where the hell are we?" he demanded.

"Well, right now we're in a gypsy vardo."

"A what?"

"A vardo. A caravan," she repeated, sitting

down beside him. "You know, one of those cute little houses on wheels that gypsies live in? It's quite colorful on the outside but not half as colorful as the gypsies themselves."

"Gypsies," Jeremiah repeated, wondering if he'd heard her correctly.

"Yes, Jeremiah, gypsies. You know, those strange people who go around telling fortunes and stealing things."

"I know what gypsies are," he grumbled. "But what are we doing here?"

"Well, they helped me bring you in here after we fell out of the balloon. Of course, it took all three of us to carry you. There's no one else here now but the two of them and us. Poor old Zonya had a devil of a time with her end, but—"

"What happened to the balloon, Charlotte?" he interrupted impatiently.

"Oh, I gave it to Zonya," she confessed.

"Zonya?"

"Yes, the old lady. I would have given her the gondola as well, but there wasn't much left of it after we put out the fire. You know, there was still a lot of kerosene left in that burner. We could have gone on for miles. But it's a darn good thing we fell out of it when we did; otherwise we might have burned up with it."

"'You gave some old woman our balloon?" he persisted doggedly.

"Well, I didn't see any harm in it. Zonya thought the silk could be used for something— what, I don't know—and we certainly won't be needing it now."

Jeremiah groaned and rubbed his aching head. It was probably the pain that was causing him to misunderstand her garbled explanation. Yes, that had to be it. Surely she wouldn't have given away their only means of transportation.

"Here, you look like you could use some of this," she said, holding a cup to his lips. "It'll make you feel better."

Jeremiah lifted his head and stared down into the chipped cup's contents. Beneath the oily surface, he could see chunks of white and green things floating about in the cloudy liquid. "What the hell is it?" he grimaced.

"Chicken broth." Charlotte pushed the cup closer to his mouth. "Francesca told me that Sandor stole the bird just last night, so it's still quite fresh."

"It looks lethal."

"Well, it's not. I had a cup myself just a moment ago, and it's quite good. Come on, take a sip. It won't kill you."

Against his better judgment, Jeremiah sipped it tentatively. The mild, herbed broth flowed smoothly down his throat, and he discovered that it was quite pleasing to his palate.

When the cup was empty, he lay back on the lumpy pillow and groaned as his ribs throbbed again. Shifting slightly to peer down the length of his bare chest, he noticed the strips of dingy white cloth that were wrapped about his waist. "What's this?"

"Oh, Zonya thought you might have broken a rib or two, so she bandaged them for you."

A deeply inhaled breath of air told Jeremiah what he wanted to know. "They may be bruised," he remarked, "but they're not broken."

"Do they hurt?" she asked with concern.

"Yes, but I can live with it. The sooner we leave here, the better off we'll be."

"Oh." Charlotte frowned and slumped dejectedly. "I thought we could stay a while. Zonya said she would tell me my fortune later."

"For heaven's sake, Charlotte. You don't honestly believe in all that mumbo-jumbo, do you? It's nothing but a pack of lies."

"I'm not so sure," she disagreed. "You didn't see the look on Francesca's face when she told me that Zonya had predicted our coming here, right down to us falling out of the sky and everything! Believe me, she wasn't half as surprised as I was. She's a witch, you know."

"Who?"

"Zonya. And you can disbelieve it if you like, but I've lived in Louisiana, and I know there are people there who can see into the future. Why, there was this old man who lived outside of Baton Rouge who could—"

"I don't want to hear it," he grumbled, pushing her out of his way so that he could sit up on the side of the bed. "You can stay here and listen to all their nonsense and lies if you want, but I'm leaving."

"Just how far do you think you'll get with those ribs?" she challenged.

"You let me worry about that." His gaze darted about the room. "Where's my shirt?"

"It's around your waist. Zonya tore it into strips for you."

"Zonya, huh? Well, I can't very well leave here half-naked. Look through that pile of stuff there beside you and see if you can't find a shirt big enough to fit me."

"Jeremiah, we can't steal their clothes!"

"Why not? You gave them our balloon. The way I look at it, it'd be an even trade."

The retort Charlotte might have made was interrupted by the rattle and squeak of door hinges. A gust of wind preceded the young girl who entered. Being a gentleman, even when in pain, Jeremiah tried to stand, but his head struck the vardo's low ceiling, and he fell back down to the bed with a grunt. One hand holding his throbbing scalp, the other gripping his aching ribs, he stared past Charlotte at their visitor.

Raven-black hair cascaded down over her slim shoulders, ending in a mass of curls at the girl's pinched-in waist. Eyes the color of dark cinnamon surrounded by heavy black lashes ensnared his gaze. He decided that she couldn't be any older than fourteen or fifteen, but she was one of the prettiest creatures he'd ever seen.

"You must be Francesca," he heard himself say as a smile tugged at his lips.

Glancing first at Francesca and then at Jeremiah, Charlotte knew in an instant that he had been captivated by the girl's exotic beauty. A nagging pang of jealousy began to uncurl within her, and she forced herself to repress it. If they were going to get away from here, they would need the girl's help. But Jeremiah didn't have to know that . . . yet.

"Francesca," Charlotte began, her voice a bit sharper than she had intended it to be. "This is Mr. Fox."

"You called him by another name." The girl's eyes remained fixed on Jeremiah while her remark was directed at Charlotte.

"You may call me Jeremiah," he smiled warmly.

"Yes, do, dear," Charlotte agreed tersely. "Even though it *is* unseemly for a child of your tender years to do so."

The girl blushed and lowered her gaze, not catching the questioning look that Jeremiah threw Charlotte. "Your woman said that you are American," Francesca remarked softly.

"My woman?" Jeremiah raised an eyebrow questioningly. "Oh, yes! Yes, my woman is right. In fact, we both are Americans."

"Good!" Francesca nodded, obviously pleased. "You will take me with you, no?"

"No!" Jeremiah jerked his head around to see Charlotte, motioning to the girl to be quiet. "What the hell? You didn't tell her she could go with us, did you?"

"Well. . . ."

"Charlotte!"

"Now, don't get upset, Jeremiah."

"My Lord, have you lost your mind? She can't go with us!"

"Why not?" Charlotte countered. "She knows the countryside much better than we do."

"Maybe she does, but that's still no reason for us to. . . . No! No, she has got to stay here with her people."

"The gypsies are not my people," Francesca informed them. "I have lived with them all my life, but I am still treated like an outsider."

99

"You see?" Charlotte nodded her head, obviously siding with the girl. "She has to come with us, Jeremiah. If we help her, she'll help us."

"I don't care," he proclaimed with a shake of his blond head. "She's not coming."

"But they stole her when she was a baby!" Charlotte argued.

"Not me," Francesca remarked. "My mother. And Mama was a young girl when they took her."

"I don't care how old your mother was!" Jeremiah was rapidly losing what little patience he had. "You still can't come with us, Francesca."

"She has to!" Charlotte countered. "I promised her that we'd take her with us when we left."

"Charlotte, will you please shut up and listen to reason? She has got to stay here!"

"Then you will not get the horses." Francesca's sudden declaration was stated with firm resolve. "Or the food, or the wagon."

"How far do you think we would make it on foot?" Charlotte challenged. "You're hurt, Jeremiah. And those ribs of yours will never heal if you don't take care of yourself."

There was some logic to Charlotte's argument, but Jeremiah didn't want to admit it. "Don't worry about me. I can make it."

"Of course you can," she jeered. "In a week, or a month. But what will Monsieur Boland and his cohorts be doing in that time? Sitting back and twiddling their thumbs? I think not. If you'll just let Francesca help us, we can make it to Cannes before next week."

"Cannes!" he snapped, growing more confused by the minute.

"Yes, Cannes! That's where Monsieur Boland is going!"

"How do you know?"

Charlotte inhaled an impatient breath. "Yesterday, when we were at the museum, I overheard Monsieur Boland talking to that woman who attacked you. She told him to be in Cannes no later than next week. Jeremiah," she paused, wanting to be sure that she had his complete attention, "Cannes is in Provence. We can leave Francesca with my great-aunt Marie in Grasse and be in Cannes at the same time, or before Monsieur Boland even gets there."

"You've known about this all along, haven't you? Why in God's name didn't you tell me this before?" he demanded, his nostrils flaring angrily.

"What good would it have done?" she countered. "After Jean-Claude and I fished you out of the Seine, you were in no condition to go chasing after Monsieur Boland and his bunch. And we were in such a big hurry to get away this morning that I forgot all about it."

"You forgot!" he growled, his lips twisting into a snarl. "You forgot! Is there anything else you forgot? Like where the hell Boland's going to be when he does get to Cannes?"

"Well, Cannes can't be that big. I mean, it shouldn't be too hard for us to hunt him down."

"Us, hell! I'll find him myself. You can stay with your aunt and Francesca."

Charlotte was suddenly all smiles. "Then you'll let her go with us?"

101

"I don't have much choice, do I?" he relented ungraciously.

Before he could prepare himself, both Charlotte and the gypsy girl pounced on him, showering him with kisses.

"You won't regret this," Charlotte promised as she released her hold on him. "I swear you won't."

"I don't know," Jeremiah grumbled, maintaining an arm about her waist. He was already beginning to have doubts.

"You'd better go tell your grandmother to get ready," Charlotte told Francesca, who was halfway out the door.

"You mean the old lady's coming too?"

"Of course," Charlotte retorted. "We can't just leave her here all by herself. And you never know, Jeremiah, we just might need a good witch."

Chapter Seven

Jeremiah held the reins loosely in his hands as he guided the horses and the vardo around the curve in the road. His mind was not on where he was going, however. It was on something else, *anything* to block out the sound of Zonya's voice. For the last five miles or so, since they'd passed through the last little French farming village, she'd been singing the same song over and over again.

"Do you think she'll ever shut up that cater-wauling?" he complained to Charlotte, who sat beside him. "I've been listening to her for the past two days, and she's beginning to get on my nerves."

"I'll get Francesca to make you some tea when we make camp for the night," Charlotte consoled him gently.

"It's not tea that I need. It's a little peace and

quiet. Lord, Charlotte, I've heard cats in heat make better noise than that."

"Well, Francesca said that Zonya likes to sing while she sews."

He mumbled something fertile and profane beneath his breath, never once taking his eyes off the road ahead. They were slowly climbing into the mountains, past narrow, uncultivated fields where wildflowers blossomed in profusion. Had he been more observant, he would have noticed how beautiful the countryside was, but he was too busy trying to figure out how he had allowed Charlotte to get him into this mess. What had started out as a simple, uncomplicated, one-man operation had somehow turned into a three-ring circus. A very *loud* three-ring circus, he amended as Zonya's voice rose another high, ear-splitting octave.

"It's so lovely here." Charlotte's soft observation drew his disbelieving gaze to her. "I've never seen anyplace quite like it before. All these mountains. All these trees. There's nothing like this back home in Texas."

"I thought you said you were from Louisiana."

"Oh, I live there now because that's where I teach school, but I was born and raised in Texas. And believe me, there has never been this much greenery in Waxahachie even in the spring."

"Waxa*what*ie?"

"Waxahachie." Charlotte's laugh was a silvery little trill that did strange things to Jeremiah's pulse rate. "It's an Indian name."

"Yeah, I figured that much. What does it mean?"

"I haven't the faintest idea. It probably translates into something like flat and fertile, because that's what it is for the most part." There was a brief pause. She turned to look at him, her head cocked at a thoughtful angle. "Where are you from? I don't believe you've ever said."

"Virginia. Dinwiddie County."

"Is that near Washington?"

"No, Richmond."

Charlotte nodded and waited for him to explain further. But when he didn't and a long stretch of silence ensued, she began to wonder if he was being close-mouthed because he didn't want her to know anything more about him, or if he just didn't want to talk. Whatever his reasons were, her curiosity was definitely aroused.

"Must have been nice there," she prompted, hoping he would add to his story.

"Mmm," was all he would reply.

"What did you do?"

"Oh, the usual things boys do."

"Do you have any brothers or sisters?"

"Yeah. One of each."

"I have two sisters. They're both older than me."

"I know. You told me."

"Did I?" This conversation wasn't telling her a thing, she thought with a heavy sigh. She knew practically nothing about him, and yet she had put her life into his hands. "How did a boy from Dinwiddie County become an agent for the United States Treasury?"

"Why do you want to know?" he countered evenly.

"Oh, no reason really. I just wondered."

"You're being awfully nosy."

"No I'm not!"

"What would you call it then?"

"Curiosity! I mean, here we are, virtually strangers. We've gone through quite a lot together since we first met five days ago, and yet we don't know a thing about each other."

"Nothing wrong with that," he drawled.

Charlotte was growing more frustrated than ever with his evasiveness. "Have you got something to hide?" she demanded suspiciously.

"No!"

"Then why won't you talk about yourself? I mean, we can't just talk about the scenery, can we?"

"Don't see why not. It's as good a subject to discuss as any."

"Jeremiah," she groaned. "If you don't want me to know about your tragic childhood, then just say so and I'll shut up."

"My childhood wasn't tragic."

"Then where's the harm in talking about it?"

"I just did!"

"You are the most infuriating—" She broke off and shook her head with an audible moan. "Oh never mind. Just forget it. How long before we can make camp?"

"I don't know." He turned his head upward, judging the time of day by the angle of the sun. "About an hour or two, I guess."

"Good," she grumbled, and stared at the road ahead of them.

Jeremiah had to repress the smile that tugged at his lips. He knew she was angry. Out of the corner of his eye, he could see her prim erectness and the sullen, almost grim set of her lovely mouth. With her dark, mahogany-colored hair hanging loose about her creamy shoulders, she looked much younger than the twenty-seven years he knew her to be. There was a somewhat childish look about her outthrust lower lip, and he longed to cover it with his own and kiss away her anger. But in her current mood she just might decide to slap him.

"My father was a farmer until the War Between the States broke out," he stated quietly. Charlotte's head turned toward him slowly, her eyes widening with surprise. "He decided he was better suited to being a legislator than tending the soil, so he moved us all to Richmond. That's where I went to school. My brother James didn't like living in the city very much, so he went back to the farm when he was old enough to leave home. My sister and I were different, though. We liked Richmond. Still do, for that matter.

"About twelve years ago, when she was seventeen, she married a young man in the diplomatic service. He's the one who got me involved with the Secret Service. I'd been out of school a few years and was practicing law with a firm in Richmond, but I didn't like my job very much. When my brother-in-law told me that the Service had an opening for new agents, I applied for one of the positions and got it.

"Washington's nothing at all like Richmond," he admitted with a chuckle. "You wouldn't believe all the wheeling and dealing that goes on among the congressmen, senators, and lobbyists. They make these counterfeiters I'm hunting look like a bunch of Sunday-school boys. But it's exciting, and I like it. Anything else you want to know?"

Charlotte's mouth, which had been hanging open during his monologue, snapped shut, and she shook her head. "No, I—I guess not." She was so surprised by his short tale that she couldn't think of anything to ask him.

"See there? Not very interesting, was it?"

"Good heavens, Jeremiah, how can you say that? You've done more and seen more than I ever have, and—"

"Well, you're a woman!" he declared.

"What has that got to do with it?"

"Oh, you know. Women are better suited to taking care of their families and teaching school than they are to wheeling and dealing."

"And chasing counterfeiters?" she added with a tenacious gleam in her eye.

"Now that was an accident. I hadn't planned on having you interfere."

"Interfere! Jeremiah Fox, I resent that! If it weren't for me, you wouldn't be where you are right now, and you know it!"

"You can say that again," he grumbled, hearing Zonya's voice once again reach that nerve-grating pitch.

"You'd probably be at the bottom of the Seine, or—or someplace far worse! And as for women only being suited to taking care of families and teaching school, well that's a lot of nonsense too! We've been fighting beside our men for centuries. Why, my own grandmother on my father's side helped fight the British during the Revolution, and she was pregnant at the time."

"How many Redcoats did she kill?"

His sudden question took a bit of the wind out of her sails. "I'm not really sure," she admitted, her shoulders slumping. "She never would say."

"Have you ever had to shoot a man?"

"No. I've never had a reason to, but—"

"Well, just be thankful that you haven't. It's not a very pleasant experience."

"You've shot a man?"

"Once," he admitted. "I didn't kill him, though, thank God. I just wounded him." The truth of the matter was that he'd caused the man to lose his arm and the man had died from infection a few weeks later, but Charlotte didn't have to know that. "I didn't like it," he continued softly. "Not one bit."

There was a moment of silence before Charlotte quietly asked, "Do you think you might have to shoot Monsieur Boland or his cohorts?"

"If it's necessary, I will. It's part of my job, Charlotte. I have to stop them any way I can. And if that means shooting and killing them—" His voice trailed off.

But he didn't have to say more. Charlotte's imagination finished his unspoken thought.

The sun was slowly setting when they made camp a few hours later. Zonya and Francesca busied themselves with preparing the evening meal, while Charlotte searched through the grove of trees nearby for the branches they would need to make their campfire. Jeremiah unharnessed the two horses and led them down to the creek, where they drank their fill of water.

Then he tethered them to a tree limb before fixing their feed bags about their enormous heads. It was a chore he was familiar with.

Supper that night consisted of a stale loaf of bread, a wedge of tangy cheese, and a pot of strange-smelling tea that Jeremiah was instantly suspicious of. With Zonya staring at him from across the fire, he half expected her to lay a curse on him if he didn't at least attempt to drink some of it. He took a tentative sip from his cup and nearly choked on its bitter taste, but he masked his grimace with a weak smile and nodded at the old lady. Her wrinkled lips parted in a toothless smile before her gums tore off a portion of the stale bread she held.

"I wonder what's in this stuff," he murmured quietly to Charlotte, who sat beside him.

"Herbs, I would imagine," she commented between bites.

"Herbs? It tastes more like bile to me."

Charlotte tossed him a look and shrugged. "Well, Francesca said there was a village nearby. Maybe we can buy some food and real tea there in the morning."

"How far away is it?"

"The village? Oh, I don't know. Why?"

"Bread and cheese might be all right for you women, but I've got to have something a little more substantial to eat." He rose to his feet and dusted off the seat of his britches.

"Are you going there now?" Her head was tilted back, and she stared up at him, her slender throat gleaming like a column of pale ivory in the firelight.

"Don't worry. I won't be gone very long," he promised, and turned to walk away.

Charlotte started to call after him as he disappeared into the darkness of the surrounding trees. But she didn't. Instead, she turned and looked back at the glowing embers of the fire. He probably wanted some time to himself, she decided, taking a small bite of her cheese. Not that she blamed him for that. More than likely, he found it quite exhausting being forced to travel with three women.

In the back of her mind, something began to eat at her conscience. She couldn't put her finger on it at first, but suddenly the thought became crystal clear, and she stiffened. He didn't have any money! He was going into the village to buy food, and all the money they both possessed was in the pouch, securely fastened to her petticoats beneath her skirt.

"Oh Lord!" she exclaimed, jumping to her feet.

Both Francesca and Zonya stared up at her, their confusion at her behavior written on their faces.

"What is the matter?" the girl asked.

"I've got to go after Jeremiah."

Zonya began to cackle. "He does not need you, child, to wipe his . . . nose."

"No, he didn't go away to do *that*. He's gone to . . . oh, never mind! I'll explain later." She turned to leave but stopped and looked back when she realized she didn't know which way to go. "Francesca? How do I get to the village from here?"

The girl's directions were simple enough: just get on the road and follow it over the hill.

Out in the open, away from the campsite, the moon cast an eerie light on the narrow dirt lane. As Charlotte passed by a thick grove of trees, she could hear owls hooting to one another, insects chirping, and little nocturnal animals scurrying through the thick underbrush. Never once, though, during her short journey into town did she think to be afraid. Her mind was too preoccupied with finding Jeremiah and giving him the money to even consider fear.

She reached the outskirts of the small farming village some time later and stopped long enough to retrieve the money. She lifted the hem of her skirt and tucked it into her waistband. Her fingers were working on the drawstrings of the coin-filled pouch, trying to open it, when she heard a loud noise erupt in a building across the street from where she stood.

"Gypsy pig!" someone, a man, growled in guttural French.

"We do not want your kind here!" shouted another.

Then she heard the sound of glass breaking. Then furniture scraped across a wooden floor before it overturned with a thud. She heard a horrible muffled grunt, as if someone had fallen or had been hit very hard, and she was galvanized into action.

The money in her pouch and her skirts forgotten, Charlotte ran toward the building, where a single lantern illuminated the doorway. Some instinct told her that Jeremiah was inside and that he was in trouble. And one look inside the tavern, when she flung open the door, assured her that she had been correct.

Four burly men with arms the size of huge hams were trying to overpower one more slightly built man—Jeremiah! But, to his credit, he was handling himself and the situation quite admirably. By weaving from side to side, he dodged one punch and then another. He rammed his fist into the fleshy midsection of one of his attackers, sending the man across the room onto a rickety table that broke instantly beneath his considerable weight. A backward kick of Jeremiah's foot connected squarely in another opponent's groin. That man doubled over to the floor and howled in pain. But the third and fourth attackers were upon Jeremiah before he had a chance to defend himself.

Knowing that she had to do something before those two men killed Jeremiah, Charlotte rushed into the tavern and grabbed for the first thing she could find—a table leg, as it happened. Wielding it like a baseball bat, she hit one of the men on the side of his head and knocked him out cold. Three down and one to go, she thought, picking up a chair that was still intact. She broke it over the head of Jeremiah's fourth attacker and then groaned in horror when she realized that it had failed to stop him. The man hadn't even been fazed, and he continued to punch and hit Jeremiah's face with all his might.

By this time, the first man had picked himself up off the table he'd broken and had waded back into the melee. He wrapped an arm around Charlotte's waist, picked her up as if she weighed no more than a feather, and flung her to one side.

Disoriented briefly, she looked around in confusion before finally locating the pile of thrashing bodies on the floor nearby.

"Get off him!" she screamed. "He's no gypsy!"

But no one paid the slightest bit of attention to her. They continued to punch and hit Jeremiah beneath them.

Gritting her teeth, Charlotte emitted a growl of frustrated anger and flew across the room, landing on the first broad masculine back in her path. She wove her fingers through the man's long, oily hair and pulled it as hard as she could, successfully dragging back his head. With a loud yelp, he jabbed her with his elbow and dislodged her from his back.

A moment later, she was sprawled on the floor, her skirts raised high over her slender legs. Not in the least deterred, she got up once more and leaped back into the fracas. This time, somehow, a bottle found itself in her hand and she used it. Glass splintered in the man's hair as the coarse red wine ran down his face, clouding his vision. When he moved aside to wipe his eyes, she kicked him and kept on kicking him until he was well away from the other two fighters.

Jeremiah threw a hard punch that connected with his opponent's jaw. The man's head flew back, and in sickening slow motion he fell to the floor, unconscious.

The salty taste of blood registered on Jeremiah's tongue as he squinted through swollen lids to see Charlotte standing over him. Her chest was heaving as she gulped in deep breaths of air. Her hair flew about her flushed face in wild disarray.

"Where the hell did *you* come from?" he demanded.

"Never mind that now," she stated, extending a hand toward him. From the corner of her eye, she saw one of the men begin to stir. "We've got to get out of here before the whole town comes after us."

Jeremiah managed to get to his feet with her help. One quick look around the tavern told him of the havoc he and the four farmers had wrought. They had literally destroyed the place. Not one piece of furniture was intact, and there were shards of glass all over the place.

As they rushed outside into the darkness, he felt anger suddenly well up within him. He was far from feeling thankful for Charlotte's well-timed interference. "Damn it, Charlotte, don't you know how to mind your own business?"

Her mouth dropped open in disbelief. "That's the most ungrateful . . . ! I just saved your mangy hide from those four giants in there, and you have the gall to—"

"I was doing okay on my own before you stepped in!" he bellowed.

"Sure you were!" she shrieked, jogging alongside him. "That's why you've got that split lip and black eye!"

By this time, they had safely reached the outskirts of the village. He stopped dead in his tracks and whirled around to glare down at her. "Look, nobody asked you to butt in."

"That's right. Nobody did. But it's a good thing I came along when I did, or you'd be mincemeat right now." Her chin tilted to a haughty angle. "You can't do anything without getting into trouble, can you? I've been fishing you out of rivers and hiding you from crooks ever since we first met, Jeremiah Fox, and, believe me, I'm getting tired of it!" She turned on her heel and stalked off down the moonlit road.

"So? Mind your own damn business from now on!"

"I will!"

Jeremiah fumed in silence as he followed her. He didn't like women fighting his battles for him. He never had, and he never would.

"The only reason I came after you tonight was because I knew you didn't have any money," he heard her say.

"What?" He increased his speed until he was even with her.

"You heard me. I was only trying to save you some embarrassment, because you gave me all your money earlier, remember? But if this is the kind of thanks I get, I'm just very sorry I didn't let those men beat the bloody hell out of you! It might have done you some good!"

"Wait a minute!" He grabbed her arm and stopped her abruptly. But she still refused to look at him. Her chest was rising and falling with each breath she inhaled. Her lips were compressed into a thin, angry line as her eyes remained fixed on the dark stretch of road ahead of them. "Are you telling me that you didn't follow me tonight to see if I was meeting someone? That you came just to give me the money?"

Her head slowly lifted to face him. "That's

right, you idiot!" she snarled through clenched teeth.

"Oh." His hand loosened its hold on her arm, and she jerked it free. "I—I thought that—that you thought that—"

"Well, you thought wrong!" she growled. "And from now on, Mr. High and Mighty Fox, if you get yourself into a tight spot, you can just get yourself out of it, because I don't ever intend to help you again!"

"That suits me just fine! I don't need a woman helping me anyway!"

"Hah!" And with that she started off again.

"What do you mean, 'hah'?" he demanded, running after her. Didn't she have any idea how emasculating it was, having her rescue him at every turn? "I did all right on my own before I ever met you!"

"Sure you did!"

"Don't use that tone of voice with me, Charlotte Atwater! I'll—I'll—"

"What?" she challenged, stopped and turned to face him. "Turn me over your knee and give me a spanking? I dare you. I just dare you to try it!"

"Don't threaten me, Charlotte," he warned, wagging a finger at her.

There was a noticeable electric charge in the air that stretched tautly between them, but its presence did nothing to stop her from antagonizing him further. "I'll threaten you all I like, Mr. Jeremiah Fox. Why Washington ever thought *you* were suitable for this job, I'll never know. You're the most inept—"

An angry growl formed in his throat as he reached out for her. He hauled her stiff body toward his, and his mouth clamped down over hers, shutting off any further remark she might have made. But the instant his lips touched her softer, more pliant ones, his anger vanished in the blink of an eye and was replaced with something far more primitive, far more urgent. Then, like a furnace being stoked, his lust blazed completely out of control.

Charlotte was so unprepared for what was happening that she found herself unable to protest. The taste of his kiss instantly transformed her anger into uncontrollable desire, and she gave herself over to the emotion willingly. With boneless fluidity, her arms floated upward and wound themselves about his strong shoulders and neck. His hand pressed hard against her back, flattening her breasts against his chest as her fingers combed through and clung to his flaxen locks.

With his lips still welded to hers in fiery passion, he slowly bent over and lifted her into his arms, cradling her like a child. Then, on unsteady legs, he carried her away from the open, hard-packed dirt road to the cushiony verge nearby. Amid the sweetly scented wildflowers there, he released her, and effortlessly, their bodies straining toward each other, they drifted down onto the patch of grass that would be their bed.

Velvety words of longing were whispered as Jeremiah pulled Charlotte's blouse over her head with agonizing slowness. "Beautiful. You're so beautiful, my love," he praised her when his hungry gaze at last feasted on her firm, coral-tipped breasts. He caressed the length of her arms with his fingers, touching them as though they were covered in fragile satin. Her back arched when his hand found the sensitive area of her ribs, but he did not linger there to tickle them. Her full, fleshy breasts beckoned to him in the moonlight, and he felt compelled to hold them cupped in his palms and to press them together while his face nuzzled their sweetly scented valley. When he could no longer restrain his need, he captured first one sleeping crest and then the other. Joy tightened in his loins as he felt her nipples harden into erotic points in his mouth.

An unnameable ache was born in the pit of Charlotte's belly as his tongue continued to excite her. That ache grew and spiraled throughout her body, turning her into a molten mass of desire. Breathing in ragged gasps, she began to tear at his shirt so that she could feel his bare skin next to hers. And when his shirt had been flung aside, the crisp, furry mat on his chest became an unexplored playground as her fingers memorized his beautiful, uncharted terrain. When her questing touch encountered his flat male nipples and she heard the groan of pleasure from deep in his throat, she lifted her head and tasted him, as he had tasted her.

What remained of their clothing became frustrating barriers as their caresses grew bolder. Manipulating Charlotte to his will, Jeremiah removed her skirts and tossed them aside. When he stood at her feet to peel off his trousers, he felt his pulse race faster at the sight of her long, slender legs and the dark nest of femininity curling at the juncture of her thighs. His gaze remained fixed on her pale body as he shoved his pants down over his hips. She was the most beautiful thing he'd ever seen—and he'd seen quite a few naked women in his lifetime.

Charlotte's breath caught in her throat when he knelt between her parted legs. Her eyes were riveted to the engorged part of him that was his manhood. As if it possessed a will of its own, her hand reached out and touched the warm, turgid staff. For something so very hard, it was incredibly smooth, she thought, and not rough at all, but soft like velvet. She caressed its length, feeling its odd-shaped head before letting her fingers follow the rigid outer vein down to the two sacs at the staff's base. And when her hand gently encircled them, she heard his pleasure-filled growl and saw him shudder uncontrollably.

Slowly, erotically, he fell atop her, his hands placed near her shoulders so that their bodies remained separated by a thin layer of air. The delicate tracing of her lips with his tongue made her open her mouth, and when it entered this honey-sweet interior his tongue touched hers with long, measured strokes.

An urgent need to know his body more intimately assailed Charlotte as Jeremiah continued to feast on her lips and throat. Her hands found his strong, muscular back, and as she explored the taut skin there she reveled in all of its curves and indentations. Upon reaching the shallow valley formed by his waist and hips, she splayed her fingers wide before boldly going forth to capture the rounded hardness of his buttocks. It took only a gentle urging to bring him into intimate contact with her. She whimpered with joy when his hot staff came to rest on the throbbing kernel that was hidden within her nest.

"Love me, Jeremiah," she moaned in a broken whisper, her hips arching as her hands pressed him closer. "Please, please love me."

"I do," he groaned into the hollow of her neck. "God help us both, but I do!"

Undulating his hips slightly, his staff rubbed against her nest as he drew it downward to poise its head at the moist opening of her heated core. Levering his chest away from her, he stared down at her and then slowly entered her velvety sheath.

Charlotte gasped, and her eyes widened with surprise when she experienced a brief flash of pain. But when he filled her completely with one quick thrust, that pain was forgotten, and she felt something wondrous and new consume her. Bathed in a golden glow of bright sensation, she found that everything but the feel of him within her was obliterated.

Time became an undefinable dimension as they possessed each other. And it was possession, Jeremiah realized. For she owned him now as much as he owned her. If only for this brief, exquisite moment, they were one, two halves of a single soul finally joined together after a lifetime of being separated.

Desire consumed them entirely. Their hips arched and undulated in a rhythm that was as old as time itself. Their breathing was inhaled and exhaled in unison; their hearts beat in the same measured tempo. And when the climax of their dance bombarded them, their world exploded into a million tiny fragments of ecstasy as each cried out the other's name into the night.

Chapter Eight

JEREMIAH FELT REBORN, AS IF HE WERE ONLY now experiencing life as it was intended to be lived. He rolled slowly off of Charlotte, unaware that his sweat-covered body was glistening like polished marble in the moonlight. His happiness welled up within him and rumbled in his broad chest. But soon the joy could no longer be contained, and it accelerated into a full shout of laughter.

Still drowsy and contented from their love-making, Charlotte was at a loss to understand his amusement. "What's so funny?" she queried in a breathy voice.

"Nothing," he chuckled. "Not a damn thing."

"Then why are you giggling like some demented idiot?" Having had only one other lover —and she would rather forget about him—

Charlotte hadn't expected Jeremiah to behave this way.

"Don't you know, my love? My sweet . . . precious . . . adorable . . . love." Jeremiah punctuated each word with a kiss on her moist face.

"No. I wouldn't have asked if I did." She levered herself away from him and sat up, not caring that her uptilted breasts were exposed to his admiring gaze.

Jeremiah's chuckles dwindled somewhat, but a smile remained etched on his mustache-framed mouth. "You were a virgin, Charlotte."

"That's nonsense!" she scoffed.

"No, it's not. You were a virgin, and I was the lucky son of a gun who received your precious treasure. Old Marvin, bless his ignorant heart, left you intact just for me."

"That's a lie, and his name was Melvin!"

"Marvin, Melvin, who really gives a damn?" Jeremiah laughed again, thoroughly enjoying her discomfort.

"You're crazy. I know I was not a virgin!"

"Charlotte . . . darling." Jeremiah sat up and faced her, his strong hand moving to rest on her bare thigh. His fingers began to inch their way closer to her curly nest, but she gasped and slapped them away.

"Stop that!" Although she knew she had no reason to be, she was confused and embarrassed nonetheless.

However, Jeremiah had succeeded in touching her intimately, and when he drew back his hand there was a slight discoloration on his fingertip. "See? This is virgin's blood, my love. Your virgin's blood."

Charlotte glanced first at his upraised hand and then at him. Feeling overwhelmed with shame, she lowered her head. "You're wrong. You have to be! Melvin . . . that is, we . . . he and I—" She broke off, unable to form into coherent words the jumble of thoughts that were spinning around in her head. "Oh Lord!"

"Charlotte, look at me." The knuckle of Jeremiah's finger pushed her chin up until she was forced to gaze into his eyes. "You were only seventeen, just a child. You didn't know what was happening, and, of course, not having been with you, I can only speculate at what transpired between you and old Melvin. He may have tried, but we both know for a fact now that he didn't succeed. You thought he had deflowered you, and you've felt like a fallen woman ever since." A soft rumble of laughter vibrated through his chest. "It's lucky for me that you didn't know, because you might have married one of those rednecks back home in Texas, and I never would have met you . . . or fallen in love with you. If old Melvin were here now, I'd thank him for what he did . . . or for what he didn't do, that is."

"Do you?" came her quiet response.

"Do I what?"

"Love me?" Her quivering voice sounded odd, even to her. "You—you're not just saying that because—because of what we just—"

"No, sweetheart." Jeremiah pulled her into his arms and held her fiercely. "I meant every word I said. I love you, and don't you ever doubt it."

"But how? Why?"

"Don't ask me to explain," he sighed, and lay back to stare up at the clear, starlit sky. He nestled her head in the hollow of his shoulder. "I won't pretend to be an expert on matters concerning the heart. I only know that what I feel for you is different from what I've ever felt for any other woman. It scared the hell out of me at first, and I tried to ignore it, but after a while you were all I could think about. In my mind I could see myself holding you, kissing you, making love to you, protecting and cherishing you. See what I mean? It doesn't make a whole lot of sense, does it?"

"No," Charlotte agreed quietly. As much as she would like to believe him, there was still one stubborn part of her that refused to admit that she had been a virgin until just moments ago. Deep down she knew she couldn't have been! And anyway, how could Jeremiah say that he loved her with such conviction when all they'd done was. . . . "We argue constantly," she pointed out, snuggling against him as her hand wove a pattern in the golden mat of hair on his chest.

"So?"

"*So*, when two people are in love, they don't quarrel all the time like we do."

"They don't?" he countered. "Where is that written?"

"What?"

"Where is it written that lovers shouldn't disagree? There isn't a book in the world that lists all

126

the rules lovers should follow, Charlotte. We all have to handle the situation differently." He opened his mouth to continue, but the words never came. It suddenly occurred to him that, in a roundabout way, she had almost said she loved him! "Now it's my turn," he chuckled. "Do you?"

"Do I what?"

"Love me?"

Her head burrowed deeper into his chest, but he didn't have to see her face to know that she was blushing. Joy filled his heart.

"How can you even ask such a thing after what we've just done?" she murmured.

"Well," he purred teasingly, "I wouldn't want you to think I'm easy. In the past, women have used my body and then gone about their merry way without ever giving a thought to what they'd done to me. How do I know that you aren't just like them?"

Charlotte's head slowly lifted from his chest, and she turned to stare at him, a smile of comprehension pulling at her lips.

"*Touché*, Jeremiah!"

"That's French for 'touch,' isn't it?" he asked, a devilish gleam in his blue eyes.

"You should know. You speak the language as well as I do."

"Mmm," he murmured, pushing and pulling her until she lay atop him. "But you're the teacher, Miss Atwater. Tell me something. How would I say, 'Make love to me, my darling,' in French?"

Coils of unrestrainable desire unwound within her as he lowered his head to kiss the breasts he cupped. In a breathy voice, she managed to whisper, *"Marque amour a moi, ma cheri."*

He growled, "I'd be delighted to," and did!

The new day was merely a promise on the horizon when Jeremiah and Charlotte rose from their grassy lovers' bed. They dressed each other with sated, languorous slowness, then made their way back to camp, arms entwined. Having made love throughout the entire night, they were pleasurably tired and more than a little reluctant to return to reality.

As they ambled down the dirt road, they were so caught up in each other that they failed to notice the strange, quite beautiful phenomenon taking place around them. The once flat, night-blackened landscape was slowly being transformed as streaks of gold and purple filled the dawn sky. Each tree, bush, and flower was taking on its own individual shape and color as the sun continued to rise higher.

More than once during their short journey, they paused to kiss and hold each other, wanting to hold on to the blissful enchantment they had experienced so many times during the night. It was only when they entered the grove of trees where they had left Francesca and Zonya that the real world managed to return with frightening clarity.

Strange, unfamiliar voices forced Jeremiah to wrench his lips from Charlotte's. He turned his head and vaguely noticed that there were several vardos where there had been only one when they had left the night before. Confused and not comprehending what he was seeing, he frowned. Then a burly, dark-skinned giant stepped into view, and Jeremiah knew without a doubt what had happened.

Standing close to seven feet in height, the giant froze as his black eyes narrowed into menacing slits, his walrus-mustache-framed mouth curling into a sneer. As he started toward them, an errant breeze blew his long black hair away from his face and exposed his large, pitcher-handle ears, one lobe graced with a golden earring.

"Oh my Lord," Jeremiah groaned, his arms tightening protectively about Charlotte. "We've got trouble, my love."

"Trouble?" she purred sleepily. Her gaze slowly drifted away from Jeremiah's bruised face until she too saw the giant who was coming toward them. Her heart suddenly constricted, and she croaked, "Who—"

"The other gypsies," Jeremiah murmured. "They've found us."

"Gadjo!" The giant's rumbling bellow attracted the attention of everyone in the camp. They all stopped what they were doing and turned to follow him.

"Papa Sandor!" Francesca called out, her skirts flying about her slender legs as she raced up behind the giant.

"You steal my daughter?" the giant accused Jeremiah, his dark face turning a mottled shade of red.

"No, Papa, he—" But Francesca's remark was never finished. Sandor's arm lashed out, striking her face with a vicious thud, and she fell to the ground.

"Go back with the other children where you belong," Sandor snarled, ignoring Francesca's pitiful whimpers. "I will deal with this–this *gadjo* thief myself."

"I knew it was a mistake to let her come along," Jeremiah muttered out of the side of his mouth so that only Charlotte could hear. He had faced bomb-toting, gun-wielding criminals in the past, but none had been half as intimidating or frightening as this one irate giant of a father.

Stepping forward, Jeremiah succeeded in placing himself between Charlotte and the big gypsy. He squared his shoulders and retorted, "I did not steal your daughter. In fact, I haven't stolen anything of yours, sir. I paid for the use of your vardo and horses, and Francesca elected to come along with us."

"You lie, *gadjo!*" Sandor growled.

"No sir, I do not. Ask the old lady if you don't believe me."

"He speaks the truth, my son." From out of the throng of onlookers, Zonya's tiny form appeared. She shuffled up beside her enormous son and exposed her toothless gums in a wizened grin. "The fine silks that I showed you before were his payment."

"He never touched Francesca?" Sandor demanded.

"No, no!" the old woman cackled. "He has no need of the girl. *She* is his woman." A gnarled finger pointed at Charlotte.

Sandor's black gaze examined Charlotte with disbelieving thoroughness before it sliced arrogantly back to Jeremiah. "My daughter is promised to Nikos. They will marry as soon as she becomes a woman. If I find that a man has known her, I will lose face. And I will kill the man who took her with my bare hands."

"I never touched Francesca," Jeremiah assured him. "My woman has been by my side every moment since we met your daughter three days ago."

"This is so?" Sandor didn't look to Charlotte for the answer. His florid face dipped to glower down at his mother.

"Look at her," Zonya grinned, undaunted by her son's dominating presence. "See for yourself. Already she carries the *gadjo*'s mark. She blooms, Sandor, like your Magda did when you first married her."

Charlotte averted her flushed face, feeling the heat rise higher in her cheeks. Everyone was staring at her. Everyone knew what she and Jeremiah had done, and it embarrassed her terribly. But with Sandor's next question, she felt like crawling into a hole and disappearing.

"You are married, no?"

"Uh, no," Jeremiah confessed reluctantly. "No, we're not married . . . uh, yet."

"This is not good!" Sandor boomed out. "Man and woman must be married before they know each other!"

"Well, yeah, I agree with you there, and one of these days, when we can get around to it, we'll take care of that little oversight," Jeremiah admitted.

"No! Not good to wait. You marry now! We have wedding celebration tonight!"

Charlotte's head jerked up, and she stared in wide-eyed confusion at Jeremiah. He looked about as surprised as she was. His bruised face seemed to be contorting into a perplexed grimace as his mouth opened and closed around garbled mutterings. Seeing how incapable he was at this point of making Sandor see reason, she tried. "Really, your interference is most uncalled for, Mr. Sandor. We—"

"No!" Sandor roared, lifting his enormous hand to stop her flow of words. "You have no say in this matter. This is between men only."

"But–but—" she sputtered.

"Go with the women. They will make you ready for the wedding. Magda!"

"But you don't understand," Charlotte began again, and she felt someone pull at her arm. She looked down into the smiling face of the voluptuous, dark-haired woman who was leading her away. "Why won't he listen? We can't get married now. We don't have time!"

"There is always time for a wedding," Magda remarked patiently.

"No there isn't!" Charlotte argued. "We have to be in Grasse by tomorrow. And in Cannes the day after."

But Magda, like Sandor, wasn't listening. She was giving instructions in Romany to the other women of the tribe, and they were carrying out her orders quite happily.

Three hours later, sitting in a tub of steaming water in one of the caravans, Charlotte cast an imploring gaze up at Francesca. "Why won't they listen to reason? We cannot stay here! If only they'd minded their own blasted business, we could have been gone from here by now."

"Gypsies are very hardheaded," the girl stated matter-of-factly. "And Sandor is worse than all the others."

"You can say that again," Charlotte agreed on a lengthy sigh as she squeezed the sponge of scented water over her skin. Her long mahogany-colored hair had been washed with a fragrant soap earlier and was now braided and pinned to the top of her head. She dipped the sponge back into the water and rubbed her neck, scrubbing it until her skin glowed pink. "What have they done with Jeremiah?"

"Oh, the men are preparing him," Francesca answered with an uncaring shrug.

"You mean they're giving him a bath?" It was such an outrageously amusing thought, Charlotte had to smile.

"No, no. There is much more to the groom's ritual than just washing. He must be prepared to come to you as a gypsy would. A gypsy who will be the leader of his tribe."

"I don't think I understand." Charlotte's dark brows knit together in a frown.

"Zonya has prepared a potion to relax him. It is not a harmful brew, but it is not good for your man to move about as Sandor puts the ring in his ear."

"Good Lord! You mean to say those men are piercing Jeremiah's ears?"

"Only one," the girl assured her, her hand coming up to tug at her left earlobe. "It is the custom in all gypsy tribes for the leader to wear a gold ring. Since your man will be the leader of his own tribe, he must wear the ring."

Charlotte hoped Zonya's potion was a strong

one, because for the life of her she couldn't imagine Jeremiah sitting still while someone drilled holes in his earlobes.

"After the ring is in place, the men will dress him in black for the ceremony," Francesca ended on an almost bored note.

"And I suppose they'll dress me in white, hmm?" Charlotte muttered, thinking how inappropriate the color would be now.

"Oh no! White is very bad luck. It is the color of the dead. You will wear red!"

Charlotte's eyes widened to clear gray pools of disbelief. A red wedding dress? Good heavens! No one back home in Waxahachie would ever accept or condone a bride wearing red on her wedding day. But, then again, no one back home in Waxahachie had ever gotten themselves into this kind of predicament.

She relaxed as another thought occurred to her. Maybe this whole situation wasn't as bad as she was building it up to be. After all, she and Jeremiah wouldn't really be getting married tonight—not legally, that is. Neither she nor Jeremiah was a gypsy, and they were only going through with this mock ceremony to appease Sandor.

"Do you think we'll be able to leave immediately after the ceremony tonight?" Charlotte cautiously asked Francesca as she stepped out of the tub and wrapped a bath sheet around her. "We've been delayed long enough as it is, and we really must be on our way."

"Do not worry," Francesca assured her with a sly smile. "Zonya and I have planned it so that you will be left alone for the entire night. No one will be able to move after the celebration, much less follow you."

Charlotte noted the secretive look on the girl's face and started to ask her what she meant by her remark. But at that moment the door of the vardo opened and interrupted her. As the tiny room began to fill with gypsy women, she knew she would just have to wait and find out the answer to that question herself . . . later on.

Chapter Nine

GNARLED, NUT-BROWN HANDS HELD CHAR-
lotte's paler one as Zonya bent her head to get a
good look at the palms in the dim lantern light.
The vardo was filled with the gaily dressed
women who had helped Charlotte get ready for
the ceremony that was soon to take place. For
something that really didn't mean a whole lot,
Charlotte thought, they had certainly spent a lot
of time and effort on her. They had woven
flowers through her long, dark-brown hair and
anointed her body with fragrant oils before helping her slip into the gaudy red and gold ruffled
dress.

"Very interesting," the old woman remarked
in a voice that crackled like dry paper. "Yes,
very, very interesting!"

"What do you see?" asked a gypsy woman who
was quite heavy with child.

Zonya's black eyes remained fixed on Charlotte's palms as she muttered, "You will go on a long journey soon. A journey filled with much excitement and adventure. More than you imagine there will be, my child. At the end of your journey, you will find much anger, much sadness . . . oh, so much pain! But then, after the pain, you will find lifelong happiness. And," she laughed dryly, "your lie will become truth."

"My lie?" Charlotte frowned at Zonya. What lie? She never told lies. Well, almost never.

"Yes," Zonya nodded. "Your lie is recent. Told in jest. Beware! Never lie again."

Charlotte stared down at her palms, seeing only the lines and wrinkles that marked every person's hands. "You see all that?"

"And more. Much more! But you are not ready to learn of it yet. You do not truly believe all that Zonya tells you. Only part. But remember this, little one; my predictions always come true. I tell you only what I see." And then she released Charlotte's hands and sat back, straightening up as much as her aged body would allow. "We are ready now," she informed the other women. "Bring her the wine."

The pregnant gypsy woman turned and produced a misshapen goblet of beaten gold. Both of her workworn hands held it with great respect while one of the other women filled it with a clear, dark liquid from a goatskin bag.

"Is there something in it?" Charlotte asked when they handed her the goblet.

"Wine," the pregnant woman said, smiling.

"And nothing else?" Charlotte was aware of the warning look in Zonya's narrowed black eyes. She blushed, knowing that she'd asked an offensive question. So, deciding to throw caution to the wind, she placed the goblet to her lips and sipped the liquid. It *was* wine, she discovered, just as they had said, but the vintage was a very sour one, and she shuddered with a noticeable grimace.

"You must remember not to speak," Zonya instructed her sternly. "After you have spoken your vows, you must remain silent until the sun rises in the east. Your man will lose face if you do not."

"It is the gypsy way," another woman assured her with a patient smile, and all of the other women nodded in agreement.

Charlotte drank the contents of the goblet and handed the empty vessel back to the pregnant woman. Her tongue tingled from the wine's bitter taste, and a pleasant, languorous warmth invaded her limbs when she tried to stand. The sensation didn't alarm her, though. She'd had wine before and knew that it always had this kind of effect on her. One glass tended to relax her, but more than one made her quite tipsy.

Someone handed her a sheer red veil, and she draped it over her head, leaving her face uncovered. Following the other women, she stepped out of the vardo and saw that night had finally descended. The sky was filled with just as many twinkling stars as there had been the night before when she and Jeremiah had—

Jeremiah!

Charlotte stopped abruptly and craned her neck, trying to find his familiar face among the crowd of gypsies. She knew he would be fairly easy to spot, because he was the only light-haired man present. But the longer she looked for him, the greater her anxiety became, until she had to wonder if he'd already left without her.

A huge bonfire blazed in the center of the clearing, casting harsh shadows on all who stood around it. Charlotte drew close to the crackling warmth and spied Sandor. When the hulking gypsy shifted his weight from one foot to the other, he inadvertently gave her a clear view of Jeremiah's leaner, more muscular form. Charlotte released a long sigh of relief.

Except for his new clothes, Jeremiah looked no different from the way he'd looked that morning. Gone was the grass-stained shirt they had used for their bed, and in its place was a black satin shirt that bloused at his lean waist and wrists and gaped down the front to expose his chest of golden curls. The black trousers he now wore were so snug-fitting that they clung to his hips and thighs like a second skin. An irrepressible smile pulled at Charlotte's lips and became even wider when Jeremiah turned, giving her a glimpse of the gold hoop that winked in his left earlobe. Lord, he was magnificent, she thought. Handsome, virile, and decidedly dangerous-looking dressed totally in black. Even more so now than the first time she'd seen him in her Paris hotel room.

But Charlotte's smile faded when she noticed the shorter, more rotund man standing beside Jeremiah. Garbed in a strange, dark, flowing robe, the man held a book in one hand and a string of beads in the other, at the end of which dangled a shiny silver crucifix. A priest? she wondered silently as a vague feeling of apprehension enveloped her. Sandor had found a priest to perform the ceremony?

Jeremiah saw Charlotte's expression alter and knew in an instant what was going through her pretty head. He hurried over to her and wrapped a comforting arm about her shoulders.

"Don't look so scared," he murmured softly, not wanting any of the others to hear. "There's nothing to be afraid of. I've got this whole situation under control." But when she didn't appear to have much outward faith in his declaration, he asked, "Uh, you're not Catholic, are you?"

At the imperceptible negative movement of her head, he released a sigh of relief. "Well, neither am I, so I guess that means we're both safe. Come on. Let's get this thing over with so we can get away from here."

The remainder of the evening had all of the characteristics of a bad dream from which there was no escape. In faltering Latin, Charlotte and Jeremiah repeated the vows that the priest requested of them. And as soon as the little man had blessed them, making the sign of the cross with his upraised hand, music began to play with nerve-jarring loudness. Violins were mournfully sawed. Tambourines were rattled and beaten. And in the background, Jeremiah's ever sensitive ears picked out Zonya's grating voice as she sang along with the gypsy musicians.

A procession of laughing, dancing gypsies led the two of them around the huge bonfire, circling it time and time again until Jeremiah and

Charlotte were abruptly wrenched apart. The women pulled Charlotte to one of the vardos, while the men continued to dance Jeremiah around the fire. And when he, too, was taken to the vardo, he saw that all of the women had formed a protective barrier in front of Charlotte and were wielding sticks, pans, and a long-handled shovel as if they were weapons.

"He cannot have her," proclaimed Magda. "She is much too valuable for us to give her away freely."

"We have a chicken we can buy her with," one of the gypsy men laughed.

"A chicken!" the pregnant gypsy woman cried indignantly. "One chicken is hardly worth her value."

"I bought you with two!" The man who said this was obviously the pregnant woman's husband, and his remark brought about an uproar of laughter from the rest of the men.

"And a goat, and a pig, and two horses," the pregnant woman reminded him smugly, drawing laughter from the women.

Neither Charlotte nor Jeremiah could understand what the devil was going on. It seemed to them as though the gypsies were bartering for Charlotte, even though they were already supposed to be man and wife. Shaking their heads in confusion, they continued to stand there, silently watching the exchange until the final deal was made.

"The use of your vardo for one night and a keg of wine for everyone!" exclaimed Magda, lifting her arms high.

Cheers were heard from all, and the music

began to play again. But Jeremiah still was not allowed to go to Charlotte. The men pulled him back to the bonfire and danced him around it one more time. *Good Lord*, he thought. *How much longer is this nonsense going to continue?*

Those exact same thoughts were passing through Charlotte's befuddled brain as each of the women, in turn, kissed her. Then, as the men had done with Jeremiah, they danced her around the blazing fire before finally leading her to a ribbon-bedecked vardo that had been moved far away from all the others. There she saw Jeremiah by the opened door, waiting for her.

The gypsy women suddenly relinquished their hold on her, and, not knowing what was expected of her, she cautiously moved toward her new husband.

"See how shyly your bride comes to you!" Sandor praised Jeremiah.

Shy, hell! thought Jeremiah. *That's pure fear on her face. She's as scared as I am!*

"Be gentle when you break her," one of the other men—who was obviously a horseman—cautioned Jeremiah huskily. "She will reward you with many fine sons if you do."

"You must have been rough with your Lina, Marcos," one of the other gypsies hooted. "She has given you nothing but daughters!"

The men, naturally, roared with laughter, causing Marcos to redden with embarrassment.

Charlotte had heard every word, and she was sorely pressed not to laugh with them. Their goodnatured jibes were as bawdy as the women's had been while they had been dressing her.

But she maintained her outward shyness and came to a halt in front of Jeremiah.

A flood of warmth invaded Jeremiah's heart as he gazed down at Charlotte's lovely, upturned face. For a moment, he wished with all of his being that this would truly be their wedding night. That the ceremony in which they had just participated had been genuine and not a fraudulent mockery of the institution he'd been taught to respect and hold sacred. That this woman, who had been by his side during the past trying days, would in fact be his wife and mate until death parted them. For only God knew how much he loved her in his own, clumsy way.

Lifting his gaze, Jeremiah saw that all the men had quietly rejoined their wives and families, and the celebration was going to continue even though he and Charlotte were no longer a part of it. Smiling down at her, he extended his hand, wordlessly asking her to join him. When she shyly placed her hand in his, they turned, mounted the steps, and entered the vardo.

Jeremiah didn't hesitate for a moment. As soon as he had shut the door behind him, sealing them off from the rest of the world, he hauled Charlotte into his arms. His mouth seared hers with a kiss so intense that it left them both breathless and shaken.

Lips mingling, they drank the passion from each other like two thirsty people. Their tongues greedily explored the feel and the taste of each other as their hands rediscovered the familiar regions of their bodies.

But then a pain began to throb in Jeremiah's neck. He was forced to pull away from her, and he cursed, "Damn this low ceiling! This vardo obviously wasn't built with a tall person in mind. I wonder what Sandor does?"

Charlotte, still glowing from the warmth of his kiss, did not respond verbally. She couldn't. But when he moved, she followed him . . . to the red, white, and blue draped bed that looked vaguely familiar.

"What's the matter with you?" Jeremiah asked when they were seated. "Cat got your tongue or something?"

Her eyes were dark gray pools of desire as she slowly shook her head and smiled.

"Then what's wrong with you?"

"I was told not to speak," she whispered huskily, "until the sun rose in the east. You would lose face if I did."

"Oh hell, Charlotte!" he grumbled. "We're not gypsies."

"I know. But they are, and I did not want to upset them."

"Yeah," he drawled, his glance sliding to the closed door. "Sounds like they're having a high old time of it, huh?"

"Weddings are very special to them."

"They're special to me, too." His blue gaze shifted back to her.

"Jeremiah," she rasped, her hand coming up to cup his unshaven jaw.

"No. Charlotte, don't say anything. I—I just want you to know that I feel like the world's biggest hypocrite. Can you ever forgive me for disgracing you?"

"Disgracing me!"

"Yes. Last night I sullied you, and then tonight you had to go through with this—this farce of a wedding. I—well, I know it's all my fault. I take full responsibility for what's happened, and I want you to know that I'm thoroughly ashamed of myself."

To Charlotte he sounded like a little boy who had been told by his parents to make an apology, and to make it sound damn convincing.

"For the last time, Jeremiah Fox, you did not sully me! I was sullied long before I ever met you, so you have not one thing to be ashamed of as far as I'm concerned!"

"Look, let's not go into all of that again. I'm too tired for one thing, and not really in the mood for another." And to prove his point, he lay back on the bed, resting his head on the pillow there.

"Well you started it!" Charlotte inhaled an impatient breath and shook her head. "Look at us. Not married an hour, and we're already having our first fight."

"That's just it. We're not really married," he remarked as his mouth widened into a yawn.

Jerking her head around to face him, Charlotte noted the lines of fatigue etched about his deep blue eyes and the difficulty he was having keeping his lids open. Oh for heaven's sake, she thought. How could she have a meaningful argument with a man who was half asleep? But then why should she bother to argue with him in the first place? His mind was so firmly set on what he wanted to believe that there was no way *she* could change it.

Charlotte decided to remain silent on the subject for the time being, or until he woke up. She sat there beside him for a while, just watching him as his breathing became deeper and more even. With no timepiece to judge by, she knew it had taken him less than a minute to fall asleep. Well, after what they'd gone through last night and all of the harrowing events they'd endured today, she could understand why he was so tired. In fact, she was beginning to feel a little weary herself.

She leaned over and blew out the candle on the small table next to the bed, throwing the room into total darkness. Stretched out next to Jeremiah, she told herself that she wasn't going to fall asleep; she was only going to rest her eyes for a minute. Then, the moment the gypsies ended their celebrating and went to bed, she would awaken Jeremiah and they would be on their way.

But the last thing Charlotte heard before sleep overtook her completely was the almost sad quality of the music that the gypsies were playing. They were laughing and singing, but the music sounded so mournful.

Jeremiah was in the middle of a very pleasant, very erotic dream. He was sitting—stark-naked —on the riverbank back home in Virginia. Beside him, just as nude as he, sat Charlotte, her lush, coral-tipped breasts glistening with beads of water. Looking down the length of his body, he saw that droplets of water were clinging to his chest hair, and he realized that they had been skinny-dipping together.

He shifted his gaze back to Charlotte and watched as her pink tongue snaked out to sensuously lick the surface of her curving lips. Then she leaned toward him, her breasts swaying dangerously close to his chest. One of her hands began to inch its way toward his thigh, and of their own accord his legs parted.

As her fingers crawled ever nearer to his sleeping staff, he felt himself fall back onto the sun-warmed grass. *Grab a handful, my love,* he said to her in his dream. *Take all you want. I've got enough for both of us.*

Then, suddenly, someone started pulling on his foot. He peered down and saw his little sister's grinning face between his parted feet.

"Go away, Judith," he muttered. "Leave us alone."

"You must wake up!" she said in a strange voice that was not altogether unfamiliar. "Please, you have to leave now!"

Jeremiah's lids protested, but he succeeded in opening them. Lying on his side as he was, the first thing he saw was Charlotte. She was curled up against him, her hand resting on his thigh, very near his groin. Then, a movement at the foot of the bed pulled his attention in that direction, and he saw, not his little sister, but Francesca, her smooth brow furrowed into a frown.

"What the—Francesca?"

"Wake up your wife. You must hurry!"

"Oh God! We fell asleep, didn't we?" he groaned. "What time is it?"

"It is still quite early. Sandor and the others have only just now settled down for the night.

Unfortunately, Zonya's potion was not as strong as she had thought. She is getting old," the girl added regretfully.

"Y'all be quiet!" Charlotte complained, and cuddled closer to Jeremiah.

"Come on, Charlotte, you've got to wake up!" He shook her shoulder gently, raising another complaint from her.

"Wanna sleep. Don't wanna wake up."

"Well, you're going to have to," Jeremiah insisted. "Come on!"

At his stern, insistent prodding, Charlotte opened her eyes and blinked at him in confusion. "What did you wake me up for? It's not even morning yet!"

"Thank God for that!" retorted Jeremiah. "Now come on. We've got to go!"

Never in a good mood when rudely awakened, Charlotte grumbled beneath her breath as Jeremiah and Francesca dragged her to her feet and led her out of the vardo. She shuddered at the chill in the air and noticed the two horses that were tethered to a nearby tree. With a groan, she realized that the four-legged hayburners were going to be their means of transportation from here on out.

Jeremiah glanced at Charlotte, who was looking over the animals with a jaundiced eye, and asked, "Don't tell me. You don't know how to ride, do you?"

"I'm from Texas, you idiot. Of course I know how to ride," came her grumpy admission. *I just don't want to, that's all,* she tacked on mentally.

With Jeremiah's assistance, she mounted one of the animals and tucked her red skirts around her legs so that only her slender ankles were exposed. But as they turned the horses and started to ride out of camp, a twinge of discomfort began to throb at the juncture of her thighs. She wiggled her bottom, trying to find a more comfortable spot on the horse's saddle-less back.

"What is the matter with you?" Jeremiah snapped when they were out on the road and away from the camp.

"Nothing," she retorted sullenly, and twitched again.

"Well something's bothering you. What is it?"

"If you must know, I'm a little bit sore from the other night. And this blanket is no protection at all! It's so blasted thin, all I can feel are the lumps in this animal's back!"

The gist of her remark registered, and Jeremiah chuckled. "Oh, is that all? Well, don't worry about it, darlin'. You'll get used to it after a while."

Chapter Ten

SHORTLY BEFORE NOON, THEY STOPPED IN A grove of trees to give their horses a well-deserved rest. They had ridden hard after leaving the gypsy camp, bypassing the medieval village of Regusse, where Jeremiah had had his previous altercation with the farmers. Then they had slowed down to a steady, less exhausting pace. Even though the horses were sleek and sturdy—the best of the gypsies' stock—Jeremiah knew they wouldn't last if he pushed them too hard.

He climbed down from his mount and tethered the animal loosely to a low-hanging tree limb near a shallow brook. He turned to help Charlotte down from her horse but paused before the gentlemanly act was completed. With a frown, he glanced back over his shoulder at the surrounding trees. It was the strangest thing; for the last hour or so, he'd had the uncomfortable feeling that someone was watching them.

With her feet finally resting on solid earth again, Charlotte groaned and rubbed the small of her back. She hadn't been on a horse in months, and the grueling pace of their morning ride was now making itself known to her unconditioned muscles.

"I wonder how much farther it is to Grasse," she pondered aloud, flexing her spine.

"We should be there before sunset if it's where I think it is," Jeremiah informed her, his blue eyes still peering off into the distance.

"Thank heavens! I don't believe I could survive another day riding this wretched animal. She may be a beauty, but she—" Charlotte broke off when she saw that Jeremiah wasn't listening to her. Her gaze followed his. "What's the matter?"

"Shh!" he ordered bruskly. "I heard a noise."

Charlotte listened with rapt intenseness but could hear nothing out of the ordinary. Birds chirped happily above them in the tree tops. Leaves rustled with the gentle urging of the breeze. Water gurgled over stones in the nearby brook.

Shrugging her shoulders slightly, Charlotte put aside Jeremiah's infectious apprehension and turned to tether her horse next to his. His overactive imagination was playing tricks on him, she decided. But she wasn't going to let his suspicious mood consume her as well.

She knelt down beside the brook and scooped up a handful of icy-cold water. It tasted very good and soothed her parched lips. After quenching her thirst, she splashed the water over her face and throat before letting her wet fingers trail down into the neckline of her gaudy red gown. Though the midsummer heat here in France was not as intense as it was back home in Texas, it was uncomfortable nonetheless. She longed to remove her shoes and dip her feet into the cold water. But she didn't. She knew that as soon as the horses had rested she and Jeremiah would be on their way again. There would be time enough for relaxation once they had safely reached her aunt's house in Grasse.

Glancing down at her unconventional gown, she had to wonder what Great-Aunt Marie would think of her dressed this way. *She'll either welcome me with open arms or turn me away from her door*, she decided with a chuckle.

A startling noise erupted behind Charlotte at that moment. She jumped to her feet and spun around to see what had caused the commotion. But there was nothing to see. Jeremiah had disappeared. Apprehension and worry guiding her, she started to go in search of him but stopped when another noise broke out.

"You little brat!" she heard Jeremiah snarl. "What the hell do you think you're doing?"

"Ouch!" cried an all-too-familiar voice.

"I ought to turn you over my knee and give you a good spanking."

Charlotte, afraid even to move, felt a wave of relief when she saw Jeremiah suddenly reappear. He was pushing Francesca ahead of him, and the girl's bodice rode high against her throat as Jeremiah's large hand held the scruff of her neck.

"Would you look at this!" came his angry declaration. "She followed us!"

"Francesca?" Charlotte moved toward them. "What are you doing here?"

"I had to come with you," the girl informed them. "I could not stay with those gypsies any longer. I am not one of them. I do not even belong with them. You saw how Sandor treats me. And Magda is not much better. I am a constant reminder to her of my mother."

"Oh hell!" Jeremiah felt his determination waver. Wanting only to get rid of Francesca, to send her back to where she belonged, he still could not forget the vicious slap Sandor had given her—and all because she had tried to explain to her stepfather about him and Charlotte.

"Maybe we should take her with us, Jeremiah," Charlotte entreated cautiously.

"Good Lord! Do you know what you're saying? It's because of her that they came after us the first time. We'd be in Grasse by now if they hadn't stopped us, and you know it. Now they'll be after us again. Hell!" He flung up his hands in exasperation. "For all we know, they could be right behind her!"

"No, they are not!" Francesca assured him. "Zonya's potion—"

"Oh, Zonya's potions be damned!" Jeremiah roared.

"What was in her potion, Francesca?" Charlotte asked patiently, and narrowed her gray eyes in warning to Jeremiah.

"The ground valerian root," Francesca responded. "Mixed with the wine, it put everyone to sleep, and it will keep them that way for quite some time." A sly little grin stole over her pretty face, deepening the dimples in her cheeks. "I added the juice of the prunes."

A soft chuckle formed in Charlotte's throat when it finally dawned on her just what the girl had said. But the chuckle soon grew into full-scale laughter. "Prune juice?" she gasped out between giggles.

Francesca, laughing with her, nodded. "Not only will they sleep until noon, they won't be able to mount their horses until some time tomorrow."

"Oh, Francesca!" Charlotte held her sides and giggled harder. "You—you are a naughty child!"

"Will somebody please tell me what the hell's so funny?" Jeremiah demanded. Here they were, stranded in the middle of France with a whole tribe of crazy gypsies behind them and a bunch of unpredictable crooks ahead of them, and these two were laughing like lunatics.

"Pr—prunes, Jeremiah," Charlotte managed to repeat, looking up at him through teary eyes. She wiped her cheeks with the backs of her fingers. "Prunes!"

"Prunes?" As he looked down into her glowing face, the frown on Jeremiah's forehead slowly cleared. "Oh Jesus, *prunes!*" Then he, too, began to howl, his laughter booming out and shattering the silence in the quiet clearing. The thought of all those gypsies being so uncomfortably incapacitated was too funny.

At last, when he was able to think clearly again, he gave silent thanks for not having had any of the doctored wine himself the night before.

"I don't guess we have to be in such a big hurry after all," he admitted some time later after his mirth began to die down. "But we do need to be on our way."

Weak from having giggled so hard, Francesca staggered away from them and disappeared into the surrounding trees, where Jeremiah had found her. In a matter of minutes she returned, pulling her dappled gray horse behind her.

After they had mounted up and made their way back to the road again, they rode silently past the fertile green fields where farmers were tending to their crops. They made an odd-looking trio and were even more odd-looking when one of them would suddenly start to chuckle softly. The other two, knowing what had caused the third's sudden bout of amusement, would soon join in the laughter. More than once, a confused farmer would stop what he was doing and stare at them as they rode past, giggling like mischievous children.

"No one ever told me," Jeremiah stated some time later when all of the laughter had finally died away, "just what a priest was doing in camp last night. Where did they dig him up?"

"Nikos found him," Francesca admitted, her lips twisting into a snarl as she spoke the other man's name.

"And he agreed to marry two Protestants?" Charlotte queried in disbelief.

"No, no," the girl negated with a shake of her head. "The good father thought that one of the tribe was in need of last rites. He did not know until he arrived that he was going to perform a marriage ceremony. But then, Nikos is very good at lying to get his way."

"Nikos." Jeremiah frowned. "Which one was he?"

"Ugh!" Francesca shuddered. "He was the oily pig who never left Sandor's side during the ceremony."

Jeremiah turned to glance over at Charlotte, who rode beside him. Her shoulders lifted in an almost imperceptible shrug, and he shook his head in confusion. Obviously, neither one of them could recall a man who fit Francesca's description.

"But I no longer have to worry about him," the gypsy girl added, her slender nose tilting smugly. "I will become a great lady. As great as my mother was. And Nikos will have to kneel at my feet. Zonya told me so."

"Oh Lord, her again," groaned Jeremiah. In the back of his mind, he could still hear the old woman's nerve-grating voice as she sang her unintelligible songs. He could see her toothless grin as clearly as if she rode before him at this very moment. But worse than that, he could still taste that awful bile-bitter tea she'd made and forced him to drink. God alone knew what she'd put in the stuff. He was just thankful that it hadn't been prunes!

"Your aunt lives here?" Jeremiah gazed up at the enormous house just beyond the iron filigree gates. "My Lord, what is she? Royalty or something?"

The gray stone building seemed to rise up from the manicured lawn and gardens for three full stories before it reached the dark slate-gray roof where towering chimneys abounded. Charlotte surveyed the imposing structure with undisguisable astonishment. She was actually related to someone who lived *here*? Lord! There had to be at least a hundred rooms inside, if the number of windows on the outside were an accurate indication.

"Royalty?" she managed to croak. "Gosh, it certainly looks that way, doesn't it?"

As awed by the size of the mansion as Jeremiah and Charlotte, Francesca suddenly smiled, her cinnamon-colored eyes glimmering with an inner fire. "This is my house," she murmured softly. "I will be a great lady in this house!"

Jeremiah shot the girl a questioning look, then flicked the reins over his horse's back, sending the animal into motion. "Come on. Let's get down there and meet the folks."

Allowing her horse to follow Jeremiah's, Charlotte began to feel very apprehensive. What if Great-Aunt Marie wasn't the lady of the manor here at all? What if she was only a servant? And if that was the case, what were the real owners going to think of her, Jeremiah, and Francesca when they knocked on their front door?

"Maybe we'd better go around to the back," Charlotte suggested timidly.

"What for?" Jeremiah asked. "Your aunt does live here, doesn't she?"

"Well, yes, but she—"

"But nothing, Charlotte," he bit out impatiently.

157

"Jeremiah, I don't think you understand. My aunt might not be—" Charlotte broke off abruptly, for at that very moment the massive front door flew open and Jean-Claude appeared. He was followed by an older man and woman, who were dressed as formally as he.

"Cousin Charlotte!" the young Frenchman cried out, hurrying toward them. "You have finally arrived! And Monsieur Fox. How good it is to see you again!"

In the process of dismounting, Charlotte slid off her horse and into her cousin's arms. He crushed her to him in a fierce embrace before kissing both her cheeks. Then he let his lips find hers, and they lingered there a little longer than polite custom dictated.

Slightly stunned, Charlotte didn't know what to do or how to behave when she felt herself suddenly released, for she was gathered up immediately in another embrace. This time, cooler lips rained kisses on her face, and when she looked up dazedly she saw an older, but just as handsome, version of Jean-Claude smiling down at her.

"Cousin Charlotte," the man proclaimed, holding her at arm's length. "I am Charles-André, Jean-Claude's father. How wonderful to have you here at last."

"Thank you," she managed to respond before he stepped aside, his gaze having found Jeremiah. Charlotte then found herself in the arms of the woman, whose embrace was much gentler than either Jean-Claude's or Charles-André's had been.

"I am Vivienne," she informed Charlotte. "Jean-Claude's mother. *Maman* is inside, waiting for you. She has been most anxious for you to arrive since Jean-Claude told us of your hasty departure from Paris. Is it really true that assassins were after Monsieur Fox?"

Charlotte's head twisted as she frantically searched for Jeremiah. How much should she tell this stranger who was her cousin's mother? But Jeremiah couldn't help her decide, she realized. At the moment he was being hugged and kissed by Jean-Claude.

"Monsieur Fox!" The young Frenchman winked devilishly. "The gold earring—it has something to do with the black mask, *n'est-ce pas?*"

Jeremiah had no chance to respond to this, because Jean-Claude had suddenly moved aside, and he found himself being welcomed by Charles-André.

"And who is this?" Jean-Claude queried over the top of Francesca's head. The girl had managed to wrap her arms about him as she slid off her horse, and she appeared quite reluctant to let him go.

"She's Francesca," Jeremiah informed him.

"Ah, Francesca," Jean-Claude nodded, trying to pry the girl's arms loose.

"Are you married?" she asked him bluntly.

"Married? Me?" Thinking the question amusing, Jean-Claude issued a dry burst of laughter.

"Jean-Claude, it appears as if you have met your match," Charles-André chuckled. "But come. We must go inside."

"Oui!" Vivienne agreed. "This night air is not good for us."

The six of them slowly filed up the vast marble steps and into the elaborate, chandelier-lit foyer, where a dozen or more servants awaited. Charles-André instructed two of the footmen to see to their horses, while Vivienne ordered her maids to prepare rooms and baths for their guests.

"We will take you in to *Maman*, and then we will let you refresh yourselves before dinner is served," Vivienne remarked as she led them toward a nearby room.

If Charlotte had been impressed by the size and grandeur of the foyer, she was truly stunned by the drawing room. Lavish paintings by a number of the old masters graced the gilt-painted and wainscoted walls, and rich carpeting cushioned the sounds of her footsteps over the polished wooden floors. The fine mahogany and silk-brocade-upholstered furniture that was decorously placed about the room reminded her of one of the museums she had toured in Paris. But then her gaze encountered the tiny, black-silk-clad woman who sat at the far end of the room. Charlotte stopped with a gasp, unable to go one step further.

"Grandmaman!" she whispered.

The old woman lifted her arms, a smile of joy stretching her wrinkled face. "Come here, my child. Let me kiss you."

Charlotte decided later that she must have floated toward the woman, because not once did she feel her feet touch the floor. And when she knelt down to embrace her elderly great-aunt, she felt hot tears sting her eyelids. Why hadn't her grandmother told her that she was an identical twin?

"Oh, you are so beautiful!" the old lady said at last, her voice thick with emotion.

"You should see my sisters," Charlotte chuckled, wiping her teary cheeks with her fingers.

"Why are you crying? This is not the time for tears."

"Well, I didn't know you would look so much like *Grandmaman*."

"Ah, Georgianna," the old woman smiled sadly. "You must tell me all about her . . . but later, of course." Her gaze slid past Charlotte to the group of people who stood nearby. "And who is this with you?"

"You remember, *Grandmere*," Jean-Claude replied engagingly. "I told you all about Cousin Charlotte's *Americain,* er, *ami.*"

"Ah, *oui*." Great-Aunt Marie's expression altered noticeably as Jeremiah stepped before her. "Monsieur Fox, I believe my grandson said you called yourself."

"Yes, ma'am." Grinning mischievously, Jeremiah bent down and planted a kiss on her wrinkled cheek. When he straightened up again and saw the iciness in the old woman's clear gray eyes, he couldn't suppress the heat that rushed to his face.

"Fox," she nodded. "*Oui*, the name fits you well, young man. Wily, cunning, and devious. And who is the child?" Never once did her gaze leave Jeremiah's face as she made her inquiry.

"Francesca," Charlotte supplied, sensing Jeremiah's discomfort. "If it weren't for her, *Tante*, we wouldn't be here now."

Francesca stepped forward and dipped into a clumsy curtsy before the old lady. Her dimples deepened, and her lashes seemed to flutter rapidly over her cinnamon-colored eyes.

But Great-Aunt Marie was more amused than she was impressed. Her smile returned once again after she had darted a glance at Jean-Claude and then looked back at the girl. "Welcome to my home, child. I think it would be best if you called me *Grandmere*."

Chapter Eleven

ALTHOUGH THE CONVERSATION AT DINNER THAT evening was bright and cheerful, Jeremiah found himself an unwilling participant. Oh, he answered and parried the others' remarks when the need arose, but on the whole he was a seething mass of inner frustrations. Cannes— and Boland—was only a short distance away, less than a day's ride from here, yet he was unable to leave. And from the looks of it, he wouldn't be leaving any time soon, either, because Charlotte's family seemed overjoyed at having him as their guest. So he sat there, staring down into his crystal goblet of wine.

Damn it! Why now? Everything had been going so smoothly. Why did fate suddenly have to turn against him?

Suddenly? What the devil was he thinking of? Hell, fate hadn't been on his side for some time, not since Lafayette Roman had decided to send him on this stupid mission. He'd lost count of the number of times he'd been delayed and side-tracked since coming to France. The only good thing to come out of this idiotic fiasco was Charlotte's ill-timed appearance in his life. If it weren't for her, he might easily be dead by now, or worse.

With the thought of Charlotte came the blood-chilling recollection of Judith, the other woman in his life. Jeremiah felt his frustrations increase. He wanted—no, he *had* to find out what Boland and his murderous cohorts had done with her. These last few days, while he and Charlotte had been on the run getting here to Grasse, he hadn't allowed his thoughts to dwell on Judith for too long. A vision of her adorable smiling face would flash through his mind at the most inopportune time, and he would be forced to dispel it quickly. But now that she was so close at hand, no matter how hard he tried, he couldn't stop himself from worrying about her.

A hell of a lot of good worrying was doing him now, though. Finding Boland and Judith wasn't going to be as easy as he'd first thought. He learned from the casual dinner gossip that Cannes, at this time of year, was the favored mecca of both artists and fashionable society. Nearly every European of any importance took up residence in the coastal resort town either to soak up the warm Mediterranean sun or to gamble long into the night. Because of this, Jeremiah knew he was going to have one devil of a time just finding a place in which to stay, much less locate Boland.

At that moment, though, Vivienne said something that intrigued him, and he turned his full attention back to the conversation.

"You said you have a villa in Cannes?" he asked. Darting a quick look at Charlotte, who sat across the table from him, he noted the quizzical lift of her brows.

"*Oui*," Vivienne smiled. "It lies just outside of Cannes, actually, in the hills. One can grow quite weary of all the noise and confusion in town. I find that it is quite pleasant just to stand on the terrace at dusk and gaze out to sea. We have a most magnificent view of the bay."

"It must be lovely," Jeremiah remarked casually, lifting his goblet to sip his wine. On the outside he appeared to be an interested observer, while on the inside his devious mind was putting a plan together.

"Oh it is!" Jean-Claude agreed. "At this time of year especially. And on Bastille Day, Cannes rivals Paris for its excitement."

"Do you go there often?" Charlotte asked.

"As often as we can," Vivienne supplied. "But this year we have been unable to go as often as we might have liked. Charles-André has had more pressing business here on the estate." She giggled at this and blushed. "*Pardonnez-moi*. I did not intend to make the—how do you say it?—the pun."

Vivienne then went on to explain that her husband's avocation of growing flowers for the manufacture of perfumes and soaps had become quite a time-consuming occupation. Not only did he personally oversee the growing of the flowers out in the fields, but he helped with the harvesting of the blooms as well. He and the estate workers spent a great amount of time in sorting the flowers—and sometimes the stems and leaves—before his chemists either dried them or blended the blooms with oils to produce the rare essences that his company was rapidly becoming noted for.

"You must allow me to show you my laboratory," Charles-André remarked with polite pride. "It is a process you might find quite interesting."

"I'm sure I would." Though Jeremiah sounded intrigued, he was far from it. The last thing he wanted to do was take a tour of this man's commercial enterprise.

Dinner came to an end shortly after everyone had consumed the last course of flaming *crêpes*. Great-Aunt Marie pleaded fatigue and had Charles-André ring for her maid, Thérèse. When the woman arrived, looking not much younger than Great-Aunt Marie herself, she helped the old woman from the room after everyone, Jeremiah included, had kissed her goodnight.

"Shall we ladies adjourn to the music room?" Vivienne suggested, rising to her feet. "The gentlemen, I am sure, would rather be left alone with their cognac and cigars."

Jeremiah noted the look of disappointment that crossed Francesca's face and suppressed a smile. It was obvious that the girl didn't want to be apart from Jean-Claude. She had all but mooned over him during dinner. Even Jean-Claude's younger sisters, Suzanne and Clothilde, had noticed her behavior; they had whispered and giggled about it behind their napkins.

As the women filed out of the room, their gowns rustling with each step they took, Francesca dutifully followed. She paused at the door long enough to glance back at the young Frenchman; then one of the footmen closed the door in her face, and the men were finally alone.

"Jean-Claude has told us of the, mmm, difficulties you encountered while in Paris, Monsieur Fox." Charles-André eyed Jeremiah cautiously as he produced a box of cigars. After Jeremiah had chosen one, he continued, "I was rather alarmed to hear that my young cousin was involved."

"If I could have avoided involving Charlotte, Monsieur Beauvais, believe me, I would have. But the situation arose so suddenly—" The remark was never completed as his shoulders lifted in a shrug.

"You can appreciate my concern, though, can you not?" Charles-André countered. "I am the girl's only adult male relative in France and therefore responsible for her while she is here."

Oh Lord, here it comes! Jeremiah groaned inwardly as he lit the end of his cheroot. *The what-are-your-intentions interrogation.*

He leaned back and blew out a stream of smoke into the air before replying, "Yes, I understand that. But you must believe that I would rather die before I would let her come to harm."

"From what I have heard," Charles-André observed, "that almost happened."

Jeremiah shot Jean-Claude a quick sidelong glance and noted how warily the young Frenchman was eyeing him. He managed to maintain his cool composure, though, and looked back at

167

the more formidable of the two men. "Monsieur Beauvais, if it makes any difference at all, I love Charlotte. Her happiness and safety have been my primary concern all along. That's one reason why we are here now. I knew you could provide better protection for her than I could."

"*Bon!*" Charles-André nodded. "That is what I wanted to hear."

"Papa!" Jean-Claude burst out. "You are not going to let him get away with what he has done to Charlotte, are you?"

"What would you have me do?" the older man countered. "Challenge him to a duel? *Non!* Charlotte is a grown woman with a mind of her own. She has decided to love this man, to be his mistress, and there is nothing I can do to stop her."

"But Papa—"

"Silence, Jean-Claude!" The order echoed about the great room, and the young Frenchman slumped dejectedly in his chair, looking duly chastised. "If Charlotte were your sister, it would be a different matter, but I am not her father. At any rate, Suzanne and Clothilde would not behave as Charlotte has. Or, if they did, be assured that they would feel the wrath of my disapproval."

The silence that ensued seemed to be charged with a volatile tension. It stretched on for an uncomfortable length of time until Jeremiah decided that he would have to be the one to say something, anything, in order to lessen the strained atmosphere. Gathering up all his courage, he cleared his throat and remarked, "I intend to marry Charlotte just as soon as it is possible."

Both men shot him a look that mirrored their astonishment.

"Divorce your wife?" Charles-André demanded.

"And abandon your twelve children?" Jean-Claude added, thoroughly outraged.

Jeremiah looked first at one man and then at the other, his mouth opening and closing around garbled mutterings. He had said the wrong thing . . . to the wrong people. It didn't matter that he wasn't really married, that he really didn't have twelve children to abandon. *They* thought he did, and being the good Catholics that they were, they obviously thought his declaration scandalous, if not downright sacrilegious.

Oh Lord! he prayed silently. *What do I do now?*

Something was wrong. Charlotte, in the solitude of her room, yielded to this uncomfortable realization as she changed out of her gown and into her wrapper. As yet, she hadn't put her finger on where the problem lay, but she knew that something wasn't as it should be.

The instant the men had joined the ladies in the music room, a tangible sensation had entered with them as noticeably as if it were a fourth entity. Charles-André sat pensively beside Vivienne, while Jean-Claude, possessing none of his usual ebullience, stared gloomily into his snifter of cognac. But it was Jeremiah who had caused Charlotte the most concern. He had approached her almost distractedly, his thoughts obviously on something far more pressing. He had lifted his gaze to acknowledge her only when he realized that she was sitting there in front of him.

She had wanted to ask him then what the matter was and had opened her mouth to do just that, but he had narrowed his blue eyes and had shaken his head, telling her wordlessly that it was not the time to make inquiries.

That had been a few hours ago. But now her curiosity demanded a few answers. She pushed her bare feet into her worn carpet slippers that she had unpacked from the trunk Jean-Claude had retrieved for her from Paris, then extinguished one of the lamps that illuminated her comfortable room. Knowing that the others had retired shortly after she had—for she heard them saying goodnight to one another as they came up to their rooms—she prayed that they were all asleep by now.

With a lighted candle held before her to guide her way, she slipped quietly out into the corridor, leaving her door slightly ajar so that she would not have any difficulty returning to it later. Jeremiah's room lay along the same passageway; she'd seen one of the maids lead him to it earlier. In the darkness, though, it was hard for her to distinguish, much less remember, exactly which room was his.

The decision about which door to open first was suddenly made for her when Jeremiah appeared in the hall. Like her, he held a candle before him, its flickering flame casting his handsome features into a shadowy mask of eerie angles.

On catlike feet, Charlotte hurried toward him, and together they entered his room.

"What are you doing wandering in the halls at this time of night?" he demanded when he'd shut the door behind them.

"I was looking for you!" she retorted. "I want to know what happened down there tonight."

"Your cousins!" Jeremiah groaned, turning toward the bed, where he placed his candle back in its silver holder. "For a while there, I thought they were going to call me out and demand satisfaction."

"What?"

"You know that preposterous lie you told Jean-Claude about me being married and having twelve kids? Well, the boy believed it! And, God help me, so did his father! Charlotte, I could gladly wring your lovely neck for that."

"But—but they're Frenchmen!"

"Yeah, and you're their cousin! I guess they think it's all right to have a mistress so long as the lady in question isn't related to them."

Well, it did make sense . . . of a sort, she thought.

"I was all set to ask Charles-André about his villa in Cannes," Jeremiah continued, wearily dropping onto the side of his bed, "but the minute you ladies walked out of the room, he let me know in no uncertain terms just how unhappy he was that I had put you in danger in Paris."

"But you told him, didn't you, about—"

"No! Are you addlepated or something? The

171

less he knows about Boland, the better. Jesus, I don't want that murderous bunch after him, too!"

Charlotte sat down beside him, sensing the frustration he felt.

"I've got to find some way of getting down to that villa," Jeremiah mused quietly. If the place had the vantage point he'd been led to believe, it would be the perfect location for him while he went about hunting for Boland.

"Well, Vivienne did say we could borrow one of their coaches if we needed it," Charlotte remarked offhandedly. Staring down at her feet, she didn't notice Jeremiah's expression as he slowly turned to stare at her. "And with a staff already in residence at the villa, we won't have to worry about opening it up. As I see it, the only real problem we're going to have is dressing to look like a pair of wealthy Americans, because only the rich can afford to go to Cannes. Neither one of us has the appropriate sort of wardrobe, you know."

"You—you mean to tell me that you've already talked Vivienne into letting me stay at their villa?" His voice was heavily laced with incredulity.

"I think I just said that, didn't I?"

An odd noise erupted from Jeremiah's throat at that moment, only to evolve into a surprised chuckle. Not knowing how else to express his gratitude, he grabbed her shoulders, hauled her to him, and kissed her soundly.

"You're one hell of a woman, Charlotte Atwater," he stated proudly when the kiss had ended. "A little strange, and maybe even a bit pushy at times, but a hell of a woman neverthe-less."

Still breathless and a little stunned from the sudden impact of his kiss, Charlotte managed to mutter a polite thank you. Then something he'd said hit her, and she stiffened. "Wait a minute!" she snapped, her brows furrowing together.

"What's wrong?"

"I think you've misunderstood something."

"Oh? What?"

"I'm going to Cannes with you."

"Oh no you're not! You're staying right here."

"Jeremiah—"

"Charles-André was right about one thing: you'll be a lot better off staying out of harm's way."

"Jeremiah!"

"I mean, Paris was one thing—that couldn't be avoided—but this is something else altogether. Why, I'd be a fool to let you come with me, not knowing what Boland and his bunch are apt to do next."

"Jeremiah Fox!" she asserted firmly. "Either I go with you or *you* don't go at all!"

"No Charlotte!"

"You need me," she insisted, getting to her feet. "Admit it."

"Yeah, well, maybe. But not for this, I don't." Blasted woman, he thought. Couldn't she see that if she stayed here with her family she would be much better off? "What are you doing?"

"I'm locking the door."

"What the hell for?"

Charlotte gave the key in the lock a resolute twist, then turned back to face him, a look of haughtiness written across her lovely features. "I'm going to show you just how much you need me."

"Charlotte, you'll be wasting both my time and yours. There's absolutely nothing you can say or do that'll make me change my mind. I've got a million things to do before—put that robe back on!"

But the sheer covering had already fallen in a whisper to the floor. With meticulous deliberation, Charlotte's fingers untied each of the bows that held her camisole together, and Jeremiah was given an enticing view of her full, curvaceous breasts. She lifted one foot and daintily placed her toes on the end of the bed, where he sat thoroughly enraptured by her performance. The white silk stocking that covered her slender leg was slowly peeled off. The second stocking soon followed, falling from her outstretched arm onto the floor.

Then Charlotte started toward him. Her hands slid up and down her hips in a most provocative manner before her knee-length cotton drawers were pushed down with infuriating slowness. It was at this point that she came to a complete stop in front of Jeremiah.

"Charlotte?" he entreated halfheartedly as she bent one knee and placed it on the mattress beside him.

"You need me, Jeremiah." Her gaze riveted to his flushed face, she leisurely shrugged her shoulders out of the camisole, letting it drop from her fingertips as his hungry gaze darted from one coral-crested breast to the other. "Say you need me."

He licked his lips, which had suddenly gone dry from his ragged breathing. "I—I need you," he repeated dazedly.

"And I can come with you."

Jeremiah's lips curled into a sly grin as his blue gaze slowly inched its way up her creamy torso. He reached out, grabbed her, and said, "Oh, you'll come all right!"

Chapter Twelve

CHARLOTTE RELUCTANTLY FLOATED OUT OF THE pleasant cocoon of slumber that she'd been long in finding the night before. Indeed, the massive clock in the downstairs hall had chimed the new day's second hour before she had finally fallen asleep in Jeremiah's arms. Their lovemaking had been so intense, so extremely satisfying, it was almost as if they really were newlyweds. Now her mind, not to mention her deliciously aching body, rebelled at having to face the morning.

A purr of sated contentment formed in her throat as a smile pulled at the corners of her lips. She stretched wide to ease the tightness in her joints, her right arm encountering nothing but an empty space in the bed beside her. Her lids flew open in alarm, and she jackknifed upright in bed.

Jeremiah was gone!

Charlotte threw back the sheet that had been covering her and bolted out of bed. She frantically searched for some sign of him, but only the dent in the pillow next to hers gave her the proof of his presence here the night before. That was all; even his clothes were gone.

Feeling panicky, she pulled on her wrapper with great haste, scooped up the rest of her things, and raced out into the hall. Unfortunately, there was no sign of Jeremiah there, either.

"Damn him!" she cursed as she headed down the empty corridor to the safety of her room. "Damn his rotten, miserable hide. If he's gone to Cannes without me, I'll kill him!"

Her anger was such that when she closed the door behind her she did not notice the bright sunlight streaming in through the opened window, nor did she hear the cheerful birds chirping outside in the trees. Her mind was totally absorbed in getting dressed and going after the scoundrel who had deserted her.

"He won't get away with loving and leaving *me!*" She jerked a dress out of her unpacked trunk and threw it on the bed. Her undergarments were donned hastily as she continued to mutter curses beneath her breath. As she fastened the row of tiny buttons down the bodice of her dress, she kept recalling all the avowals of love and adoration Jeremiah had whispered so earnestly to her in the heat of passion. She knew now that they had only been a smokescreen to throw her off guard.

"Well, this is one time that wily Fox isn't going

to elude *this* hunter. I'll chase him to hell and back if I have to!"

Fully dressed and with her hair carelessly arranged, she hurried downstairs to find that the family had already gathered. Seated at the small breakfast table in the sunny morning room, they all turned and smiled up at her when she entered.

"*Bonjour,* Charlotte," Great-Aunt Marie beamed. "Did you have a pleasant night?"

"*Oui, Tante, tres bien!*" She dropped a kiss on the old lady's wrinkled cheek and thought, *If you knew how pleasant it really was, you'd probably be quite shocked!*

"Come sit beside me, Charlotte," Vivienne beckoned, indicating the empty chair next to her. "Maurice? Tea and *croissants, s'il vous plaît.*"

The somber-looking footman, standing silently near the food-laden sideboard, turned to fulfill his mistress's order.

Charlotte slipped into the chair and unfolded her linen napkin with as much decorum as she could muster. "Have any of you seen Jeremiah this morning?"

"He and Papa were the first to leave," Suzanne replied.

"Oh?" Charlotte fluttered her lashes, hoping that maybe he hadn't left after all. "Are they taking a tour of Charles-André's laboratory?"

A puzzled frown formed on Jean-Claude's brow. "Did not Monsieur Fox tell you, cousin? He decided to leave for Cannes this morning."

The small surge of hope that Charlotte had felt died an uneasy death, but she carried off her disappointment with great aplomb. "That's right. I had forgotten. Oh, *merci*," she murmured as the footman placed a filled plate and cup before her.

While the others went about discussing their plans for the day, Charlotte pretended an interest in her flaky *croissant* by breaking it apart and spreading it with jam. Taking a tiny bite of it, she failed to taste its light, buttery sweetness.

"Jean-Claude?" she began when there was a lull in the conversation. "Have you made any special plans for today?"

Francesca, who had been sitting quietly beside the young Frenchman, lifted her cinnamon eyes and glanced across the table at Charlotte. Noting the look of anticipation in the gypsy girl's face, Charlotte had the feeling that Francesca knew what she was thinking.

"*Non*," Jean-Claude responded with a shake of his head. "Nothing that cannot wait."

"Then, if you wouldn't mind, perhaps you could take Francesca and me on a tour of the estate. You'd like that, wouldn't you, Francesca?"

"Yes, I would!" the girl remarked brightly.

For Charlotte, the remainder of breakfast continued at a snail's pace. More than a little anxious, she knew that the longer she was delayed in leaving Grasse, the closer to Cannes Jeremiah was getting. Heavens, for all she knew he was there by now, and getting into God knows what kind of trouble.

At last, when Vivienne and her daughters excused themselves from the table to go about their duties, Charlotte breathed an inner sigh of relief. She gulped down the remains of her now cold tea and was about to excuse herself as well, but Great-Aunt Marie stopped her.

"You are going after your Monsieur Fox, are you not, child?" the old woman asked.

Charlotte felt heat rush to her face as she turned to look at her elderly relative. The thought of lying to her aunt was briefly considered but then forgotten. "I have to, *Tante*," she admitted softly.

"Ah, I expected as much." Great-Aunt Marie shook her head and sighed. "When he left so hurriedly this morning, I knew you would not be satisfied remaining here with us. But what is so urgent that you both have to go? You have only just arrived, child, and I would like to have more time to get acquainted with you."

"I—I wish I could explain, *Tante*, but I can't. Just believe this: it is vitally important that I be with Jeremiah right now. Otherwise I wouldn't even consider leaving."

The old woman seemed to accept Charlotte's earnest declaration, because she nodded again, a sadly patient smile appearing on her lips. "You are so like your grandmother Georgianna. You rush after your Monsieur Fox just as she did her *Americain* so long ago. He was a spy, you know."

"Grandpa was a spy?" To say that Charlotte was surprised by this remark would be an understatement. She was totally flabbergasted! The grandfather she remembered hadn't been an intriguing sort of person at all. He had been a gentle, white-haired old man who had bounced her on his knee while she stole hard candies from his coat pocket.

"*Oui!*" Great-Aunt Marie chuckled. "He came to France not long after that rascal Bonaparte proclaimed himself emperor. Georgianna and I were still living in Paris then, but I can remember it as clearly as if it were only yesterday. Daniel was so dashing, so handsome, so impressive that both Georgianna and I could not help but fall a little in love with him. But, of course, my sister was the one to win his heart.

"Ah, but that was long ago," she sighed reminiscently, "and you do not have the time to listen to my tale. You want to be after your *Americain, non?*"

Charlotte continued to gaze at the old woman. She wanted to learn more about her grandparents, yet her anxiety to get to Cannes refused to let her linger. "I'll be back," she promised, rising to her feet. "I don't know how long I'll be gone, but I swear I'll be back as soon as I can." She dropped a kiss on her great-aunt's cheek and hugged her fiercely.

"*Bon.* We will talk then," the old woman agreed. "You be on your way now. And Charlotte? Take great care!"

"I will, *Tante.*"

"Do not worry, *Grandmere*," Jean-Claude remarked, coming to embrace his grandmother. "I will see that no harm comes to her."

"What do you mean, *you'll* see to it?" Charlotte demanded, her gray eyes widening with alarm.

"Why, only that I shall be going with you," Jean-Claude proclaimed.

"And I too!" Francesca piped up excitedly.

"Oh no! No, you're both staying right here," Charlotte retorted adamantly.

Everyone began talking at once then. Jean-Claude tried to convince his cousin that she would become lost in Cannes if he did not accompany her about the crowded coastal town. Francesca, not to be left out, babbled something about Charlotte needing a maid. But then Jean-Claude turned on the girl and scolded her for having such a foolish notion. She was too young, he said, and would only get in the way. Francesca naturally took exception to this and told him that she was a lot older and more experienced than he thought. And all the while they were arguing, Charlotte kept shaking her head and saying, "No, no, no!"

"Silence!" Great-Aunt Marie's shout abruptly ended the trio's quarrel. Three heads turned at once to stare at her. "Your childish bickering has given me a headache. If you wish to disagree with one another, do so somewhere else. I am too old to be disturbed in such a manner. Jean-Claude, ring for Thérèse *tout de suite!* Charlotte, go prepare yourself for the journey. And Francesca? See to it that they do not kill each other before you all get to Cannes."

Chapter Thirteen

ELEGANT. THAT WAS THE FIRST IMPRESSION JER-
emiah had of the pink-washed villa perched
high above the coastal town of Cannes. Elegant
and decidedly more lavish than he'd imagined it
would be.

He puckered up his lips and emitted a soft
whistle. Lord, these folks had money! They *had*
to, to have a chateau the size of a castle, a villa
that was almost as big as the White House in
Washington, and, as he'd learned earlier from
Charles-André, a "comfortable" townhouse in
Paris. And Charlotte, who professed to be just a
schoolteacher from some unpronounceable
town in Texas, was related to them!

"The perfume business sure must be lucra-
tive," he assumed, drawing closer to the mansion.

He rode past the side entrance steps and circled around the villa to the back, where Charles-André had told him the carriage house would be. There he found three men, dressed in leather aprons, polishing harnesses in the bright sunlight, while in the shade of the stables a young boy curried a sleek black Arabian stallion.

An avid horseman since his youth, Jeremiah admired the animal as he climbed down from his own mount. Though somewhat smaller than some other breeds he'd seen, the Arabian possessed a regal quality that marked him a champion. He could probably outrace the wind, Jeremiah decided, handing his horse over to one of the men.

As he started toward the house, a frown formed on his forehead. No one had seemed surprised that he was here. In fact, they hadn't even questioned his arrival. Oh well, he concluded while mounting the steps, maybe they were used to receiving unexpected visitors.

Upon entering the villa, Jeremiah was met by a tall, somewhat burly-looking gentleman dressed in dark trousers, white shirt, and striped waistcoat.

"Monsieur Fox?" the man queried, his accent sounding odd to Jeremiah. *"Bienvenue. Monsieur le comte* informed us by wire that you would be arriving."

"Monsieur le who?" was Jeremiah's confused response.

"Fox," the man repeated. "You are Monsieur Fox, are you not?"

"No—er, I mean yes. Yes I am! But did you say *monsieur le comte?"*

"*Oui.* Comte André Charles Robert Beauvais."

Charles-André was a comte? Lord, no wonder the man could afford three fully staffed residences. He wasn't just wealthy from the perfume business, he was royalty! Or the next best thing to it.

"You seem surprised, *monsieur,*" the man observed in that strange dialect of his. He turned and began to lead Jeremiah toward the front of the villa, where a grand staircase climbed to the second floor.

"Yeah, you could say that," Jeremiah retorted dryly. "Charles-André didn't tell me that he had a title."

The man lifted his shoulders in a gallic shrug. "With certain, mmm, people, *monsieur le comte* does not like to boast of his rank. He is a very modest man, as I am sure you have discovered."

Eyeing the opulence surrounding him—the marble statues lined against the corridor walls, the crystal-prismed sconces, the rich Persian carpet running underfoot—Jeremiah murmured, "Yeah, modest."

Casting Jeremiah a puzzled sidelong glance, the man stopped before a pair of gilt-edged doors, twisted the ornate knobs, and pushed both panels open wide. "These will be your quarters while you are here, *monsieur.*" He led Jeremiah inside the massive chamber. "Should you require anything more, just ring for the maid and she will be up to assist you."

Jeremiah gave the room a cursory perusal before he turned to look back at the burly man-

185

servant. "Well, there is one thing. What do I call you?"

"Emil, *monsieur*. I hold the position of major domo."

Again Jeremiah detected the man's strange accent and frowned slightly. He'd been in France long enough to know that each region had its own distinctive dialect, but Emil's was one he was unfamiliar with. It was partly cultured, almost Parisian in fact, and partly . . . he didn't know what.

"Emil," Jeremiah began, placing a hand on the man's shoulder.

The major domo glanced pointedly down at the hand then back into Jeremiah's face. His disapproval of Jeremiah's familiarity was clearly written on his rough-hewn features. But Jeremiah paid no notice as he led Emil further into the room and closed the door behind them.

"I don't know what you've been told about my reason for coming here," Jeremiah stated, and purposefully broke off, waiting for Emil to comment.

"Nothing, *monsieur*," the man admitted after a short pause. "We only received the one wire, telling us to expect you some time today."

"And that was all?"

"*Oui*. Should there have been more?"

"No," Jeremiah negated with a shake of his blond head. "You see, Charles-André—I mean, *monsieur le comte*—well, he doesn't know the real reason why I was in such a hurry to get here to Cannes. I've, er, ah, I've got a problem of sorts."

"Problem, *monsieur*?" Emil eyed him warily, one dark bushy brow arching inquisitively.

"Business," Jeremiah nodded.

"Ah, business!" Emil looked almost relieved at this admission.

"Yes. You see, I'm sort of involved in a—a transaction that is, er, well, it's not quite legal." He was doing a very bad job of skirting the truth, and he knew it, but he had to have some assistance while he was here or he wouldn't be able to find Boland.

"What's your problem, mate?"

Mate? Jeremiah shot Emil a surprised look. "I beg your pardon?" he queried with astonishment.

"Look, if we're gonna be honest wif one another, let's drop all this French bull and get right down to the meat of the matter. You're up to somethin' shady and you need me help. Right?"

"Well, er, yes, you could say that, I suppose."

"Right. Well, you've come to the right bloke. I know everythin' what goes on in this bloody little hamlet, and I don't mind tellin' you, some of it's right shockin'! Curl old Queen Vick's hair, it would."

Jeremiah was dumbfounded, to say the least. He watched Emil cross to one of the silk-upholstered chairs and fall into it as his hand dipped into his vest pocket to pull out a cigar. From another pocket he produced a match and lit the tip of his tobacco wand, puffing on it a few times until smoke curled about his unruly dark head.

"'Ere, mate, sit your arse down and let's get on

wif it. Tell me what kind of scam you're up to, an' I'll see if I can help you wif it. Them bloody little wenches downstairs won't miss me for a while yet. Probably have themselves a bit of a holiday, if I know them. We got time to talk before they decide to bring up high bleedin' tea."

"You're not French, are you?" was all Jeremiah could think of to say.

"French! Me?" Emil guffawed. "I should say not. I'm as English as Queen Vick herself. Maybe even more, since she's one of them Hanovers. Were you taken in by me accent then?" He chuckled again. "I must be better at it than I thought. I don't mind tellin' you, I had a right bloody job of convincin' *monsieur le comte*." This last was issued in the deep-throated accent he'd affected earlier. "'Course, the old lady was a bit harder to convince, but I soon got her to come round. Did me job better'n they expected me to, I did. Right finicky lot, these Frenchies are."

Jeremiah dropped into the chair next to Emil's and tried to organize his thoughts. Learning of Emil's true nationality was enough to make anyone go blank. But little by little he tried to explain the importance of his mission in Cannes, while not revealing the entire truth of the situation. After a while the Cockney seemed to grasp what he was saying.

"Let me get this straight," Emil responded. "You say this chap Boland's got somethin' of yours and you want to get it back wifout him knowin' about it." At Jeremiah's nod, he asked, "What exactly is it that he's got? I mean, is it a bleedin' elephant or a bloody little stick pin? I got to know, mate, so's I can figure out how to help."

Jeremiah took a deep breath, knowing that the time for the truth was at hand. "They're plates."

"You mean china? The kind what you eat off of?"

"No, no! Engraving plates."

"Bloody hell!" Emil's mouth dropped open, and his black eyes widened. "Engravin' plates! For makin' money? Just who the hell are you, mate?"

"I'm a special agent for the United States Treasury," Jeremiah confessed reluctantly. "But you aren't to breathe a word of this to anyone! Do I make myself clear? Boland and his accomplices have already tried to eliminate me once, and they've succeeded in incapacitating an associate of mine. I certainly don't want anyone else to follow his fate."

"Right nasty buggers, are they?" Emil assumed with a distasteful grimace.

"*Very* nasty. The woman most especially."

"They got a wench wif 'em? Gor! You really got trouble wif that lot. Wenches ain't nothin' like men. They're nastier! At least wif a man, you can sort of expect what they'll do, but *women*—" He shook his head, leaving the rest of his thought unsaid.

"Yes, I know!" Jeremiah nodded sagely. It wasn't Boland's feminine cohort he was thinking of, though. It was Charlotte. Knowing her as well as he did—which wasn't well at all—he knew she wasn't going to be satisfied staying behind in Grasse. The chances were she was on her way to Cannes right now. But with the head

start he had on her, he would have the wheels of
this mission set well into motion before she
made her appearance, which, if he'd timed it
right, wouldn't be before nightfall, or tomorrow
morning if he was lucky.

"We'd better get down to business, Emil,"
Jeremiah said, leaning forward and resting his
elbows on his knees. "You say you're familiar
with Cannes. . . ."

The better part of an hour had passed before
their intricate plotting was interrupted by a
knock at the door. Emil stiffened at the sound,
his head jerking around to face the closed doors.
And when he looked back at Jeremiah, his lips
were twisted into a disapproving line.

"Bloody wench is a half-hour late wif the high
bleedin' tea," he grumbled. "No tellin' what
they've been up to while me back was turned.
No good, most likely. Can't trust 'em a bloody
inch."

"Well, we can finish this later," Jeremiah
stated, and thrust the papers he'd been writing
on into his hip pocket.

Emil nodded in agreement and stood up, his
shoulders squaring as his mantle of a haughty
manservant slipped back into place. He walked
to the door and opened it to admit the young
housemaid, who carried a heavily laden tray.
Small and not uncomely, she merely glanced up
at Emil before brushing past him.

Always the gentleman, Jeremiah got to his
feet and smiled at the girl as she moved toward
him. She placed the tray down on the table, and
he noticed how her gaze seemed to shift for a

moment onto the glass dish where his and Emil's cigar butts were crushed. She didn't comment on this odd sight, though. Instead, she straightened and smiled at him, giving her lashes a flirtatious flutter before she dipped into a curtsy and turned to leave the room.

Emil stopped her at the door and muttered something harsh to her in French. Jeremiah caught only part of what the man said, but he knew that the girl was being chastised for her impertinence.

"You shouldn't have been so hard on her," Jeremiah said after the maid had disappeared, red-faced, down the hall. "She's just a child, and she was only trying to be nice."

"Nice! Gor, mate, if you only knew. If you don't keep the likes of her in line, she'll be tryin' to climb into your bed come nightfall. Then tomorrow mornin' she'll be demandin' you set her up in her own lodgin's wif an allowance to keep her and her family goin'." He inhaled a deep breath and shook his head. "You don't know what I have to put up wif wi' this lot."

Poor Emil, Jeremiah thought as he closed the door behind the Cockney. He had his hands full with the maids below stairs. But something told Jeremiah that the major domo could more than adequately handle what his "wenches" dished out.

Jeremiah stood before the tall mirror in his room, surveying the quite dashing image he presented in the clothes he'd borrowed. The bit of improvising he'd done—choosing the coat, vest, and shirt from Charles-André's wardrobe and finding the trousers and shoes in Jean-Claude's—caused him to look more than satisfactory. With his face clean-shaven, his mustache trimmed, and his blond hair washed and slicked back, he looked every inch the wealthy American. The only disconcerting part of his appearance was the damn gold ring still stuck in his lobe. He'd tried to pull it out but found he couldn't. It was in there for good.

He was in the process of inserting a small diamond stick pin into his cravat when he heard carriage wheels crunch to a halt in the gravel forecourt down below. Since his room was at the front of the villa, he was sorely tempted to peer down out the window and see for himself just who had arrived. But he repressed his curiosity and finished dressing, knowing that, whoever it was, it couldn't be Charlotte. She couldn't possibly get here before nightfall.

His certainty wavered slightly when he heard Jean-Claude's familiar voice ring out a greeting to Emil, and it vanished altogether when he heard Charlotte phrase a sweet hello. It *was* her, damn it! They must have left Grasse right after he had. But his disappointment at their sudden arrival was soon replaced with intense anger when he heard another feminine voice call out to Jean-Claude, and the young Frenchman responded with undisguisable impatience.

Jesus Christ, they'd brought Francesca with them!

"Get two of the men to help you with our trunks, Emil," Jean-Claude directed the man-servant distractedly as he led Charlotte up the front steps. "There are too many of them to handle on your own."

"*Oui, monsieur,*" Emil responded.

"Oh, and the ladies will require hot baths, so have the maids tend to that as well."

"*Oui, monsieur.*"

"I don't need a bath," Francesca protested quietly.

"Yes you do," Charlotte informed her.

"But I had one just last month," the girl complained.

"Well, it's time you had another."

"But—"

"If you're going to be *my* maid, Francesca, you will take a bath. Otherwise you'll go right back to Grasse."

"Oh all right," the girl relented sullenly, and followed Charlotte into the villa's vast foyer.

"And you're going to behave yourself while you're here, aren't you? You're not going to traipse around after Jean-Claude and make a nuisance of yourself. He's got enough on his mind without you adding to his worries."

To this, Francesca neither agreed nor disagreed. She lifted her chin at a defiant angle and set her full lips into a stubborn, unwavering line.

"Francesca!" Charlotte hissed warningly.

"I will not get in his way," was all the girl would promise.

"Well, that's better than nothing, I suppose." Charlotte groaned inwardly, rueing the fact that they'd let Francesca come with them at all. It hadn't been *her* idea. Great-Aunt Marie had insisted!

"Would you care for some tea before you go up to your rooms?" Jean-Claude asked when he joined them a moment later.

"No thank you," Charlotte demurred. "The sooner we can wash all this grime away, the better we'll—" She broke off abruptly, a movement at the head of the stairs having captured her attention.

Jeremiah stood there in his elegant evening clothes, looking down at her with that smile she'd come to love. Her heart literally skipped a beat, and she almost smiled back at him, but then she remembered what he'd done to her and quickly jerked her gaze away to glare back at Jean-Claude. She was not going to let herself be taken in by Jeremiah Fox's pretentious charm ever again.

"As I was saying," she continued, "the sooner we can bathe, the better we'll feel."

"Aren't you even going to say hello to me, Charlotte?" There was a hint of amusement in Jeremiah's voice as he casually sauntered down the stairs.

"I would like to get to the casino and try my hand at roulette." Charlotte addressed Jean-Claude, ignoring Jeremiah's presence completely. "I feel very lucky today. And you did say you would show me how to play the game."

"Come, come, Charlotte," Jeremiah chuckled. "Surely you're not *that* angry with me."

"Jean-Claude, would you please inform this— this *person* that I don't wish to speak to him?"

The young Frenchman darted a confused look at Jeremiah, then glanced back at his cousin. "But he is—"

"Just *tell* him, Jean-Claude!"

"Monsieur Fox, she does not—"

"I heard her, Jean-Claude." Jeremiah shook his head disappointedly. "Charlotte, you're being very childish about this."

Charlotte still refused to look at him. "Jean-Claude, ask him what he considers running away to be if not the epitome of childishness."

"I call it having good sense," Jeremiah retorted. "You were better off in Grasse, and you know it!"

A growl of frustration formed in Charlotte's throat, but she suppressed it by taking a deep breath. "Jean-Claude, tell this idiot that if I had stayed in Grasse he wouldn't be able to get to Boland like he wants to."

"For God's sake, Charlotte," Jeremiah cringed. "Watch what you're saying. They shouldn't know about—"

"And why not?" she challenged, turning to address him herself. "How in heaven's name do you think you're going to find that man if we don't have some help?"

"*We! I* have all the help I need, thank you!"

"There's no need to raise your voice to me, Jeremiah Fox. I won't stand for it. It was embarrassing enough to find that you'd left without me this morning. I certainly don't have to take your petty insolence as well."

"Insolence! Damn it, Charlotte, I left you there for your own good!"

"I'll be the judge of that," she countered loftily.

Jeremiah's face suddenly suffused with red as his features contorted into a grimace. His teeth, clenched tightly together, were bared, and the veins in his neck became taut and prominent as he tried to repress a scream. As it was, he sounded as though he were on the verge of having a fit.

Charlotte glanced down her nose at him, a part of her thoroughly enjoying his rage. "Come, Francesca. We have a million things to do before we can go to the casino."

They turned, mounted the stairs, and had reached the upper landing at the top when Jeremiah's rage was finally released in an angry roar.

"Women!" he bellowed, his voice echoing off the walls.

Charlotte merely smiled and swished off down the hall.

Chapter Fourteen

"YOU LOOK UTTERLY RIDICULOUS, YOU KNOW."
Charlotte observed Jeremiah from her corner of
the carriage. "No one in their right mind is ever
going to believe you're my father."

"Husband, Charlotte. Remember, we decided
I was to be your much older husband. For God's
sake, do try and get it straight. Anyway, it's all
your fault."

"My fault?"

"Yes. If you had stayed behind at the villa like
I wanted you to, I wouldn't have to look like this.
But no, you just *had* to go to the casino tonight."

"Well, you could have stayed at the villa. You
didn't have to come with me. Jean-Claude was
more than willing to—"

"Why do you think I insisted on coming?"
Jeremiah asserted. "There's no telling what the
two of you would have gotten yourselves into."

Silence fell between them, a silence that was just as tense and angry as it had been earlier. Jeremiah glanced down at his clothes, which were years out of date and nothing at all like the dapper ensemble he'd put together earlier. Then he lifted a hand and touched the paint-stiffened strands of hair just above his temples.

The disguise had been Emil's idea, not his. The silver streaks in his blond hair and the wire-framed spectacles perched on his nose were intended to make him appear older, more distinguished. Instead he felt like some aged *roué* who was out to prove he still had some life left in him.

However, if Charlotte thought *he* looked ridiculous, *she* looked downright cheap! Her dark brown hair had been dressed with too many ringlets and feathers. Her cheeks bloomed too rosily with the same garish shade of rouge that was smeared on her naturally pink lips. Her gown dipped so daringly low in front that anyone who chanced to meet her would have an enticing, unobstructed view of her well-shaped bosom. Lord, he hadn't seen that much bare flesh in years! Not since he was fifteen, in fact, when his older brother had taken him to Madam Flora's place outside Richmond.

"I hope Monsieur Boland doesn't come to the casino tonight," murmured Charlotte as she tried to pull the gown up over a rounded portion of her bosom. When Jean-Claude had brought her the dress, he'd told her that it was *de rigueur*, that all of the women at the casino tonight would be wearing gowns similar to this one. But in truth Charlotte felt rather like a trollop.

"It's a little late to be thinking about him now, don't you think? Anyway, worrying is a waste of time. From what I've heard, only the wealthy can afford to frequent the casino. Artistic and scholarly types don't have the money it takes to throw away at the gaming tables."

Their carriage pulled to a stop before the large, Italianate building that housed the casino. Jeremiah painstakingly stepped down, moving with the exaggerated slowness of an elderly gentleman, then turned back to assist Charlotte.

"Can't you stand up? You're slouching," she chided quietly. Other casino patrons were milling about the front steps of the establishment, and she didn't want them to overhear her.

"No, I can't," he murmured near her ear. "Emil's got the bottom of my shirt pinned to my pants. If I try to straighten up, I'll rip the whole damn thing to shreds."

Charlotte cast him an astounded look. "What on earth did he do that for?"

"Oh, the fool had some misguided notion that I should really look like an old man. He said that only young men stand tall and proud. Old men sort of stoop over and dodder around a lot."

Their carriage pulled away, but it was soon replaced by another. The door to this conveyance swung open, and its occupant, a man obviously in his late seventies, hopped out. After carelessly tossing a coin to his driver, he turned and sprinted up the casino steps, taking them two at a time.

Charlotte, having stood there silently watching the old man's rapid ascension, shook her head in dismay and turned to face Jeremiah. "You know, there's something a little strange about Emil."

"If you only knew," Jeremiah growled.

With her arm looped through his, they mounted the steps and entered the casino. Charlotte was more awed by the casino's patrons than she was by the lavish interior. The men were dressed in their finest evening wear; a few even sported broad, colorful ribbons across their chests, marking them as foreign dignitaries. The women, with diamonds and other precious jewels glittering in their ears and at their throats, paraded about the main salon as if they were in competition with one another. But it was the cut of their gowns that astonished Charlotte the most. They were even more daring than her own!

"Would you care for some champagne?" Jeremiah asked when he spied a waiter nearby.

"No thank you. Where's the roulette table? I'm dying to try my hand at it."

"I wouldn't advise it, Charlotte. You're liable to lose your shirt . . . what there is of it."

"Oh, don't be such an old fuddy-duddy. Let me have some money."

Reluctantly, Jeremiah delved into his trousers pocket and produced a coin. So far they had been quite frugal with the little money they possessed between them. After tonight, he thought dismally, they would probably be flat broke.

Charlotte eyed the coin he'd pressed into her gloved palm. "Is this all I get?"

"If you want more, you're going to have to win it. That's all we can spare."

"I knew Jean-Claude should have come with me," she muttered, and walked away.

There were more women at the roulette table than there were men. Charlotte slid in between two expensively gowned ladies and watched the game for a moment to see how it was played. It looked quite easy to her. One only had to place one's money on a number painted on the table and wait for a little marble to spin around on the wheel. Then it would either fall into a corresponding slot or it wouldn't.

But which number to choose was her biggest problem. On the first play, the marble landed in the black thirteen slot. On the second, the winner was red twenty-two.

Throwing caution to the wind, Charlotte placed her coin on the table and slid it onto the red square marked with the number twelve. Why not? she thought. It was as good a number as any.

The *croupier* spun the wheel, then sent the marble into motion in the opposite direction. Charlotte watched pensively as it went round and round, the numbers and colors all blurring together. The wheel finally began to slow down, and the marble bounced off one slot to another. When the wheel stopped turning, she was surprised to see that the marble had landed in her slot.

"I won!" she exclaimed excitedly, and watched as the *croupier* placed a coin of equal value beside hers.

Almost immediately he called for the next

round of bets. Not knowing what else to do, Charlotte left her money alone. *What the hell,* she thought. *I'll let it ride.*

Twenty minutes later, she walked away from the table with her beaded reticule full of coins and the smile of a winner etched across her face. She wanted to find Jeremiah and show him what she had accomplished. He had thought she would lose at roulette, but instead she'd turned her one single coin into almost a thousand dollars.

From behind the potted palm where he had been hiding, Jeremiah saw Charlotte leave the roulette table. Knowing that she was looking for him, he cautiously stepped out from behind the plant and was about to raise his hand to get her attention when he was suddenly addressed by a woman in her early fifties.

"Do you have a light, *monsieur?*" The woman lifted a long ebony holder in which a slender cigarette had been placed.

Jeremiah felt in his coat and made a show of searching through his pockets. "Alas, *madame*, I do not," he apologized.

"Ah, *n'importe,*" she shrugged. "I did not wish to smoke anyway. I use my unlit cigarette only as an excuse to meet you." The wrinkles about her sparkling hazel eyes deepened as she smiled up at him winsomely. "You have not been here before, *monsieur?*"

"No, this is my first time," he admitted, and looked past her to see where Charlotte had gotten off to. He saw her milling with the crowd at the crap table. *Oh hell, Charlotte,* he groaned inwardly. *Whatever you do, don't bet on snake-eyes!*

"I am wondering, *monsieur*," the woman began, bringing Jeremiah's attention back to her. "What is the purpose of the gold ring you wear in your ear?"

Jeremiah's hand flew up to cover his still sensitive lobe. He felt heat suffuse his face and voiced the first lie he could think of. "I was a sailor in my youth."

The woman's eyes widened, and her painted mouth dropped open in a gasp. "Your ship went down? *Comme affreaux!*"

"Yes," he nodded dramatically. "It was rather horrible. Not many of us managed to survive. Our captain, God rest his soul, went down with the ship."

"You are *Anglais, n'est-ce pas?*"

"American," he corrected her.

"Ah, *Americain!* But tell me, *monsieur* . . .?"

"Renard." Jeremiah supplied the equivalent of "Fox" in French. "Jerome Renard."

"Renard! Ah, *bon, bon!* A Frenchman of the heart, if not by birth. I am Héloïse Lambert. But you may call me Héloïse."

And with this, she moved in closer to him—so close, in fact, that Jeremiah was almost overwhelmed by the odor of her powerful perfume.

Lord, Charlotte, he cried out silently, again searching for his companion over Heloise's head. *Get me out of this! Where are you when I need you?*

Charlotte was too absorbed in her latest discovery even to consider what sort of dilemma

Jeremiah might be involved in. She had watched the dice table's activity for a few minutes before deciding that it was far too risky a game for her. She'd won all this money, and by golly she was going to keep it as long as she could!

As she turned to walk away, she caught sight of an oddly familiar-looking woman dressed in deep burgundy silk. It didn't occur to her at first where she'd seen the woman before, but the longer she looked at her, the clearer Charlotte's memory became. Then it hit her. Her breath caught in her throat, and her heart thudded painfully against her ribs. The woman was Boland's accomplice! The one Charlotte had seen the old man talking to in the Paris museum. The same one who had attacked Jeremiah and pushed him into the Seine!

Charlotte was forced to avert her gaze when the woman glanced in her direction. She stared blindly at the table before her, not noticing what was happening. Then she chanced a second look and saw that the woman had turned her attention back to the young man who stood beside her.

So far so good, she thought, knowing now that the woman hadn't recognized her. A quick glance down at her dress brought a smile to her lips. There was nothing unusual about her not being recognized. Why, even her own mother wouldn't know her in this getup.

Charlotte wanted to get closer to the two people. She just might learn something of Boland's whereabouts.

She began wandering about the crowded salon, always keeping the pair in sight. The longer she looked at them, though, the more she realized how similar their features were. Like the woman, the young man possessed dark, slanted Magyar eyes and a nose that was shaped like a hawk's beak. They were obviously related. But were they brother and sister or mother and son? Probably the latter, she decided, because the woman looked years older than the young man.

Staring blindly back down at the table before her, she thought, *I've got to get to Jeremiah and warn him that she's here. If they see through his disguise and recognize him, there's no telling what they might do.*

Charlotte never got the opportunity to carry through her plan—not at that moment, at any rate. She started to turn away from the table, but the young man she'd been watching so warily suddenly appeared beside her and gave her a smile that made her heart go cold. At a distance he appeared rather threatening. Up close, though, he looked positively dangerous. There was an aura of cruelty about him that was hard to ignore.

"An interesting game," he observed casually. "Do you intend to play, *mademoiselle?*"

Unable to speak because of the intenseness of her apprehension, Charlotte could only shake her head.

"I have not seen you here before," he went on, the smile about his mouth deepening. "Is this your first visit to the casino?"

"Yes." Through the blood pounding in her ears, her voice sounded high-pitched and unnatural.

"Ah, well, you must not let all of this opulence intimidate you, little one. Come, I will get you a glass of champagne."

"No!" she ejaculated, and stepped away from the hand he stretched out to her. "I mean, no thank you. I—I'm not thirsty."

"You are playing a game with me, no? I saw the way you were watching me earlier, and now you pretend to be repelled by my attention."

Oh good heavens! He thought she had been flirting with him. Not knowing what else to do, she did not correct him on his false assumption.

"I—I didn't think you had noticed," she murmured, letting her gaze drop from his as her mind grappled for what to say, what to do next.

An ominous chuckle rumbled through his chest. "Oh, I noticed, *mademoiselle*. It *is mademoiselle*, is it not?"

"Yes. I'm not married." Only after Charlotte had admitted this did she realize that she should have told him she *was* married. If she had, he might have gone away and left her alone. But it was too late now to correct the error.

"But I take it you did not come alone tonight, did you?" he drawled.

"No, I'm here with my—" She broke off, her mind suddenly going blank. What relationship had she and Jeremiah agreed upon? "My uncle," she ended, almost panicky. It wasn't the right relative, but it would have to do.

"Your . . . uncle is a very possessive man, I take it."

By the tone of his voice, she knew he hadn't believed her, that he assumed her "uncle" to be her lover. "Yes he is," she agreed. "If he sees us talking, he'll . . . well, there's no telling what he might do."

"Surely he would not mind if we took a cup of punch together. With so many people about, where would the harm be?"

"You don't know him like I do. He can become insanely jealous if he suspects that I'm even thinking about another man."

"I can understand that," the young man professed huskily. "With a woman like you, I can easily see myself becoming jealous as well."

With a woman like her? What on earth did he mean by that? Was he blind or something? Couldn't he see that she was nowhere near as beautiful as the other women in the casino? But whatever the case, she pretended to be embarrassed by his compliment and thanked him shyly.

"Come," he stated, and offered her his arm. "Let us brave your 'uncle's' wrath and have that cup of punch."

Jeremiah didn't see Charlotte place her hand on the stranger's arm. In truth, from his place behind the potted palm, he couldn't see much of anything or anyone except the three women who swayed unsteadily before him. And their presence was about to drive him crazy!

Madame Héloïse Lambert hadn't been satisfied with torturing him all by herself; she'd called over a couple of her cronies, "to keep him entertained," as she'd so aptly phrased it. But the way he looked at it, there was nothing at all entertaining about witnessing a trio of middle-aged women drink themselves into oblivion as they rehashed their husbands' peccadillos.

"It does not surprise me," one of them was saying when he turned his attention back to them. "My Georges was the same way. I had a wonderful *modiste*, Fifi her name was. She could sew like a dream. But when I found her in the closet with Georges, I had no choice but to dismiss her from my employment. Her replacement, Roxanne, was just as good a seamstress, but she too ended up like her predecessor . . . in the closet with Georges."

"Did you get rid of her too?" one of the other women asked.

"Yes, I had to."

The other two women commiserated with the wronged wife before downing their drinks. Jeremiah, having listened quietly to this pitiful dialogue, thought the woman would have been better off getting rid of Georges—either that or nailing shut the damn closet.

"You are not the unfaithful type, are you, Monsieur Renard?"

Hearing his name, Jeremiah glanced up with a jerk. "Huh? Oh no! No, certainly not!"

"That is because you are a man of honor," Madame Lambert praised him with a noticeable slur. Obviously well into her cups, she was still capable of waylaying a passing waiter who carried a full tray of fresh drinks. *"Merci, garcon,"* she murmured, and handed each of the other women a new glass. When the waiter had wandered away, she continued, *"Americains* pos-

208

sess integrity where our Frenchmen do not. I wanted to marry an *Americain* once."

"Héloïse!" the soberest of the remaining two cried out. "*Vraiment*? Why have you not told me of this before?"

And then the trio launched into woeful tales of the men they could have married but hadn't.

Leaning his shoulder against a pillar, Jeremiah knew he must look every inch the tired old man he was pretending to be. He felt like he'd aged a good ten years in this one night alone. He'd never spent a more boring evening in his whole life. Even those times when he'd been forced as a boy to endure the unending gossip of his mother and assorted female relatives, he hadn't been half as weary as he was now.

So to say he was relieved when he saw Charlotte weaving her way toward him would be a gross understatement. He looked upon her as his very own angel of mercy, come to rescue him from this torment. But then, when he noticed how her bosom jiggled, how her saucy ringlets bounced with each step she took, and the expression of excitement that was plastered on her face, he decided she wasn't angelic at all. She was the cause of all he had suffered through.

"We have to leave," she said without preamble, stopping before him.

"Oh? But I'm having *such* a good time," he jeered.

"I don't care. We have to go—now!" A quick glance away from Jeremiah took Charlotte's gaze to the trio of middle-aged ladies who were listening avidly to their exchange. "Oh, you will forgive him, won't you? It's way past his bed-time."

"But I don't want to leave now," Jeremiah protested stubbornly, wanting to give her a dose of her own medicine.

"Come along, Uncle. Don't be difficult," she ordered, linking her arm in his before leading him out from behind the potted palm. "We'll come back again some other time, I promise."

As soon as they were out of the trio's hearing range, she leaned close to Jeremiah and whispered, "Keep your head down! Don't look around. Don't say anything. Just keep quiet and follow me."

"What the—"

"Shh!" she hissed. "Just keep walking. No, not so fast. Go a little slower and shuffle your feet more. You're an old man, remember? I don't want them getting suspicious."

"Them? Who?"

"I'll tell you when we get out of this place."

It took them a few moments to collect their evening capes and Jeremiah's shiny top hat, and for the doorman to hail a carriage. But as soon as they were safely inside the conveyance, Jeremiah turned to her and demanded angrily, "Just what the hell happened back there?"

"You'll never believe it in a million years."

"Probably not, but try me anyway."

"I know where Boland is."

"You *what*?"

"Yes, I know where Boland is," she beamed, obviously pleased with herself. "I let one of his accomplices make a play for me. Well, he only bought me a cup of punch and talked to me for a little bit, but he inadvertently told me where Boland has set up his studio." She then repeated the street name the young man had mentioned. "Aren't you proud of me?"

"Good God, no! You could've gotten yourself killed."

"Oh for heaven's sake. I was never in any danger. There were too many people around for him to do anything to me. And anyway, he doesn't even know who I really am." She giggled suddenly. "He thought I was some jealous old man's young mistress. He kept trying to get me to leave the casino with him and go to his place, but when he realized he was wasting his time, he—" She broke off as a low-pitched growl filled the carriage.

She'd heard that growl before—earlier that day, as a matter of fact—when Jeremiah had unleashed his fury in an ear-splitting roar.

"Oh, you're not going to yell, are you?" she asked, cringing as the sound continued. "I can't stand it when you do that. And you'll frighten the living daylights out of the driver."

Jeremiah's clenched fists were turning his knuckles white. His even white teeth were bared in a snarl beneath his mustache. And she knew, even though she couldn't see him clearly in the dark, that the veins in his neck were standing out like tree roots. So she waited silently, pensively, for his fury to diminish.

In due time, Jeremiah did manage to calm down. His fists slowly unclenched at the same moment his snarl disappeared. He wiped his sweaty palms down his trouser legs and began to inhale deep gulps of air. But the silence remained with them for a long while.

They were almost to the outskirts of Cannes before he finally asked, "Just where is Boland's studio?" in a voice that was tight with control.

Charlotte quietly told him, then cringed when he lunged toward the door. At first she thought he was going to attack her. She'd certainly provoked him enough. But when he didn't, when he only leaned across her to stick his head out the window and bark out an order to their driver, she felt a wave of relief wash over her.

"Why are we going to his studio tonight?" she asked cautiously after he'd settled his long frame back into his corner.

"We aren't," came his wooden reply. "We're just going to drive past it . . . very slowly. I want to see for myself what the place looks like at night."

"Whatever on earth for?"

"Look! Don't push me too far, Charlotte. I've had about all I can take for one night."

"You've had! Well, if that isn't the most ungrateful thing I've ever heard! I went to a lot of trouble to get that information for you. I risked my life, not to mention my reputation, by letting that—that man fawn all over me, and then you have the unmitigated nerve to sit there and—"

Jeremiah did attack her then. But it wasn't a malicious kind of attack at all. He hauled her toward him and pressed his mouth to hers, successfully ending her tirade. And after a few moments, when the headiness of his kiss began to spread through her body, when her arms wound their way about his neck, she began to make tiny whimpering sounds of pleasure deep in her throat.

The kiss had been intended only to shut her up, but it soon evolved into something far more delightful than Jeremiah had anticipated. Driven by the same old hunger that had drawn him to her in the beginning, he rejoiced in the power her response unleashed within him. As it had done before, when he'd been angry, his heart beat a ragged tempo, sending his blood coursing through his veins until, this time, the urgency settled in his loins.

He moved, manipulating her, guiding her so that her back lay flat upon the carriage seat. The exposed portion of her bosom grew greater as he pushed the fabric of her gown down and aside, his questing fingers gaining freer access to her sweetly scented flesh. Where his hands touched, caressed, explored, his mouth soon followed until they reached and covered her rigid coral nipples. He bathed them with kisses so hot and feverish that Charlotte began to writhe wildly beneath him.

Her skirts were soon pushed up about her waist, letting her experience the rough sensation of Jeremiah's trousers against her legs. She parted her long limbs instinctively, planting one foot on the seat as the other dangled to the floor, and cradled his weight between her thighs. When the bulging hardness of his manhood came to rest against her feminine counterpart, she inhaled a sharp gasp at the pleasure its presence elicited. Her hips arched, as did his, and there began the rhythm that carried them farther and farther away from reality.

Though they were still separated by the thin barriers of their clothes, the zenith of their passion was almost upon them when the carriage suddenly swayed and came jerking to a halt. Jeremiah fell to the floor in a heap, and Charlotte would have followed him had she not braced herself in time. Feeling shaken and bereft without him, she could see the expression of surprise mixed with noticeable discomfort on his features in the dimly lit carriage.

Neither of them was capable of movement for a moment, so overcome were they by the frustration of having been so rudely, so shockingly separated. But then, realizing what state her gown was in, Charlotte covered her breasts and adjusted her skirts before she tremulously settled herself back into her corner.

Outside, voices were raised in anger. However, Charlotte was far more concerned with Jeremiah and his obvious discomfort than she was with what had happened elsewhere.

"Jesus," he swore at long last on a harshly expelled breath. He pulled himself up into the seat with great effort, being careful not to touch her. "Now I know what they mean by *coitus interruptus.*"

"C—*coitus interruptus,*" she repeated in a trembling voice, groping for some sense of normality. "Th—that's Latin, isn't it?"

"No," he groaned, moving to open the door. "It's pure hell!"

"Where are you going?"

"Out. I want to see what's happened. I'll be back in a few minutes."

"I'll come with you." She made a move to do just that, but he turned around and stopped her with a firm, insistent hand to her shoulder.

"You're not going anywhere. You're going to stay right here and wait!"

Jeremiah stepped out into the darkened street and slammed the carriage door behind him. The night air, possessing a salty tang of the ocean nearby, invaded his overwrought senses, enabling him to think coherently once again. He managed to make mental notes of one or two of the local landmarks before he joined the driver, who was in the process of helping another man replace crates of produce on a wagon that had overturned.

"I am sorry for the inconvenience, *monsieur*," the carriage driver remarked distractedly.

"Oh, that's quite all right," Jeremiah retorted with much more conviction than he felt. "No one was hurt, were they?"

"Only my fruit," the wagon driver complained. "I harvest it early for the celebration tomorrow, and now look at it."

The two men began to squabble again, each accusing the other of carelessness, and Jeremiah grew weary of listening to their inane prattle. He interrupted them and asked the driver exactly where they were. The man told him, gesturing with a pointed finger, that they were not far from the street he'd requested earlier. And as Jeremiah struck off down the street on foot, the two men returned to their arguing with as much fervor as before.

If Charlotte's informant had been correct, Boland's studio ought to be close by, Jeremiah thought. But which building housed it? They all looked the same to him—tall and stuccoed, with two or three stories to their height. He muttered a curse beneath his breath, feeling the futility of his ignorance. What good was a street name going to do him if he didn't know the location of the house as well?

And then, as if his guardian angel had suddenly heard his thoughts, a carriage entered the street from the opposite end. Not wanting the driver of the carriage to see him, Jeremiah quickly darted into a nearby alleyway and waited for the conveyance to pass.

But it didn't pass. It slowly pulled to a halt almost directly across from where he stood.

Sinking into the shadows, he pressed his body against the wall and cautiously watched as the carriage door swung open. He was so close that even the darkness of the night did not deter him from clearly seeing the young man who descended to the pavement. Nor did it conceal the identity of the older woman who followed.

The shock of recognition was so great that it caused the blood in Jeremiah's veins to freeze momentarily. But while he felt cold on the inside, beads of sweat formed on his palms and brow. He thought the sound of his thudding heart would surely be heard in the silence around him.

He guessed that Boland's house was the one the couple was now standing before, for the woman was without doubt the same one who had attacked him in Paris. For all he knew, they could be the same pair who had bound poor Albert to his wheelchair after so brutally beating him and leaving him for dead those many months before.

The couple entered the house, and their carriage pulled away, disappearing into the darkness. Jeremiah remained in the alley for a while longer, his mind racing ahead to the possible problems that his plan might entail. Then, stealthily, he started back to where his own carriage awaited, a smug smile playing about his lips.

Chapter Fifteen

"No!" CHARLOTTE REFUSED EMPHATICALLY AS she swished down the corridor toward her bedroom. "I will not be used like that, so you can just forget it!"

"Who's using?" Jeremiah persisted, not understanding her refusal. "You certainly didn't seem opposed to the idea earlier."

"That was before you left me in the carriage to twiddle my thumbs for a good half-hour. I might have been in the mood then, but I'm not now."

Twiddle her thumbs? She'd been doing everything but that, as he recalled. He had returned to the carriage from his highly successful reconnaissance of Boland's studio to find Charlotte sitting rigidly in her corner, her foot tapping out an angry beat against the floor as her arms hugged her body. He had known she was a bit perturbed, but he hadn't thought it was to the extent of denying him.

"Oh come on, Charlotte," he coaxed plaintively as he came to a halt behind her. "Just because I wouldn't tell you what happened back there—and nothing did!—you suddenly decide to play the outraged virgin."

"Now that isn't so, and we both know it! Besides, Jean-Claude and Francesca are in the house. I would feel very uncomfortable. . . ."

"You weren't very uncomfortable last night at the *chateau* when your whole damn family was right down the hall," he pointed out when her voice trailed off.

"That was last night," she retorted. "This is now. I don't want the two of them thinking that we're . . . well, you know."

"Yeah, you don't want them thinking that we're lovers, which is exactly what we are!"

"Not tonight we're not. Look, Jeremiah, it's one thing to be lovers in private but quite another to flaunt it openly."

Jeremiah blinked at her for a few moments, then gave his head a quick shake, hoping the movement would jar loose his thinking capability. "Your reasoning escapes me."

"That doesn't surprise me." She gave him a beatific smile and turned to open her door. "Anyway, it's been a very long day, and I'm tired. All I want to do now is go to bed—alone!" And with that she entered her room and closed the door firmly behind her.

Left facing the panel, Jeremiah had a sudden urge to kick the door down, march inside, and show her just who was the boss around here. But he didn't. Another, more intriguing idea came to mind, and he decided to follow through with it.

Humming happily if a bit off key beneath his breath, he ambled off down the corridor to his own room and changed out of his formal clothes. He slipped on the black satin robe that Jean-Claude had let him borrow earlier and then went in search of the young Frenchman.

Jean-Claude, sitting upright in the middle of his bed with a boring book, had spent the better part of the evening worrying about his cousin's fate at the casino while at the same time trying to avoid the bothersome clutches of Francesca. Oh, she was a pleasant enough child and in a few years might even prove to be an enjoyable *petite amie*, but he'd had enough of her following him around like a soulful puppy for one evening.

Hearing the light knock on his door, he called out, *"Entrer!"* somewhat reluctantly, hoping it wasn't Francesca on the other side.

"You weren't sleeping, were you?" Jeremiah asked, sticking his head inside the door.

"Oh, *non, monsieur.*" With a snap, Jean-Claude closed his book and set it aside. "Tomorrow is Bastille Day, and I decided to retire early."

"Bastille Day," Jeremiah repeated, coming further into the room. "I had forgotten."

"Have you ever celebrated our nation's greatest holiday before?"

"No, can't say that I have. Though I understand that you French put as much enthusiasm into it as we Americans do our Fourth of July."

Jean-Claude's expression brightened. "Ah, then you can appreciate why we honor our Fourteenth of July so highly. It is strange, is it not, how different our two countries are in some respects and yet so alike in others. We both celebrate the freedom of our nations within the same month; yours from the tyranny of British dogs and ours from the despotism of pompous, uncaring fools."

Jeremiah was taken aback slightly. He hadn't anticipated a history lesson. He'd come for something far more important. "Er, Jean-Claude, did you by any chance bring that black mask with you?"

"Black mask, *monsieur?*" Looking a little confused, Jean-Claude wondered what a black mask had to do with Bastille Day? But in a matter of seconds Jeremiah's question registered, and Jean-Claude's expression changed. His gray eyes grew wide. The furrows in his brow disappeared. His breath was indrawn on a sharp gasp. "Oh, *oui!* I have it right here."

The sheet atop him was suddenly thrust aside as he leaped out of bed. He bounded across the room, his nightshirt flapping about his bare ankles, and flung open the doors to his armoire. He reached inside for his leather valise, and when he found it he held it in his arms and began pulling out articles of clothing, letting them fly about his head as he dug into the depths of the bag. With a joyous exclamation, he produced the item he'd been searching for.

"You are going to tell me of its use now, are you not, *monsieur?*" he asked eagerly.

"Its use?" Jeremiah took the folded cloth from Jean-Claude. "It's just a mask."

"Oh, but surely it is more than that! I may not be as well versed as you, *monsieur,* in the art of *amour,* but I do know that even the most innocent-looking things have other, quite delightful uses."

Jeremiah's confusion grew. *Being illogical must run in the family,* he thought. *First Charlotte and now Jean-Claude. Neither one of them makes any sense.*

As if to prove his point, Jean-Claude went on to explain, "My friend Philippe has told me of one rather special game that he enjoys playing with his *petite amie.* Only he does not use a mask. He told me that he has velvet ropes, so long—" he measured an invisible length between his outstretched hands—"with which to bind his lover to a bed. Then he—"

"Wait a minute!" Jeremiah's forceful interjection halted the young man's flow of words. "I've heard of that before, but you can believe me, I've never done it! This mask is just a mask and nothing more."

"If you say so, *monsieur,*" Jean-Claude agreed with a sly wink. "But you know you do not have to pretend to be the backward provincial with me. I know you are as much a man of the world as am I. You can tell me. Who wears the mask in the heat of passion? You or Cousin Charlotte?"

Jeremiah mumbled an "Oh my God!" beneath his breath and turned toward the door. He had to get out of here and back to sanity, where he belonged.

But Jean-Claude wouldn't be put off. "Your secret will be safe with me," he persisted. "I promise to tell no one!"

"Damnit, boy, it's just a mask!" Jeremiah reiterated firmly, and marched into the hall.

"And if I were you, I'd forget all that other nonsense about velvet bonds and—and just go back to bed. God help us all!"

"But *monsieur!*" Jean-Claude called out to him from his doorway. "If you do not wish to enlighten me about the mask, at least tell me about the gold earring!"

Jeremiah's progress faltered, but he refused to turn around and address Jean-Claude. He squared his shoulders, gave his head a firm negative shake, and continued deliberately down the hall.

"What's happened to young people today?" he mumbled, closing his door behind him and locking it. "Have they all gone sick in the head or something?" The black mask was shaken out and placed over his head, the eye-slits adjusted so that he could see through them. Tying the scarf in back, he muttered, "Velvet ropes, for heaven's sake. What's happened to good, old-fashioned courting?"

With a negative shake of his head and a disgusted sigh, he opened his window and climbed out onto the ledge, the length of his black dressing gown hampering his way somewhat. Only as he proceeded cautiously toward the back of the house, where he knew Charlotte's room to be, did it occur to him to wonder if maybe his method of wooing her into bed tonight wasn't a bit unorthodox as well.

But how could it be? he mused before dispelling the notion as ridiculous. His mask wasn't an article of perversion like Philippe's velvet ropes. It was merely a romantic reminder of the first time he and Charlotte had met. Once she got a look at him wearing it as he came through her window like he had done that night in Paris a week ago, she would fall into his arms and shower him with unbridled passion.

Jeremiah soon learned that even the best-laid schemes don't always end as they are planned to.

As he neared Charlotte's window, where a dim pool of light shone, his bare foot encountered something soft and warm that cooed. He flinched at the unexpected contact and began to lose his balance. Only by flattening his back against the cool stone wall did he save himself from falling.

Aroused from its peaceful slumber, the pigeon flapped its wings in protest before flying off to a nearby tree. Unfortunately, its route went directly up into and past Jeremiah's face.

Naturally startled by the bird's sudden flight, Jeremiah lifted his hands in front of his face in an age-old protective gesture. The jerky movement destroyed what precarious footing he had, and he felt himself sway dangerously away from the wall and out into space.

With a need born of desperation, he managed to twist his body to the left and lunged toward the pool of light. His hands grabbed frantically for something, anything to hold on to, and he felt splinters pierce his fingertips as they curled around the wooden window sill. His knees, unfortunately, were not so lucky. They scraped over the rough stone wall as his body swung down to dangle against the side of the building.

Oh Jesus! he prayed. *Help me!* And then, on a

different note, *What am I doing out here anyway? Hell, I'm afraid of heights!*

"Who's out there?" a voice demanded from inside.

Charlotte!

Relieved more than he cared to admit, Jeremiah opened his mouth to identify himself, but all that came out was a breathy grunt. He tried unsuccessfully to lift one of his dangling feet onto the ledge so that he could lever his long body into the room. Each time he moved, though, his fingers slipped a little more off the sill.

"I know you're out there, because I can hear your heavy breathing!" he heard Charlotte proclaim, her voice a little louder this time, telling him she was coming toward the window. "I must warn you, I—I have a gun. If you try to come into my room, I won't hesitate to use it."

"Charlotte!" His cry for help came out in a thready croak.

Charlotte's lovely form suddenly filled the dimly lit window. Her hair was falling about her shoulders in wanton disarray, but to him it looked like a halo.

"Jeremiah?" She looked down at him, not believing what she·saw. "What on earth are you doing out there at this time of night? And what's that you've got on?"

"Don't ask. Just help me. I'm falling!"

As if some higher authority wanted to reinforce his statement, Jeremiah's fingers slipped off the wooden sill, and he found himself clawing at bare stone.

Guided by instinct, Charlotte reached out and

grabbed both of Jeremiah's arms just as he was about to disappear down into the darkness. Then she began pulling him, using more strength than she'd ever thought she possessed, until his stomach rested halfway across the ridge of the sill. Never one to leave a job half done, she pulled him completely into the room with one more jerk. Unfortunately, her bare foot had encountered the edge of a small throw rug during her struggles, and as he toppled inside she felt her backside slap painfully against the polished hardwood floor.

Jeremiah lay there for a long, breathless moment, his heart beating loudly in his ears. He'd come so close to falling to his death; he had to take a few moments to thank the Almighty for sparing him.

"Do you know something?" Charlotte asked. "You are crazy!"

Her rather biased observation of his actions caused him to lift his head and look at her. He discovered, much to his enjoyment, that she was sprawled on the floor near him, her slender calves and knees exposed below the hem of her nightgown. He let his gaze travel up to the full breasts that were rising and falling with each breath she inhaled, and on to the flushed countenance of her lovely face. His reckless escapade suddenly seemed to have been well worth the risk. After all, he was in her room, just where he wanted to be, wasn't he?

"No, not crazy," he managed to respond, levering his body closer to hers. "Just horny."

"What?" She sat upright and laughed. "Do you

mean to tell me you put on that silly mask and that horrible robe, then climbed out on that ledge just so you could seduce me?"

He didn't answer immediately. It had seemed like a good idea at the time. But the way she had phrased her question, he wasn't so sure now.

"Why didn't you use the hall?" she chuckled. "Or the door, for heaven's sake?"

"Would it have done me any good?" he countered, inching closer to her. His face was almost even with hers, and he could smell the fragrance of her skin. He found it a very stimulating scent. Her eyes, brimming with mirth, were two clear pools of dark gray ringed in charcoal. "Would you have let me in here if I'd knocked?"

The mirth disappeared and was replaced with an emotion he'd seen in her eyes before—desire!

"Probably not," she admitted. "But then you'll never know for sure, will you?"

"Charlotte." He expelled her name on a sigh and watched her lips part enticingly. "Darling, kiss me."

Her head moved slowly from side to side. "I don't like kissing men in masks. Take it off."

"You take it off."

And she did. Slowly, provocatively, her fingers untied the knot at the back of his head before she pulled the scarf free. Then her other hand came up off the floor, where it had been balancing her, and combed through his pale golden locks.

"You are crazy," she repeated in a husky purr. "But I love you anyway."

He had been slowly leaning toward her, his

mouth gradually opening in anticipation of the kiss they were about to share, but her unexpected confession caused him to stop and draw back. "What did you say?"

"You heard me. You're not deaf. I said I love you."

"That's what I thought you said."

He did kiss her then, the pressure of his chest pushing her back onto the floor. Her arms wound about his neck, her fingers massaging his scalp as their tongues met and stroked. The whimpers that formed in her throat caused tiny sparks of desire to blaze out of control within his loins. Astounded by the immense pleasure of the ache there, he knew for certain that he loved this woman. And, thank God, she loved him as well!

The urge to get closer, to feel her silky-smooth skin against his, caused him to roll onto his back. He dragged her with him until she lay on top. His mouth, no longer satisfied with the taste of hers and demanding further appeasement, trailed down to the soft inviting curve of her throat.

"Why the hell did it take you so long to admit it?" he growled against her skin. "I've loved you for ages."

"Well, we've only known each other a week," she replied as his lips nibbled her flesh. "I didn't want to rush into anything until I was certain."

"And now you are?"

"Uh-huh!"

Of their own volition, her hands began pushing and pulling the robe from his shoulders, while at the same time his fingers were undoing the row of tiny pearl buttons down the bodice of her nightgown. Jeremiah sat up, shrugged out of his robe, and then lay down again to watch with heated admiration as Charlotte whisked her nightgown over her head and tossed it aside.

As had happened all the other times he'd seen her beautifully upturned, coral-tipped breasts, his breath caught in a gasp. Releasing it in a long, agonized groan, he let his hand drift upward over her hips to her waist and on to capture her weighty fullness in his palms. He realized dazedly that even the most gifted of painters could never do justice to their true loveliness.

Charlotte's head fell back weakly as his fingers encircled and toyed with her nipples. Her mouth opened, and tiny moans escaped her throat as her lids grew so heavy she could no longer hold them open. After a moment it became impossible for her to maintain her balance, her head was spinning so, and she fell forward slowly. The warmth of his lips as they closed over one of her peaks caused her to whimper with joy, and his teeth and tongue began to incite unnameable pleasure. Heat swirled through her, settling in that strange, sensitive spot between her legs.

His hunger had been momentarily sated by the taste of her breasts, but Jeremiah felt compelled to sample other, more erotic portions of her beautiful body. Letting his lips nibble their way down the satiny flesh of her ribs, he gently rolled over with her and slipped his hand beneath the soft mounds of her buttocks. He lifted them and then braved that more precious, protected region below.

An unrestrainable cry of joy escaped from Charlotte as she felt him possess her femininity. Instantly catapulted beyond the realm of rational thought, she found herself incapable of protesting his tender invasion. She moaned with the sensations his lips elicited, and, before she could stop it from happening, jolts of ecstasy began to pulsate within her. Her body arched as she reached the sublime summit that before she'd only experienced while Jeremiah was inside her.

Basking in the afterglow of her climax, she drifted slowly back to reality, still feeling Jeremiah's mouth working, teasing, caressing her willing flesh. With a wordless gesture, she beckoned him upward. At last his mouth closed over hers, and she hungrily welcomed his kiss.

Their bodies still entwined, she rolled over with him and paid homage to his body as he'd done to hers. She knelt between his thighs and trailed a path of feathery kisses down the length of his golden torso. His nipples felt like leathery buttons against her tongue, the crisp hairs on his chest and belly a tickling irritant to her nose. But she continued on, undaunted, gradually being made aware of the noticeable change in his breathing. Tiny gasps followed by guttural moans escaped from him as she drew ever closer to his engorged staff. His body trembled as if from some unknown malady as she reached her objective and paused for a brief moment to hold it lovingly in her hands. She admired its proudness, its shape, its remarkable texture and hue, and then, without a qualm, her head slowly descended.

Jeremiah knew a wonder so immense that time came to a complete standstill. Her mouth engulfed and consumed him like a tight, velvet sheath, her lips and tongue working an unbelievable magic. Her manner of loving him was systematically destroying what little self-control he had.

Wanting only to stop her before the inevitable happened, he grasped her upper arms and forcefully pulled her upward. His mouth captured hers in a fiery kiss, his tongue penetrating the slickened surface of her lips. He slid his hands down the silkiness of her flesh and curled his fingers around her hips. Rocking her gently, he maneuvered her until she was impaled on his rigid manhood.

As he reentered the spinning maelstrom, blood raced through his veins, causing his ears to ring. Lights of every imaginable color flashed sporadically inside his head with each beat of his heart. Shudders began to wrack his body. Heaven was so close at hand, he only had to reach out to touch it. Then, in one magnificent explosion, his world shattered about him. His seed shot out of his body in rapid spurts, filling her completely and leaving him totally, thoroughly, blissfully drained.

In the aftermath, he felt lighter than air, brighter than the sun. With his mouth still fused to hers, he gradually became aware that there was moistness on his cheeks, and he knew that it was tears—Charlotte's tears.

Holding her head away from his, he opened

his eyes and saw the rapt expression of passion on her face. With a smile, he wrapped her in a loving embrace and held her as close to him as was humanly possible.

"I love you," he murmured softly in her ear.

Chapter Sixteen

BASTILLE DAY, ALWAYS THE MOST HIGH-SPIR-
ited holiday for the French, unfortunately
dawned gray and somber. Dark clouds lum-
bered across the Mediterranean and settled over
Cannes just shortly after sunrise, threatening to
put a damper on the annual observance of
France's freedom from tyranny. But if the sky
was gloomy and overcast, the temperament of
the people certainly was not. In fact, they didn't
even seem to notice the condition of the
weather.

Shopkeepers bustled about happily, exchang-
ing pleasantries with their neighbors and early
patrons as they made preparations for the up-
coming festivities. At various points about the
town, a small army of civil servants was busy
draping gay red, white, and blue banners on
posts, buildings, and whatever else they could

find. Anchored out in the bay was a large boat, where men were setting up an elaborate display of fireworks that would be discharged at nightfall.

In the villa on top of the hill, the elated mood was evident as well. The entire household staff, due to be released from their duties at noon, went about with smiles on their faces. Some of the braver ones even had the courage to hum catchy little tunes under their breath. And those who usually cowered or were surly in kind to the major domo, Emil, when he barked out an order, managed to maintain their good humor despite his less than cheerful disposition.

"Bloody wenches," Emil grumbled as he made his way toward Jeremiah's room, a large tray of freshly baked *croissants* and a pot of tea in his hands. "The longer I stay at this job, the less I like it. Rather be in charge of a Turkish bleedin' harem, I would, than that lot in the kitchen."

By balancing the tray on one knee, he freed a hand to rap lightly on Jeremiah's door. But when no one bade him to enter, he knocked again, more firmly this time.

"Oh come on, mate," he mumbled impatiently. "I ain't got all bloody day."

A sound at the other end of the corridor caused Emil to turn and look in that direction. He saw Jeremiah beckoning to him. "What the hell?" he muttered in soft dismay. Then, more loudly, he asked, "Bed wasn't soft enough for you, guv?"

"Oh, it was soft enough," Jeremiah replied with a smile. "But this one was a lot nicer."

Emil entered the room and saw Charlotte sitting up in bed, the sheets draped decorously about her nearly nude body. *Oh, it's like this, is it?* he thought, but maintained a blank expression.

"*Bonjour, mademoiselle,*" Emil remarked politely as he placed the tray down on a table near the bed.

"*Bonjour,* Emil." There was a glimmer of surprise in Charlotte's wide gray eyes. "Were my ears deceiving me, or did I just hear you speak English? And with a Cockney accent?"

Emil's broad chest expanded as he inhaled a deep breath and nodded.

"My word! You aren't French at all, are you?" At the slow, shrugging motion of his shoulders, she shot a look at Jeremiah, who was grinning at her, his mustache tilted upward at one corner. "*That's* what was so. . . . And you knew the whole time, didn't you?"

Jeremiah opened his mouth to respond, but Charlotte had already turned her attention back to the major domo and was asking, "But why are you pretending to be French?"

"Oh, I ain't pretendin', ma'am. I am French. Well, half of me, anyway. You see, me mum was French, but I was raised in London."

That would certainly account for his strange accent, she concluded, still staring at him.

"Mum was a proper lady's maid, she was," Emil went on to explain, "until some bloke planted me in her belly. If you ask me, it was that old duke Mum worked for. But she never would say for sure. Protected the old bugger, she did, till the day she died. 'Course, when the old duchess learned that I was on the way, she dismissed Mum *tout de suite.* Can't rightly blame her, though. Wouldn't want me spouse's by-blow a runnin' about underfoot neither."

"It must have been very difficult for your mother, having to raise you on her own without any help from your father," Charlotte observed sympathetically.

"Oh, but he didn't forget us," Emil retorted. "Well, that is, the old duke didn't. You see, that's why I think he was me dad. He set us up in real nice digs and came to see us quite often, twice a week or more. He even had plans to send me to school. Wanted to educate me all proper like, you know. But when Mum took sick and died, the old bugger just sort of forgot me and . . . well, here I am."

"Emil, your courage in the face of adversity is to be commended," Jeremiah remarked, "but, uh, I think the tea is starting to get cold."

"Oh! Right you are, guv." Emil turned, intending to leave, but at the door he stopped and looked back. "If you'll be wantin' anything else, you'd best ring for it quick. Them bloody wenches down in the kitchen are bein' right hard to handle this mornin'. It's all this Bastille Day nonsense. They get to rememberin' the Revolution and become right uncooperative, they do. I even heard one of them say somethin' like 'off wif his head.' And they were lookin' straight at *me* when they said it!" He released a weary sigh and shook his head. "Gor, this is a nasty job."

"Yes, but somebody's got to do it," Jeremiah commiserated. "I have faith in you, though. Just keep your guard up, go back down there, and give those women hell." Then he slapped an encouraging hand on Emil's broad shoulder and gently shoved him through the doorway. He closed the door and turned back around to face Charlotte, his body vibrating with mirth.

"What's so funny?" she asked.

"Emil. Who do you think?"

"Well, I for one can understand his position." She tossed the covers aside and slipped out of bed. "It isn't all that easy keeping a staff as large as this one in line. Especially when most of them happen to be female."

"You've been in charge of a large household staff, huh?" he challenged, watching her pad naked across the room to where her nightgown lay.

"No, but I'm a teacher! There's not much difference between my job and his. Trying to keep a dozen silly little rich girls in line is quite a chore, believe me! All they do most of the time is bicker and squabble. They're never satisfied unless they're hurting someone else's feelings."

As she bent over at the waist to retrieve her gown, Jeremiah noticed how her full breasts swayed provocatively downward. Yet when she straightened they lay heavy against her ribs, their rosy tips pointing upward. Her waist, narrow and slightly pinched, gave way to the delightful curve of her hips, and at the juncture of her thighs was the inviting nest of dark curls that he'd explored so thoroughly throughout the night.

In a husky voice, he asked, "If you hate teaching so much, why do you do it?" Then, as if suddenly magnetized, his legs began to carry him toward her.

"Well, I *do* have to earn a living, you know. Unmarried women my age can't depend on anyone but themselves for support. What are you doing? Give me back my gown!"

One large hand slipped around her waist and pulled her to him as the other stole her garment and dropped it to the floor. His lips descended to the enticing curve of her shoulder, where they began to nibble. "Mmm, you taste good in the morning."

"Do I?" As before, a warm glow spiraled in the pit of her stomach. With only a slight urging, she let him insinuate one of his muscular, trouser-clad thighs between her legs, and she had the wanton audacity to undulate her hips against its sublime pressure. The tips of her pleasantly sore breasts chafed against the roughness of his hairy chest.

"Mmm-hmm," he murmured, nibbling up the column of her throat to capture her earlobe between his teeth. "Almost as good as you did last night." Then he gave her backside a playful swat and stepped away, knowing that if they continued on this way he would never get away from the villa and down to Boland's as he'd planned. There would be plenty of time for loving Charlotte when his mission was completed.

"You're being very mean this morning, Jeremiah," she scolded huskily. "Why?"

"I've got a lot to do."

"Boland, you mean."

"Er, no," he lied. "I need to let my superiors back in Washington know where I'm at and what I've accomplished. They haven't heard from me in over a week. I don't want them to get worried." That much was true. He intended to send Roman a wire by way of the Paris office to let him know what progress he'd made. And to inform Roman of his suspicions regarding Judith. He just prayed that they wouldn't inform Albert. "What are your plans for the day?"

"Oh, I thought I'd go shopping," Charlotte replied brightly. "All that money I won last night is just begging to be spent. I'm surprised it hasn't burned a hole in my purse."

Jeremiah chuckled. "Well, have fun."

"I intend to," she vowed with a smile.

Jeremiah started for the door but stopped and looked back just as she was about to step behind her dressing screen. "Do me one favor, will you?"

"What's that?"

"If you happen to meet what's-his-name from the casino last night, try and avoid him if it's at all possible."

"But he doesn't know who I am. I certainly didn't give him my name!"

"I don't care. Just stay out of his way. And if that woman is with him, avoid her too."

Charlotte looked at Jeremiah for a moment, then sighed and nodded in agreement. "If that's the way you want it."

"It is." And he opened the door and departed.

Francesca trudged silently and sullenly behind Charlotte as they made their way from one shop to another. She'd voiced her complaints on more than one occasion during their morning's buying expedition. She didn't like the clothes Charlotte had made her wear. They were too dull and ordinary-looking for what she was used to. She didn't like the shoes that were pinching her feet or the black stockings that scratched her legs. And she certainly didn't like the idea of leaving the villa, and Jean-Claude, behind.

Having listened to all of the girl's grievances, Charlotte continued to hold fast to her beliefs. "If you want to be something other than a gypsy, Francesca, you're going to have to start dressing and behaving like it. And you cannot go around chasing after Jean-Claude, either. He's much too old for you."

"No, he is not!" Francesca countered. "There are more years separating you and Monsieur Fox than there are separating Jean-Claude and me."

Realizing that the girl was correct about that, Charlotte felt compelled to clarify what she meant. "I'm not talking about age, dear. I'm talking about experience. My cousin has seen and done more than you've ever dreamed of."

"You mean women."

"That . . . and other things."

"Well, I do not mind. A man should have more experience than his woman. It is only right."

Charlotte shot the girl an astonished look. "Jean-Claude hasn't . . . that is, the two of you haven't . . . become intimate, have you?" The very idea was mind-boggling.

"Not yet," Francesca confessed, her head cocking to a haughty angle. "But we will. When the time is right."

"Good Lord!" Charlotte ejaculated. "Well, you can just get that idea right out of your head, young lady. It's—it's positively indecent, not to mention—"

"Mademoiselle Atwater?"

Hearing her name, Charlotte jerked her head around and discovered Monsieur Boland, dressed in a white linen suit and dapper straw hat, standing right behind her. Half of her mind was still spinning from the shock of Francesca's statement, while the other half was trying to absorb the fact that she was staring at Boland. Needless to say, she was utterly speechless for a moment.

"Monsieur Boland!" she managed to exclaim when her jumbled thoughts finally meshed once again. "What a—a pleasant surprise!"

"I was just about to say the same thing," the elderly gentleman chuckled. "I certainly didn't expect to find you here in Cannes. I understood that you were to be visiting your great-aunt."

"Oh, I did! I mean, I *am*, still."

"She is in Cannes?"

Charlotte opened her mouth to negate this but decided that a lie was safer at this point than the truth, and she nodded her head stiffly.

"And who is this young lady?" Boland turned his gaze to Francesca. "Another of your French cousins?"

"*Oui, monsieur,*" Francesca remarked, and dipped into a demure curtsy. The look Charlotte shot her could only be described as alarmed. "I am Francesca."

"*Enchanté, mademoiselle.*" Smiling, Boland lowered his chin in a polite nod. Had she been older, he would have taken her hand and kissed it.

"*Merci, monsieur.*" Francesca fluttered her black lashes and smiled back at him.

241

"You have been shopping, I see." Boland glanced down at the packages Charlotte held. "That is a very becoming frock, Mademoiselle Atwater."

Charlotte glanced down at the creamy *voile* dress she'd bought just moments earlier—a lucky purchase indeed, since she hadn't had to be fitted for it. *"Merci,"* she responded distractedly, jerking her gaze back to Boland. "Are you shopping too?"

"Alas, I am only out for a breath of fresh air. I had thought to be confined to my studio for the remainder of the day, due to the threat of rain this morning. But when the sun came out, I knew I had to join it. It appears as though quite a number of others have had the same idea." His pointed glance encompassed the well-dressed men and women who were parading up and down the street past them.

Charlotte turned to look at them but did not pay attention to anything other than the thoughts racing through her mind. She had half a notion to send Francesca back to the villa before the girl let something slip about Jeremiah. Heaven only knew what would happen if Boland discovered she was in league with the American agent.

"What are your plans for this evening, Mademoiselle Atwater?"

As she had been by his unexpected appearance, Charlotte was caught off guard by his question. "This evening? Oh, well, I have no plans at all." At least, she didn't think she did. But with the tailspin her mind was in at the moment, she couldn't remember.

"You are not going to participate in the celebration with your family?"

"No, they—they've made other arrangements," she responded.

"Ah! Then perhaps you would do me the honor of dining with me this evening. I realize it is rather presumptuous of me, wanting you to—"

"Oh no, *monsieur!* It isn't presumptuous at all," she responded hastily. He might be a counterfeiter—indeed, a hardened criminal—but he was still an old man. If she could ease his loneliness, even for a little while, she wanted to do it. "I would be honored to have dinner with you."

"Tres bien!" he smiled warmly. "Shall I meet you at your aunt's house at, shall we say, seven?"

"Uh, no. No, I think it would be better if I met you. My aunt, regretfully, lives in a rather, mmm, out-of-the-way part of town."

"If that is what you wish." Boland then proceeded to give her the address of a nice little restaurant that he swore served the most fantastic food in all of France. He tipped his straw hat, smiled at Francesca, and then shuffled off down the street, humming an odd little tune under his breath.

Charlotte continued to stand there, oblivious of the girl at her side and the others who walked past her. What in the world was she going to say to Jeremiah? Knowing him, he would probably have another fit at the thought of her consorting with the enemy. But she didn't think of Monsieur Boland as the enemy—not really.

"My feet hurt."

Hearing Francesca's sullen complaint, Charlotte jerked her gaze around and saw the girl fidgeting, lifting one foot off the pavement and then the other as if to prove her statement.

"Can we go home now?"

"No, not yet," Charlotte replied. She dragged her thoughts away from her current dilemma and back to the present, noticing the shop they had been standing in front of. "I want to get some gifts for my mother and sisters."

But she would have been better off going back to the villa, she realized later. The gifts she purchased in her distracted state probably wouldn't please her family one bit. After all, what possible use could they have for books printed in Russian?

Chapter Seventeen

"I DON'T CARE WHAT YOU HAVE TO DO! LOCK HER up in her room, knock her over the head when her back is turned—" Jeremiah abruptly halted his pacing and noted the appalled look that came over Emil. "No, on second thought, don't do that. But do whatever it takes to keep Charlotte here and out of my way."

"You're gonna steal them plates." It came out as more of a statement of fact than a question.

"Either steal them or destroy them," Jeremiah responded.

Emil cocked his head to one side as if accepting the answer. Then he slouched back in the chair, which was dwarfed by his large frame.

"The fact is," Jeremiah continued, "I won't know what I'll do until I see what stage of development they're in. You just keep Charlotte tied up here."

It was these last few words that Francesca overheard. She jumped away from the door, where she'd been listening, as if her ear had suddenly been burned.

Coming up the stairs, Jean-Claude saw her and demanded, "What are you doing?"

A rapid movement of Francesca's hand and the horrified look on her face told the young Frenchman to keep his voice down. Then she took one last look at the door, shivered, and started toward him. "They are making plans to tie up Charlotte," she whispered.

"What?" Jean-Claude was shocked, visions of velvet ropes and black masks immediately flashing through his mind.

"I cannot believe it either! But that is what I just heard them say. Monsieur Fox ordered Emil to—"

"Emil! *Mon Dieu*, they have a *ménage à trois*?"

Not really knowing what a "household of three" had to do with anything, Francesca merely stared at Jean-Claude for a moment before pulling him toward his room. "We must do something to stop them," she hissed, closing the door behind them.

"We will do nothing of the kind!" Jean-Claude retorted. "And you will forget what you have heard just now. You are too young to understand matters of *amour*."

"*Amour!* They said nothing about *amour*. They were discussing plates!"

Jean-Claude was taken aback for a moment, and his fertile imagination could not comprehend what dinner plates had to do with erotic love. "Perhaps it is something new that the *Americain* has discovered," he murmured with a frown.

"Are you not going to do anything to stop them?" Francesca demanded. "Are you just going to stand by and allow them to mistreat your cousin?"

"Cherie, you do not understand." Jean-Claude heaved an indulgent sigh and shook his head, much like a patient father would do with an offspring. "But then I would not expect you to. You are only a child. You see, this is a matter of the heart; desires and passions are involved here. I have no right to interfere."

Francesca's lovely face slowly suffused with color. She could not believe what Jean-Claude was saying. True, gypsies were different from most other people, but they did not condone the mistreatment of innocents. And Charlotte—though a bit too concerned with taking baths and wearing shoes—was just that, an innocent, in her opinion.

Francesca's full lips compressed into a thin, disapproving line. An angry fire burned in the depths of her cinnamon eyes. "Well, if you will not do anything to stop them, I will!"

"Non, you will not!" Jean-Claude reached out and grasped her arm as she started to walk away. "You will leave well enough alone and stay out of their affair."

"Is that what you call it? An affair?" Her eyes met his in a straightforward stare. Her nostrils flared. Her rounded breasts heaved beneath the sheer fabric of her cotton dress. "It is more than that! It is . . . per-se-cu-tion." She drew the word out slowly, as if savoring the flavor of each syllable as it rolled across her tongue.

"Where did you hear that word?" Surprised by the extent of her vocabulary, Jean-Claude chuckled.

"Ah, you did not think that a stupid gypsy girl could say something so intelligent, eh?" she challenged, jerking her arm free from his grasp. "I would tell you a lot more, but *you* would not understand." An eerie-sounding laugh bubbled forth from her parted lips as she cocked her head to one side and stared up at him through half-opened lids. "You would be the stupid one then, *gadjo*."

"Don't be ridiculous," Jean-Claude scoffed. "I speak three languages, including my own. Of course I would understand. What has come over you, Francesca?" More than a little alarmed by this new, unknown side of the girl, he began to back away.

"You, *gadjo*. You have come over me. From the first I have known that you were the one man who would fulfill my destiny." Her hands floated up from her sides, and she began pulling out the pins that held her waist-length hair in place atop her head. With a gentle shake, ebony curls cascaded down over her shoulders. And then, riveting her gaze to his, she began to recite an incantation in Romany, her native tongue, as she moved closer to him.

Not knowing what was happening, Jean-Claude felt himself rapidly withdrawing from the world with which he was familiar, only to enter an extraordinary dimension where he and Francesca were the soul occupants. He could no longer hear the humming of the bees or the chirping of the birds outside his bedroom window. The sounds emanating from the kitchen below receded far into the distance as well and were replaced by deafening silence. The coolness in his room was replaced by a stifling heat that made him claw at his clothing. And all the while Francesca continued to chant her Romany litany as the distance closed between them and her garments disappeared with as much haste as his own.

"I come to you a virgin," she confessed huskily when they both stood naked. "But I will not leave you as one. We will be united forever, for all eternity."

Jean-Claude could not explain the things that happened next, nor was he able to suppress the urges that drove him onto the bed with her. He was a pliant puppet, bending to Francesca's will. She had spun a spell around him that was so complete, so undeniably wonderful, that after a while he had no wish to escape.

He took the precious gift from her that she so willingly offered and found himself drained and exhausted from the experience.

It was only afterward, when he felt the cool breeze drift across his sweat-dampened flesh, when he heard the birds outside his window, that he realized what had happened, what he had done. Glancing over at Francesca, who purred contentedly beside him, he knew a shame so great that it astounded him.

"Mon Dieu!" he groaned, and rolled away from her to curl up into a fetal ball. "I have compromised a fourteen-year-old child."

"No," Francesca soothed him. "Thanks to you, I am a woman now. *Your* woman . . . forever!"

Charlotte hurried through the heavily congested streets toward the restaurant where she had promised to meet Monsieur Boland. Gaily dressed merrymakers laughed and danced about her, jostling her and trying to draw her into their merriment. Deftly managing to elude them, she found herself glancing back over her shoulder as prickles of apprehension crawled up her spine.

Jeremiah would be furious if he knew she was out here. She had promised him, with her fingers crossed behind her back, that she would remain at the villa tonight. He and Emil had seemed unnaturally preoccupied with the idea of detaining her there. Neither of them was going out, or so they had said, but they didn't want her to join the celebrants either.

If it hadn't been for Francesca and Jean-Claude, she might still be back at the villa. They had come to her rescue, so to speak, when Emil refused to leave her side after Jeremiah had mysteriously vanished upstairs. But once the burly major domo was out of her sight, she had grabbed her shawl and slipped out of the house, she hoped, unobserved.

Now, weaving her way through the press of people, she finally caught sight of the restaurant sign and exhaled a sigh of relief. Only a few more feet to go and she would be out of this madness. It seemed to her that everyone in Cannes and its environs had converged onto this one street to hamper her progress. She was all but pushed through the restaurant's door as a wave of revelers collided with her.

Inside at last and able to get her bearings, she noticed Monsieur Boland sitting at a small table in the far corner of the room. He spied her and smiled.

She rushed over to him and dropped gratefully into the chair that he held out for her. "I'm so sorry I'm late," she apologized. "I had no idea that the streets were going to be so crowded."

"No need to worry, my child. From what I understand, it gets worse every year."

"You've been here before?"

"Not in Cannes, no. But I have been in Paris on Bastille Day." He sat down after she had made herself comfortable. "You must relax and catch your breath before we order."

She tried to do just that, but her frazzled nerves and that imp of apprehension she'd been feeling kept her tense for quite some time. Whenever a new customer entered the restaurant, she would dart a furtive glance toward the door to see if it was Jeremiah or Emil. After a few minutes, though, when their bottle of wine was brought to the table and she had sipped some of the fruity brew, she found herself paying less attention to the entrance and more to Monsieur Boland.

"Did your aunt not object to your leaving her alone this evening?"

"Oh no," Charlotte demurred with a shake of her head. "Great-Aunt Marie retires very early these days. Her age, you know."

"Ah yes," the old man nodded sagely. "I had forgotten that you told me she was your great-aunt."

There was a momentary lull in the conversation, and then he asked, "Has she enjoyed your visit?"

"I don't know. It's a little difficult to say at this point," Charlotte replied, thinking of the small amount of time she had actually spent with her elderly relative. "I know that *I've* enjoyed my time here. I got to hear a lot of stories about my grandmother. She and Great-Aunt Marie were twins, you know. Identical!"

He seemed surprised by this, for his old eyes brightened. "I knew a pair of identical twins once, when I was a boy in Hungary."

"Then you aren't French by birth?"

"No. Austrian, actually. My father traveled a great deal and took us with him. I've lived all over the continent and even spent some time in the north of Africa."

"Oh, that sounds so exciting. Much more so than my childhood."

She then proceeded to give him a sketchy outline of her life in Waxahachie—leaving out the part that involved Melvin, of course—and her move to Baton Rouge at the age of eighteen.

"So you see," she ended just as the waiter arrived with their steaming bowls of soup, "this is the first time I've ever really been away from home. Oooh! What is this? It smells delicious!"

"It is." Monsieur Boland nodded in agreement. "It is *bouillabaisse*."

Charlotte's appetite was whetted by the not too subtle aroma of garlic, onions, and herbs that wafted past her nostrils. They had been artfully blended with the succulent, white-fleshed fish and pink shrimp, which bobbed about in the broth. She dipped her spoon slowly into the bowl, then lifted it to her mouth and tasted its spicy and unusual flavor. The look that instantly crossed her face told Monsieur Boland that she was more than pleased with what she was eating.

Crusty rolls and a crock of butter rounded out the meal, which consisted of a second bowl of bouillabaisse and another bottle of dry white wine.

"I don't know when I've enjoyed a finer meal," she remarked, blotting her lips with her napkin. "Or better company."

"You are being too kind, but I thank you."

"Kindness has nothing to do with it," she countered. "I'm being very honest. You are delightful company, *monsieur*."

A pink blush stained the old man's pale cheeks. As she noted his embarrassment, she was suddenly reminded of the fact that he was a counterfeiter, out to bankrupt the United States Treasury. The notion was still so inconceivable, though; she felt like laughing—or crying. How could he have gotten himself involved with such a larcenous gang in the first place? That's what she couldn't understand. For he was the most unlikely looking criminal she'd ever met.

After the check had been paid, the two of them wandered out into the street to discover that it was even more congested than before with merrymakers. Music filled the air about them. It seemed to come from every direction at once and clashed horribly. Those who were celebrating, though, didn't seem to notice or care.

One large group of people, dressed in elaborate evening gowns, formal suits, and exotic-looking masks, laughed and danced their way down the center of the narrow street. One couple in particular danced closer and beckoned to Charlotte and Monsieur Boland to join them. She declined with a smile and a shake of her head and clung even more closely to the old man beside her.

"It's like Mardi Gras!" she shouted above the din, wanting Monsieur Boland to hear her.

"Is it?" he shouted back.

Charlotte flinched as an explosion suddenly rent the air. The night-darkened sky was filled with a thousand shooting stars that projected outward from a central sunburst and died before they hit the ground. Another shot rang out, and a second display of stars illuminated the sky.

Feeling the gentle tug on her arm, she dropped her gaze back to Monsieur Boland and saw that he wanted her to follow him.

Francesca and Jean-Claude huddled close to each other like two frightened children caught in the midst of a full-fledged riot. They stood pinned against the wall of a building while a gang of noisy revelers paraded down the street, singing to their own accompaniment of music.

"Can you see him now?" Francesca all but shouted when the musicians had passed.

"No," Jean-Claude responded. "But he was headed down that way just a moment ago."

Without stopping to consider what perils she

might encounter ahead, Francesca tore off in the direction Jean-Claude had indicated. Not knowing what else to do, Jean-Claude followed her. He felt a strange, unexplainable compulsion to protect this precocious woman-child who, just hours before, had made herself his. And he was still unsure about how *that* had happened.

Following the American this way was utter insanity, and he knew it. He'd come up with a dozen different reasons why they should remain at the villa tonight, but Francesca had ignored them all, flatly refusing to be deterred. They had succeeded in diverting Emil by telling him some tall tale about a catastrophe in the cellar. Then, after they'd locked the major domo inside the dark, dank room, they had spied Monsieur Fox slipping out of the servants' entrance near the stables. Just before they'd dashed out into the night after him, Jean-Claude had heard the major domo beating on the cellar door, swearing all kinds of wrath if he ever got his hands on them.

Jean-Claude gave his head an almost imperceptible shake and shuddered. He could just imagine what condition that door was in now, for surely Emil had broken it down after they'd left.

"Look!" Francesca stopped so abruptly that Jean-Claude almost plowed into her. "Is that him?"

"Who?" His gaze searched the throng of merrymakers.

"Him!" she pointed. "That man over there."

Dressed completely in black, as Monsieur Fox

had been, the man in question turned at that moment and presented them with his profile. Much to Jean-Claude's dismay, he saw that it wasn't the American at all but a total stranger.

"Merde!" Francesca spat. "We'll never find him in this crowd."

"Good! If we can't find *him,* then the chances are fairly obvious that *he* won't be able to find Cousin Charlotte."

"But what if he does?" Francesca challenged.

"Well, if he finds her . . . then he finds her! I doubt that he would beat her, much as she deserves it for disobeying him."

"How can you say that?"

Jean-Claude stiffened and asserted his masculine superiority. "Women do have their place. You and Cousin Charlotte would do well to remember that."

Francesca rolled her cinnamon eyes heavenward and growled, "Men!" through clenched teeth. When she looked back at Jean-Claude to make a scathing retort, a shadowy movement behind him caught her attention.

"There he is!" she cried, clutching at Jean-Claude's arm. There was no mistaking that flaxen head of hair and that lean, muscular body. It was definitely the American.

Jean-Claude turned sharply just as Jeremiah entered a darkened alleyway. He made a frantic grab for Francesca's hand, and the two raced after him.

Chapter Eighteen

Jeremiah stepped out of the alley, saw how crowded the street was, and released a groan of frustration. Damn it, where had everybody come from? Not only did he feel pinned in by all these people, but by the looks of it he was totally lost as well! For such a small community, Cannes possessed enough twisting, turning, dead-end streets to bewilder even one who was native born.

He stood there for a moment trying to decide in which direction to go first. Hell, just getting to Boland's studio was proving to be quite an undertaking, much more so than he'd imagined. Getting inside the place was going to be easy—at least, easier than finding it again. Since leaving the villa, he'd been sidetracked no less than half a dozen times by the deluge of revelers. The fates had been on his side, though, because no one had seemed even mildly interested in his suspicious-looking costume. But why should they? Hell, most of them were garbed in costumes that were far more outlandish than his.

He let his gaze scour the length of the street in both directions until it encountered a landmark that looked vaguely familiar. Of course, he admitted silently, his befuddled memory could be playing tricks on him, but he was almost certain that he'd been on this very same street just last night. It looked a lot different now from the way it had then, but he would be willing to bet a month's pay that his carriage had intercepted and overturned the farmer's cart on that far corner to his right. And if that were true, Boland's place ought to be just around the corner from where that band of gypsies was entertaining.

Gypsies!

Oh Lord, he prayed, starting cautiously toward the group as a wave of apprehension threatened to engulf him. *Don't let them be part of Francesca's family.*

God must have heard him, because when he passed by the gypsies a moment later he didn't recognize a single face in the tribe. Making his way on up the street, his mustache twitched before he broke into a relieved grin. So far, so good!

Jeremiah finally reached the house that he knew was Boland's, but he elected to stay hidden in the shadows as he tried to assess the situation. Going through the front door was out

immediately transpired afterward. "Counterfeiters use engraving plates," he murmured thoughtfully. "But what reason could Monsieur Fox have for wanting them?"

Francesca's shoulders lifted in a slight shrug as she turned to look back at the house. A light suddenly illuminated one of the second-story windows, one that Jeremiah had just passed. "Oh no!"

"What is it now?"

"Someone is inside the house!"

Jerking his head around, Jean-Claude also saw the light and groaned. "It looks to me as if he is headed straight for trouble."

"Well, we cannot just stand here and do nothing. We have to help him!"

"How? If you think I am going up there after him, you—"

"No, of course not! But—" Francesca's voice trailed off as an idea suddenly came to mind. Her eyes gleamed with excitement as she bent over and scooped up one side of her skirts and petticoats. She tucked the hems securely under her waistband before proceeding to unbutton her blouse, arranging it so that her creamy shoulders and a portion of her full round breasts were revealed.

"What the hell do you think you are doing?" Jean-Claude demanded, appalled at her behavior.

"I am going to help Monsieur Fox."

"By undressing?"

"No! If we cannot stop him from going inside the house, then maybe we can get whoever is inside of it out! Now unbutton your shirt."

"My shirt? What for?"

"Because you do not look like a gypsy with it buttoned up!"

Jean-Claude just stood there, confusion etched on his young face. "I do not know what you are getting at, Francesca."

"You will." And with an impatient click of her tongue, she grabbed the front of his shirt and gave it a vicious yank. Pearl buttons were sent flying off into the night, dropping like small pebbles onto the cobblestone pavement as the expensive fabric was ripped open to Jean-Claude's waist. Francesca grasped his arm with hers. "Come on!"

One of her long, pale thighs gleamed indecently in the moonlight as she raced around the building and reentered the crowded street. Jean-Claude, painfully aware of the way her shapely limb flashed with each step she took, wanted to throttle her for being so immodest. *Mon Dieu*, he was going to have a job on his hands making a lady out of this one!

He watched Francesca as she headed straight for one of the gypsies who stood with the rest of his tribe on the street corner. The man, a tall, dark-skinned fellow, wore a gold ring in his ear. Not knowing that the ring denoted the man as the tribe's leader, Jean-Claude was amazed at how like Monsieur Fox's ring it was. But he quickly brushed aside the thought with a shake of his head. There was something far more important at stake here than the similarity of two gold earrings.

Drawing close to Francesca, Jean-Claude

heard her speak to the tall gypsy in a strange yet slightly familiar tongue. It was Romany, of course, and though he couldn't understand what she was saying, the gypsies obviously could. They listened intently to her excited pleas, and one of the women handed Francesca a tambourine just before the whole tribe turned and followed the girl back up the street.

"What are you going to do now?" Jean-Claude asked Francesca when she drew even with him.

"You will see," was all she would say.

A noisy group of celebrators had been enjoying the gypsies' entertainment. When the tribe left their post on the corner, the onlookers naturally decided to follow. They even copied the gypsies' lead when members of the tribe began to go from door to door, pounding on them as they called for the people inside to come out and join in the celebration.

A lively tune was being played by the gypsy violinist as Francesca approached one door in particular. She rapped loudly on the panel, then stepped back and rattled her tambourine, striking it on her hip as she kept time with the music. For all outward appearances, she looked just like one of the revelers.

When the door finally swung open, Francesca bestowed her most provocative smile upon the young man who stood framed there in the light. "It is Bastille Day!" she cried excitedly, and reached out for his hand. "Come, enjoy it with us!"

"Stefan!" A voice inside the house called out to the young man, and he turned. "Who is it?"

Glancing past the young man called Stefan, Francesca saw a tall, dark-haired woman standing on the stairs. The woman's eyes were strangely slanted, like Stefan's, and filled with annoyance.

"Gypsies, Eva." With a chuckle, Stefan turned and looked back at Francesca. "They want us to join them."

"But we cannot!" the woman called Eva protested. "Tell them to go away and leave us alone."

"Oh, surely there cannot be any harm in dancing with a few gypsies," Stefan retorted.

"The house will be empty if we leave it now!" argued Eva.

"You worry too much," Stefan chided. "Boland will be returning soon, and I promise we will not go far. Come, it will be like the old days in Budapest."

Francesca knew a moment of relief when she saw the woman's expression alter at the mention of the Hungarian city. She had been afraid that she would not be able to lure the two of them out of the house. And if she hadn't, Monsieur Fox would surely have been discovered.

With a sigh and a shake of her head, Eva finally relented and descended the last few steps to join Stefan at the door. The gypsies and the onlookers were creating such a din that neither she nor Stefan heard the thud that sounded at that moment in one of the upstairs rooms.

Jean-Claude, singing at the top of his lungs, rushed up and grabbed Eva's hand. Then, with great pomp, he led her out into the street. Once there, she seemed to shed her mantle of apprehension and doubt, for she soon joined everyone else in laughing and dancing.

Stefan chuckled at the sight of Eva finally enjoying herself and closed the door slowly behind him. The lovely gypsy girl at his side gave him a very flirtatious smile, and he returned it, almost leeringly, before allowing her to whisk him away.

In the upstairs room, Jeremiah lay on the floor trying to recapture his breath, not to mention his nerve. He had heard the loud commotion at the front door just as he had literally fallen through the third-story window. For a brief moment, he'd wanted to turn around and leave again, even though it would mean going down the same way he'd come up. But he didn't, and with the sound of the front door being closed and the house suddenly quiet, he realized that Boland's accomplices had left.

Hope managed to overtake his exhaustion and fear. Maybe his luck hadn't deserted him after all. If they were gone, and the house was indeed as empty as it sounded, then he would be able to go about freely in his search for the plates.

Or would he?

Knowing that there was only one way to be sure—and it wouldn't be by sitting here on his butt—he got to his feet and cautiously made his way out into the hall.

"It is not very far from here," Boland assured Charlotte. "Hold my hand so we will not be separated."

"Are you sure you don't mind?" she queried, taking his proffered arm.

"No, of course not, my child. My collection is not very big, you understand, but I am quite proud of it."

"I'm sure you are!" Charlotte hoped she sounded sincere and not too excited, for when Boland had invited her to see his engravings, she'd all but jumped at the chance to go with him. She was actually going to get inside the man's house. And, who knew, she might possibly even find his counterfeit plates. If she did, wouldn't Jeremiah be surprised? Why, she could already see the expression on his face when she told him of what she had accomplished. Oh, he was going to be so pleased!

Charlotte and Monsieur Boland wound their way down one street, bypassing a large group of slightly inebriated merrymakers, before turning a corner and starting up another that was just as congested as all the others had been. She didn't pay much attention to the people, though, for she was much too concerned with getting into Boland's house.

They were halfway up the street when Boland's footsteps faltered. "Is that gypsy music I hear?"

"Gypsies?" Icy fear instantly flooded Charlotte's veins, and her head jerked around to look behind her.

"Yes." Boland peered around her, his old eyes narrowing into slits as he squinted into the distance. "Tell me, child, are they? My eyesight is not what it used to be. I cannot see very well in the dark. It is all of that close, detailed work that I do, you know."

Charlotte's gaze frantically scanned the gaily dressed tribe for some sign of a familiar face. If Sandor, Zonya, or any of the others were here and they saw her, she didn't know what she would do if they recognized her or if they asked about Jeremiah. Then her heart suddenly began to knock against her ribs when she spotted Francesca. The girl was undulating her lithe young body in a most provocative manner. And if Francesca wasn't bad enough, Charlotte saw Jean-Claude standing close by and glowering at the way Francesca was behaving.

God help me, Charlotte prayed. *What do I do now?*

Her feet had taken root in the spot where she stood. After a few moments, though, when neither of the two young people saw her, she knew she couldn't press her luck any further. She tightened her hold on Monsieur Boland's arm and hurried him along.

"They were gypsies all right," she announced in a strained voice. "But I don't think it would be a good idea for us to linger. I understand they are notorious for picking pockets."

"You are quite right, my child," Boland agreed. "But we must try and be tolerant of their shortcomings. They do not have an easy life, you know. Oh!" He stopped abruptly. "Here we are now. This is my house, and we almost passed it."

Francesca rattled her tambourine and, lifting

her arms high over her head, spun around so that her skirts flared out away from her legs. When she stopped spinning, she let her gaze land deliberately on Stefan, who hadn't been looking at her at all, she realized. He was staring at the couple who was just now entering his house. Recognizing Charlotte immediately, Francesca knew that the old man who was with her was the same one they had met earlier that day outside the Russian book store.

Stefan, too, had recognized Charlotte. Being of a suspicious nature anyway, he wondered what she was doing with Boland. With an ominous groan, he decided to answer that question for himself and started to walk away from the merrymakers. But a hand on his arm delayed his departure.

"Where are you going, handsome man?"

Turning only his head around, Stefan looked down into Francesca's beguiling face. "I just remembered, I have to do something back in the house."

"Do not go!" she implored, pursing her full lips into a pout. "You leave now, and I will be hurt. We dance some more, no?"

"No!" Stefan countered firmly. "Go play up to somebody else, *cherie*."

Jean-Claude witnessed this interchange and became furious. He didn't know why Francesca had suddenly stopped dancing or why she was now clinging to Stefan, but he was damn sure going to find out! He stalked over to her and managed to block Stefan's departure.

"Leave my woman alone!" he snarled with all the credibility of an outraged lover, which is what he was.

"Is she yours? Take her, with my blessings," Stefan replied, and turned to walk away again.

"No!" Francesca shot Jean-Claude a wide-eyed, beseeching look. "He cannot leave!"

"What is the matter here?"

Eva had joined them, and Stefan stepped close to her. "Boland is back, and he has that girl from the casino with him."

"What girl?" Eva asked.

It was then that Jean-Claude realized what had caused Francesca's rather odd behavior. She must have seen Charlotte. And the other man must have seen her too!

"Is one woman not good enough for you?" Jean-Claude challenged savagely. "You have one of your own, and now you want to take mine as well!"

"I do not know what you are talking about," Stefan remarked with a shake of his head. "I was not trying to take her away from you."

"What girl, Stefan?" Eva insisted again.

"Last night at the casino, I told you—"

"You are saying that you do not like my woman?" Jean-Claude hastily interrupted.

Stefan whirled around to glare at him. "Stay out of this! Take the girl and be gone with her. I do not really give a damn!"

When it appeared as if Stefan was going to turn away again, Jean-Claude did the first thing he could think of. He doubled up his fist and punched Stefan in the stomach. The blow, unfortunately, wasn't as powerful as Jean-Claude hoped, for Stefan quickly lashed out with a fist of his own, striking Jean-Claude's chin painfully.

Francesca screamed out something in Romany, and the gypsies began to converge.

Chapter Nineteen

"My goodness! It sounds as though we got inside just in time." Boland left Charlotte standing in the center of the small, sparsely furnished drawing room to wander over to the window. He pushed the heavy brocade drapes to one side and squinted out into the dark street. "I cannot tell what they are doing out there. Can you?"

Charlotte had heard the loud shouts and screams too. She peered through the slit in the drapes and had to stifle a gasp at what she saw there. Francesca was no longer dancing flirtatiously but had leaped onto the back of the young man Charlotte had met at the casino last night, while Boland's Magyar-eyed accomplice was trying to pull her off.

"Oh, they're . . . they're just celebrating," she replied, and quickly closed the drapes, almost hitting Boland's nose in the process. "Why don't we go see your lithographs? It's getting rather late, you know, and I wouldn't want my Great-Aunt Marie to worry about me too much."

"But I thought you said she had already retired for the evening."

"Oh, er, yes, I did! But she doesn't sleep well some nights. And when she can't sleep, she gets up and wanders about the house. If she finds that I'm not there, she just might decide to come looking for me in her nightgown. She's done it before and was almost arrested."

"Oh. Well all right. Come this way then. I would not want your aunt to worry . . . or get arrested."

Boland turned toward the stairs and preceded Charlotte up the two flights to the third floor. During their ascent, he described some of his lithographs to her. His pride in his collection was evident in the tone of his voice.

Charlotte only half listened to him. She was too preoccupied with wondering what the devil Jean-Claude and Francesca were doing outside. They shouldn't even be there! They ought to be back at the villa with Jeremiah. Good Lord! Maybe Jeremiah wasn't at the villa either!

Stepping onto the third-floor landing, she suddenly froze, unable to follow Boland any further. She heard a sound in the room that Boland was heading for.

Boland heard it too. "What was that?" he asked, his hand twisting the knob. Then he quickly shook his head and said, "Oh, it is probably mice. This old place is full of them."

"Mice?" Charlotte pounced on the assumption. "Maybe we shouldn't go in there then. I'm deathly afraid of mice!"

"There is no need for you to be afraid, my child," Boland murmured solicitously. "The little things are more afraid of us than we are of them. They will not hurt you." And with that he opened the door and entered the room.

A half-step behind him, Charlotte watched anxiously while he lit an oil lamp, then let her gaze sweep quickly and thoroughly over the entire room. Seeing nothing but clutter around the floor, she released her breath in a long sigh of relief. This agenting business was a lot more nerve-wracking than she'd imagined it would be.

Glancing back over the room once again, she noted the huge packing crate that was the size of a large steamer trunk sitting on the floor. A few of the thick boards—two by sixes, they appeared to be—had been removed from the crate's top and were leaning against the wall. She didn't have to look inside to know that it was probably Boland's printing press. An imperceptible shudder passed through her before she moved across to join the old man at his work table.

While he dug around in a carton on the floor, busily searching for something there, she managed to get a good look at the litter of papers that was scattered across the top. One drawing in particular caught her eye, and she couldn't suppress the wave of sadness that washed over her. It was a strange-looking sketch of an American twenty-dollar bill. Right next to it was a thin sheet of metal, and covering three-quarters of its smooth surface was the sketch's likeness.

"Ah, here they are!" Boland straightened up and placed a large, hardbound portfolio on top of the table.

Charlotte forced her thoughts off the sketches and metal plates that were now hidden beneath Boland's prized collection of lithographs and tried to pay attention to the pictures he was now showing her. At first glance they looked to her to be crudely done and not very interesting. But the longer she looked at them, the more of the painstaking detail that had gone into their creation could she see. She knew next to nothing about the art form but concluded that they were really quite lovely.

"How old are these?" she asked, bending over to examine the sheet of aged parchment.

"The one you are looking at now is almost a hundred years old," Boland remarked. "It is one of Aloys Senefelder's earliest works."

"Aloys Senefelder?"

"The father of lithography as we know it," Boland supplied.

"Mmm!" Wanting to see what the next lithograph looked like, Charlotte reached out to move the top sheet of parchment aside. In doing so, her hand accidentally brushed against a stoppered bottle and almost knocked it over.

"Do be careful!" warned Boland, grasping the bottle before it had a chance to spill. He set it aside and added, "This is acid, my child. I would not want you to burn your hand."

"No, neither would I!" Quickly jerking her hands away, she clasped them together before her and let Monsieur Boland turn the pages.

"I have some others in my room," he remarked when they had seen the last lithograph in the portfolio. "Wait here. I will see if I can find them."

He stepped out into the hall, and Charlotte watched his head slowly disappear out of sight down the stairwell. Not knowing how long he would be gone or how much time she had, she quickly turned back to the work table and lifted the portfolio, being very careful not to get near the bottle of acid.

The first look she'd had of the sketches had piqued her curiosity. Something hadn't been right about them. Now, getting a second look, she knew what had been wrong. The sketches themselves were all right; they were exact copies of the American currency that she knew so well. It was the thin sheets of metal that were all wrong; they were done in reverse of what they should be. All of the lettering, the numbers, and the pictures were directly opposite from the way the sketches looked.

"*Pssst!*"

Charlotte flinched at the sound. Her head turned to see if a mouse had scurried past. She wasn't really afraid of them, but she would rather avoid the little nuisances if she could.

"*Pssst!*"

Hearing the sound again, and this time from behind the huge packing crate, she had a sinking feeling that a mouse hadn't been responsible for the noise. Indeed, no mouse she had ever encountered had a finger to wiggle at her as this one was doing now above the crate's top. A mouse couldn't, she decided, and started across the room, but a six-foot-three-inch, two-legged *rat* could.

"What are you doing here?" she demanded impatiently.

From his crouched position on the floor, where he was wedged between the wall and the crate, Jeremiah countered, "What are *you* doing here?"

"I came to find the counterfeit plates. And I did!"

"So did I! Now get Boland out of the house so I can destroy them."

"How?"

"I don't know. That's your problem. You got yourself into this mess, now you can just get yourself out!"

"No, I didn't mean how do I get Boland out? I mean, how are you going to destroy the plates?"

"He is not, *mademoiselle!*"

Charlotte pivoted sharply, feeling the bouillabaisse she'd eaten for dinner churn in her stomach. Standing in the doorway, his once fine clothes now nearly torn to shreds, was the man she had met in the casino the night before, and clutched in his left hand was a very big, very deadly looking revolver.

"I, er, how nice to see you again," she all but whimpered. "St—Stefan, wasn't it?"

"Yes, you have a very good memory. Unfortunately, you do not have the intelligence to go with it. Tell your friend to show himself."

"My friend?"

"Do not play the fool with me, *mademoiselle*. I know that your comrade is hiding behind the crate. I heard him speaking to you. If he does not come out now, I will be forced to shoot you." Then he lifted the gun and aimed it directly at her as if to prove his statement.

"Oh Lord!" Charlotte prayed, slowly moving to one side so that Jeremiah could do as he'd been ordered.

And he did, much to her relief.

Jeremiah stood up and stepped out from behind the crate, moving slowly so as not to alarm the gun-wielding Stefan. An easy, seemingly unconcerned brush of his hand dislodged the dirt and dust that clung to the back of his black trousers. After he'd straightened his black shirt, tucking it back into place beneath his waistband, he folded his arms across his chest and allowed his gaze to match the malevolence of Stefan's, who was glaring back at him.

Charlotte had to marvel at Jeremiah's indifference to the situation they were in. He was behaving as though he didn't have a care in the world, as though they weren't going to have their heads blown off at any moment. How did he do it? she wondered. How did he appear so untroubled when she was nothing but a quivering mass of anxiety?

"So, Steadman, we meet again," Stefan proclaimed on a soft, mirthless chuckle.

Steadman? Charlotte frowned in confusion at Jeremiah.

"I thought Eva had gotten rid of you permanently back in Paris."

"Sorry to disappoint you," Jeremiah replied, the harshness in his voice belying the politeness of his words.

"Yes, I can see that you are. But I must tell you, what Eva failed to do, I will accomplish," Stefan vowed. "It is a pity that your lovely, er, lady here will have to be destroyed with you. Such a waste for one so pretty. But she will have to go. We cannot let anything stand in our way."

"Like you didn't let Albert stand in your way?" Jeremiah countered. A muscle throbbed in his jaw, and Charlotte could see the slight narrowing of his blue eyes.

"Albert? Ah yes!" Stefan nodded. "I vaguely remember a nuisance by that name."

"He's still alive, you know," Jeremiah informed him.

"Is he?" Stefan appeared neither alarmed nor surprised by this. He crossed the room to Boland's work table, never once taking his eyes, or his revolver, off the two of them. "Now, that is interesting."

"Interesting that you didn't kill him, or interesting that I know about him?" Jeremiah challenged.

"It matters not," shrugged Stefan. "I will just have to make sure that this time we do not fail in getting rid of you. You Americans are far more trouble than you are worth."

"Stefan?" a feminine voice called from outside the room.

"We are up here, Eva!" Stefan informed her loudly. "You might want to bring the old man with you!"

They stood there—Charlotte with her churning stomach, Jeremiah with his supposed indifference, Stefan with his big, shiny gun—and waited until the Magyar-eyed woman and Boland entered the room.

"What is this?" Boland asked, appalled at what he saw. "Stefan, have you gone mad? Mademoiselle Atwater happens to be my guest! She has nothing to do with—"

"Shut up, you old fool!" Stefan interrupted, his well-chiseled lips curling into a snarl. "Of course she is involved. She has been all along, only you have been too blind to see it."

"Mademoiselle Atwater?" Boland looked at Charlotte, his expression one of pleading confusion, as if he wanted her to contradict Stefan.

"I—I—" she stammered, unable to find the right words to say.

Jeremiah came to her rescue. He dropped a comforting arm about her shoulders and pulled her close to him. "She's an innocent bystander in all of this. She knew nothing of you three or of your activities until I informed her."

"That is most unfortunate." Eva shook her head slowly, her black eyes narrowing to deadly slits as they remained focused on Jeremiah. "But then, you seem to be forever involving innocent people in our business, do you not, Monsieur Steadman?"

"Steadman?" This time, Charlotte voiced her thoughts aloud.

Jeremiah shot her a furtive, not-now look and turned his gaze back to Eva. "Since you seem to know so much about me, perhaps you wouldn't mind telling me what you've done with Judith. I mean, you are planning to kill us. Before I die, I want to know what's happened to her."

"Judith," Stefan repeated thoughtfully, his brow furrowing. "Ah yes! The lovely blonde you were with in Paris. Eva, set his mind at rest, will you? You know more about his wife than I do."

"She is safe, I suppose," the Magyar-eyed woman replied offhandedly.

"You only suppose?" Jeremiah challenged. If it was the very last thing he ever did, he had to know about Judith. She had plagued his thoughts for far too long now, and he knew he wouldn't be able to take control of this situation until his mind was at rest concerning her.

"Yes," nodded Eva. "Because I do not know for sure. I did go to your hotel to—"

"Was this before or after you shoved me into the Seine?" Jeremiah interrupted.

"After," Eva confessed. "You see, we knew about the two of you almost from the very beginning, but until that night you were only petty annoyances and no real threat. But after I got rid of you—or I *thought* I got rid of you—I knew we would not be safe until we had disposed of your Judith as well. However, when I got to the hotel, she had already left, and the desk clerk could not tell me where she had gone."

Jeremiah masked his overwhelming relief and gave a fleeting thought to Judith's whereabouts. He could only assume that she had returned to Albert and the children. Then he let his mind focus on getting himself and Charlotte out of this impossible situation. All wasn't lost, even though it looked like it. They could still get out of this mess. He was certain of it.

But then he became aware of Charlotte. At

some point within the last few moments, she had moved away from him, her back becoming stiff with anger. He looked down at her and noticed the strange, almost accusing expression on her face.

"Your wife?" she all but whispered.

"Be quiet," Jeremiah ordered, not having the time to explain the truth to her now when he had to focus all his thoughts and all his energies on subduing the gun-wielding Stefan.

"Don't tell me to be quiet!" she raged, and stepped further away from him. Her gray eyes flashed with fury. Her nostrils flared. Her lips curled back in a snarl, and her chest heaved with each deeply indrawn breath she took. "All this time. . . . We've been lovers! We've been through hell together! Only last night you said that you loved me. . . . And you've had a *wife*?"

"Charlotte," Jeremiah pleaded, vaguely hearing Stefan's amused chuckle. "You've got to listen to me. I—"

"No! I don't want to hear a damn thing you've got to say!" She retreated from his revolting outstretched hand. Her body became stiffer, her arms more rigid at her side, her hands balled into tight fists.

Jeremiah wanted to calm her down, but she stepped further out of his reach and, in doing so, brushed against the packing crate boards that were leaning against the wall. One fell to the floor, raising a clatter and a cloud of dust. A second threatened to follow suit, but she grabbed it before it could fall.

"I was used *once*," she snarled, hauling the huge two-by-six-inch board in front of her, "by a miserable bastard like you. I thought you were different from Melvin, but you're not! Well, I won't be used again!"

Seeing the way she held the board, Jeremiah was instantly reminded of the first time they'd met. That time she had used her parasol to overpower him. There was no telling what kind of mortal damage she could inflict with the weapon she was wielding now!

"Charlotte, don't!" he cried out, and ducked his head in time to avoid her lethal swing.

Charlotte missed Jeremiah by a mile. But she hit Stefan's right hand, the hand that held his revolver. The gun sailed across the room and landed in the corner behind some unopened boxes marked "Paper" and "Ink, green." As needles of pain shot up Stefan's arm, he yelped and stumbled back against the work table.

Crouched low to the floor, Jeremiah had only a moment to note the path the gun had taken before he was forced to evade Charlotte's second attack. *Keep it up, sweetheart. That's right, swing that board as hard as you can. But for God's sake, don't hit me!*

This time it was Eva who was hit. The end of the board struck the side of her head, its rough edge tearing into the soft flesh of her face. She pressed a hand to her bleeding cheek and dropped to her knees with a whimper.

Only Boland had enough presence of mind to retreat. Three backward steps took him to the safety of the hallway, where he vaguely heard voices coming from downstairs. With both hands clutching his chest, he stood there while

Charlotte snarled and swung the board again in Jeremiah's direction.

Wanting only to get out of her way, Jeremiah crawled across the floor, deliberately putting Stefan back into Charlotte's line of fire. Standing at the work table, clutching his bloody right hand, the man received a second blow, this time to his muscled arm. The force of the blow knocked him sideways, and as he fell he overturned the bottle of acid. The already loosened stopper fell out, allowing the colorless liquid to splash across the top of the work table, which was still littered with Boland's work. A strange odor filled the air as vapors rose up. The acid ate its way through the paper sketches, the partially completed metal plates, and the table top, and then dripped onto the floor below.

With her back to the door, Charlotte closed in on the still crouching, still retreating Jeremiah. She had the two-timing bastard in her sights now, and she was going to exterminate him just like one would get rid of an offensive rodent. By the time she was through with him, he wouldn't want to cheat on his wife or break another innocent woman's heart. By the time she was through with him, he would be lucky if he could breathe!

But just as she drew the board back and stepped toward him, a pair of arms wrapped themselves around her, and a bodiless pair of hands jerked the board away from her.

"*No!*" she screamed in outraged fury. "Don't stop me now! He's married!"

"Charlotte! Get a hold of yourself!"

Jean-Claude's familiar voice penetrated through Charlotte's dazed senses. She stopped struggling and allowed him to turn her around in his arms. As the fury that had been clouding her brain gradually evaporated, she noted the startled expression on her cousin's face. What had happened to her? What had caused her to suddenly go berserk that way?

"He's married," she whispered.

"Well, of course he is," Jean-Claude agreed patiently. "But that is no reason to kill him."

"But he's married, Jean-Claude. He has a wife!"

"*Oui.* I know, *cherie,* and twelve children too! Ah, you *Americains,*" he sighed sadly. "You simply are not equipped with the emotional wherewithal to handle the *affaires d'amour.* Francesca, I think you had better take her back to the villa."

Charlotte allowed herself to be passed into the waiting arms of the gypsy girl, vaguely noting the presence of uniformed *gendarmes* in the room. "He's married," she mumbled again as she and Francesca stepped out into the hall past Monsieur Boland, who was still gasping for breath and clutching at his chest. "All this time he's been married, and I didn't even know it!"

Chapter Twenty

THE MOMENT CHARLOTTE STEPPED OUT OF THE
house and into the warm summer night, she felt
herself thankfully return to normal, her disoriented state at an end. As she and Francesca
made their way back through the crowded
streets to the villa, she tried to rationalize what
had happened to her, what had made her go so
mad. Momentary insanity, she thought. That's
the only thing it could have been, for she certainly had never behaved that way before!

"Were you really going to kill him?" Francesca
asked after they had left the more crowded
section of the city and were climbing the hill.

"No, I don't think I was," Charlotte admitted
with some confusion. "I just wanted to pay him
back for all the pain he'd caused me."

"What happened?"

"I don't really know, Francesca. One moment I thought we were going to be killed, and the next thing I knew I was trying to decapitate Jeremiah. He's married!"

"Yes," the girl agreed, nodding her head. "To you."

"No, Francesca, not to me. His wife's name is Judith. Stefan and Eva knew that much . . . Boland too, probably. I was the only one ignorant of the fact."

"But how can he be married to you *and* to that Judith woman?"

"That's just it, dear. He can't! He and I were never really married. That wedding ceremony your stepfather forced us to participate in was a sham, a mockery of the real thing. Neither one of us is a Catholic, you see." A mirthless chuckle passed her dry lips. "A lot of good it would have done us if we had been."

Francesca shook her head and sighed with confusion. "I do not understand."

"It's just as well that you don't. I feel like such a fool." For ever having believed him, for ever having loved him so wantonly as she'd done, for ever having met him at all! He had ruined her life, what there had been of it, and she knew that nothing would ever be the same again.

Feeling angry, used, and bitter beyond belief, Charlotte walked silently alongside Francesca until the villa loomed into sight. The first-floor windows sparkled with inviting, beckoning light as they mounted the steps of the wide marble terrace. They let themselves in through the front door, and Charlotte heard voices coming from the nearby drawing room. Not knowing or caring who was inside, she started toward the stairs, wanting only to reach the solitude of her room, where she intended to weep her broken heart out.

However, she was not allowed that privilege. Charles-André heard them enter the villa. He stepped to the drawing room doorway and called to her just as she was about to mount the stairs.

"Not now, Charles-André. I just want to go to my room."

"What has happened, child?" He approached her, all but ignoring Francesca's presence and the girl's outlandish manner of dress. He touched Charlotte's arm and turned her around to face him, noting the pallor of her skin and the sadness about her lovely gray eyes. "You look ill."

"Do I? I'm not surprised."

"We will get to the bottom of this in a moment. But first there are some people inside whom I would like for you to meet."

"Can't it wait?" Charlotte pleaded.

"No, it cannot." And he pulled her with him into the lavishly appointed room, where the rest of the family waited.

At first glance, Charlotte saw her Great-Aunt Marie and her cousin Vivienne sitting on the silk brocade settee. But when her gaze wandered farther, she noted the large dark-haired man who stood next to the fireplace, a snifter of brandy held in his huge hand. Near him, seated in a wing-back chair, was one of the most beautiful women Charlotte had ever seen. Blond and blue-eyed, with the innocent look of a child, the woman smiled at her.

"Charlotte, I would like for you to meet Monsieur Lafayette Roman."

Charles-André led her across to the man at the fireplace, and Charlotte politely took his outstretched hand.

"Nice to meet you," she mumbled woodenly.

"It's my pleasure, I assure you, *mademoiselle*." Lafayette Roman brought her moist hand up to his lips and slowly kissed it, his black eyes never once leaving her face.

Any other time, Charlotte would have been thrilled to receive such attention from a handsome man like Roman. But not now. Jeremiah's duplicity still weighed heavily on her heart, and all she could think of was him.

Charles-André waited until Roman released Charlotte's hand, then turned her toward the petite blonde, who smiled up at her angelically. "And this is Monsieur Roman's, er, companion, Mrs. Judith Steadman."

"Nice to m—" Charlotte broke off with an audible gasp as the woman's name registered. "Oh God!" The guilt and pain that was bottled up inside her burst through the barrier of her self-control. Her face, having been held in a tight, expressionless mask, contorted as tears welled up in her eyes. She began to sob, her shoulders shaking, her tears pouring out of her eyes and down her cheeks in torrents.

"Forgive me!" she wept, sinking to her knees in front of the startled Judith. "Please, you must forgive me. I didn't know until just a few minutes ago that you even existed."

"Jeremiah didn't tell you about me?" Judith queried with surprise.

"No!" Charlotte wailed. "If he had, I wouldn't have . . . oh, I'm so sorry!"

Judith gasped, her lovely porcelain complexion draining of all its natural color. "Charlotte, Jeremiah isn't . . . oh Lord, he isn't dead, is he?"

"No. I tried, but—"

Judith's loud sigh of relief cut off what Charlotte would have said. "Thank heavens for that! But if he's all right, then why are you going on this way?"

Charlotte couldn't answer. Each time she tried to speak, great sobs wracked her body, and her words came out in an incoherent jumble of noises. She could only make gestures with her hands as her mouth continued to contort idiotically.

"There, there," Judith soothed her, reaching into her reticule for the handkerchief she always kept there. "It was probably just an honest oversight on Jeremiah's part."

"Honest?" Charlotte jerked back and glared at Judith as if stunned. "You can sit there, after what we've done to you, and say it was *honest*? Oh, you poor thing!" And her tears and her sobbing began anew.

Over Charlotte's bent head, Judith gazed up in complete bewilderment at Lafayette Roman. "Maybe you should go find Jeremiah. This child is obviously at her wit's end. He might know what to do to calm her down."

"I don't want to ever set eyes on that—that *man* again!" Charlotte suddenly snarled. "He's ruined my life . . . and yours! How can you be so—so understanding, after what he's done, after what *we've* done to you?"

"But you haven't done anything to me, dear," Judith insisted patiently. "At least . . . I don't think you have."

"Oh, if you only knew!" Charlotte wailed.

"This has gone far enough!" Great-Aunt Marie's curt words caught the attention of everyone —with the exception of Charlotte, of course, who was still sobbing into Judith's lap. "Charles-André, you are letting that poor child suffer for no good reason. I am quite ashamed of you!"

"*Maman*—" Charles-André began, but the old lady threw up a hand and stopped him.

"*Non!* You will hear me out! We all knew, or presumed, that Charlotte and her *Americain* were lovers, yet we all kept our counsel and ignored it. Now that she is in pain because of her *affaire d'amour*, I will not see her tormented in such a sadistic fashion. You will go down into Cannes, find the *roué* who has broken her heart, and bring him back here *tout de suite!*"

"But I would not know where to begin to look for him, *Maman!*" exclaimed Charles-André.

"Er, Madame Beauvais," Lafayette Roman cautiously asserted. "If you don't mind me saying so, it might be dangerous for your son to go hunting Fox at this time. I know for a fact that he's dealing with some pretty rough characters, and I certainly wouldn't want to see Charles-André get himself hurt. You see, they've already done a passable job of trying to get rid of Mrs. Steadman's husband. The poor man's in a wheelchair."

"Jeremiah is *not* in a wheelchair!" Charlotte suddenly spoke up, her tears ceasing somewhat. "Not that he doesn't deserve to be!"

"Well, of course, Jeremiah isn't, dear," Judith agreed with a patient smile. "My *husband* is in a wheelchair."

"But Jeremiah *is* your—"

Her words were abruptly interrupted by the blood-curdling scream that split the air. Every head in the room, even Charlotte's, turned toward the sound, which had come from the doorway. They all watched in horrified astonishment as Jean-Claude suddenly flew across the room and leaped upon the unsuspecting Lafayette Roman.

As the two of them fell to the floor in a tangle of arms and legs, Vivienne gasped and fell back against the settee, a hand pressed to her heart.

Great-Aunt Marie issued a disappointed groan and shook her snowy-white head.

Charles-André, thoroughly bewildered by the behavior of his only male offspring, could only stand there with his mouth open and gape at the boy.

Judith, having been so intent on listening to Charlotte, managed to lift her head at the last moment to see the young stranger tackle her American companion.

Wrestling the big man, Jean-Claude made demonic sounds as he straddled his opponent's back. "You will not get him now!" he proclaimed, pressing Roman's face into the rich Persian carpet. "Papa, help me!"

"Jean-Claude!" Charles-André exclaimed, looking down at the two bodies on the floor. "Have you gone mad?"

"*Non*, Papa." Jean-Claude beamed up proudly at his father. "I have saved you all from this criminal! He is after Charlotte's lover, Monsieur Fox. You see, he is in cahoots with the others."

"*Cahoots?* What others, Jean-Claude?" Charles-André queried with unabashed impatience.

"The other counterfeiters, Papa! I saw their printing press and everything when the *gendarmes* were arresting them."

"They're arrested?" This on a surprised gasp from Judith.

"*Oui!*" Jean-Claude proclaimed with a nod.

"Oh, thank God!" With a sigh, Judith slumped back against her chair.

"And this one will soon join them!" Jean-Claude tightened his hold on Roman's drawn-back arms.

"No, I don't think he will," Charlotte countered. "You'd better let him go, Jean-Claude. He isn't one of the counterfeiters."

"But he is!" Jean-Claude insisted. "He was the one who was asking for Monsieur Fox in the village the morning after we saved him from drowning in the Seine."

"He was?" Charlotte's surprised gaze sliced to Roman, then back to her cousin again.

"Of course!" proclaimed Jean-Claude. "I recognized him from the description Monsieur Fox gave us. Do you not remember? Tall, slanted eyes, very dangerous-looking. I knew the instant I saw him that he was the man who had hit Monsieur Fox over the head while his wife stood by watching."

"No, you misunderstood us, Jean-Claude,"

Charlotte explained. "It wasn't a man who hit Jeremiah over the head that night and shoved him in the river. It was a woman! The same woman who was with Stefan and Monsieur Boland tonight."

"That *woman* is the lover of Monsieur Fox's wife?" Jean-Claude appeared appalled at the thought.

With an audible groan, Charlotte shook her head. "No dear. Jeremiah's wife wasn't even there that night. We only said she was because we knew that you would think . . . well, anyway, we were really referring to Monsieur Boland."

Jean-Claude, growing more confused by the minute, jerked his head around and glared down at the man trapped beneath him. "Let me get this straight." One hand released its hold on Roman's arm and pointed to his head. "He is *Boland's* lover?"

Roman's large body began to vibrate with mirth as a chuckle rumbled out of his broad chest. "I'm no one's lover, young man. But I *am* Jeremiah Fox's superior."

"Jean-Claude," Charles-André snapped. "Let Monsieur Roman up this instant, and stop behaving like such an ass!"

"I do not think I understand," the young man murmured, reluctantly doing as his father had ordered. He fell to the floor beside Roman and turned a pleading gaze up to Charlotte. "If he is not who I thought he was . . . then who is he?"

"It's really quite simple," Charlotte began.

Then she proceeded to bewilder them all with her confusing explanation of what had actually happened to her and Jeremiah their last night in Paris; of their short, hair-raising flight in Philippe's balloon and its subsequent demise; and, lastly, of their encounter with Francesca's family. During her monologue, Lafayette Roman rose from the floor, his dark head nodding periodically.

"We were one day behind you," he admitted when she paused to take a breath. "Judith and I saw the balloon ascend into the sky, and she recognized Jeremiah in the gondola. By the time we had tracked your flight and came to the gypsy encampment, the two of you had already gone. I'm surprised, though, that you didn't come down with the same sort of stomach disorder the gypsies were suffering. They were all quite ill. They kept running off into the bushes at the oddest times. Diarrhea, I believe it was."

"I wouldn't know," Charlotte remarked somewhat sheepishly. "You'll have to ask Francesca about that. She's the one who helped Zonya spike the wine."

"Ah yes, Zonya!" Roman rolled his eyes and cocked his head. "A strange but interesting old lady, wouldn't you agree, Judith?"

"Yes, very interesting!" Judith nodded. "The dear old thing insisted on reading my palm, when she wasn't dispensing some vile-smelling tea to her family, that is. She told me some of the most fascinating things."

"They will all come true, you know." This

from Francesca, who had been standing silently behind the settee. She gazed directly at Jean-Claude and smiled. "My fortune has."

"I couldn't quite understand the language they were speaking," Roman continued. "The dialect was one I'd never heard before. But they kept rambling on about a bride and groom having disappeared before the celebration was over. Were they by any chance referring to you and Jeremiah?"

"Yes . . . unfortunately," Charlotte affirmed. "It was all a sham, though. Neither one of us is a Catholic, so the ceremony wasn't valid. But even if it were—"

"What do you mean?" Great-Aunt Marie suddenly asserted.

"Well, you see, they found this nice little priest to officiate at the ceremony, but both Jeremiah and I are Protestants. Even if we had been Catholics—"

"You are still married!" the old lady declared angrily. "Do you think that we Roman Catholics have been living in sin for all these centuries because we were not married by some upstart Protestant minister?"

"That's not what I meant at all, *Tante*," Charlotte hastily replied, fearing the fury in her great-aunt's voice.

"Then what did you mean, child? I can assure you that when a priest pronounces you man and wife, you *are,* in the eyes of God, man and wife! And whether you are Catholic or Protestant, you are still married!"

"But I *can't* be married to Jeremiah," Charlotte sadly confessed. "Not legally, anyway. He's already married . . . to Judith here."

"No he isn't, dear." At Judith's softly spoken words, Charlotte whirled around and stared at her. "That's what I was trying to tell you when your cousin came charging into the room and attacked poor Mr. Roman. I'm not Jeremiah's wife. I'm his sister!"

Chapter Twenty-one

"HIS—" CHARLOTTE GULPED— "SISTER?"

"Yes dear. As I tried to tell you before, *my* husband is Albert Steadman. Jeremiah has been using the Steadman name as an alias, and we've been posing as man and wife."

"His . . . sister," Charlotte repeated once again, the newfound knowledge finally sinking deep into her brain.

Judith nodded, an angelic smile making her features even more beautiful. "I guess that makes *us* sisters now, doesn't it? Why Charlotte, whatever is the matter? You don't seem at all pleased that—"

"Oh my God!" Charlotte nearly swooned. She pressed a hand to her pale, clammy forehead and gasped for breath. "What have I done?"

"You married my brother," Judith informed

her, her gold-tipped lashes blinking over her pretty blue eyes.

"And I almost killed him! I finally get married to a man, and then I try to kill him!"

"You *what*?" Judith, too, paled, all of her former happiness vanishing as she sank back against her chair, a tiny hand pressed to her heart.

"Oh, but she did not succeed, Madame Steadman," Jean-Claude hastily reassured her. On his knees, he crawled to Judith's side and took her hand in his. "We stopped her just in time, did we not, Francesca?"

The gypsy girl, still smiling at Jean-Claude, nodded.

Only Great-Aunt Marie caught the secretive interchange between the two young people and smiled slyly.

Vivienne, who had had about all she could stand for one evening, slowly got to her feet and extended a hand toward her husband. "I cannot take any more of this, Charles-André. We find Emil locked in the cellar. My son attacks an innocent man right before my eyes. Charlotte admits to trying to kill a man. . . ." She shook her head dramatically. "I should quit without notice like Emil did. I must lie down. Please, take me to our room."

"Of course, *cherie*." And Charles-André dutifully caught her arm before turning to lead her out of the drawing room.

Upon learning of her brother's survival, Judith managed to regain some of her former self-composure. Gracefully sitting forward again, she peered into Charlotte's face. "But why would you want to kill my brother?"

"She thought he was married to another," Jean-Claude supplied when Charlotte appeared not to have heard. "In truth, *madame*, I thought it too!"

"But to try and *kill* him," Judith reasserted, looking utterly dumbfounded.

"She is *Americain, madame*." This, Jean-Claude thought, should explain it all.

Charlotte suddenly shot to her feet and headed for the doorway. "I've got to go to him," she murmured. "I left him at Boland's house with all those criminals. I've got to go to him and clear up this horrible misunderstanding."

As she passed Great-Aunt Marie, the old woman chuckled and shook her head. "Just like Georgianna. History is repeating itself." Her gaze lifted heavenward. "You should be proud of your granddaughter, my sister. She is just like you."

Charlotte got no further than the front door. She started to wrench it open and dash out into the predawn darkness when Jeremiah suddenly raced into the house. He entered with such force that he knocked Charlotte flat onto the cold marble floor.

"Good God Almighty!" he roared, glaring down at her.

"Jeremiah?" Charlotte struggled up to her elbows as he sank down to the floor beside her. "Oh Jeremiah. I've been such a fool."

"Are you all right?" He cupped the back of her head with his hands, concern filling his eyes.

"I didn't know she was your sister."

"There don't seem to be any bumps," he exclaimed, not having heard her apology. "But when I came in just now, I had no idea you were standing on the other side of the door."

"Stefan said you were married, and I just suddenly lost all control! I don't know what happened to me, I swear it!"

"What are you talking about?" he queried with a frown.

"Stefan!"

"Oh, he's been arrested and taken to prison along with Boland and the woman." Then he wrapped Charlotte in a tight embrace and pressed her head to his chest. "I'm so proud of what you did, my love."

"Proud? Of me?" She had to push away from him to stare into his face. "For trying to kill you?"

"No," he chuckled. "For eliminating Stefan and Eva the way you did. I've got to tell you, sweetheart, I was really worried there for a minute. I thought we'd had it for sure. But you certainly surprised us all. You swing a mean board, darling!"

"But I wasn't trying to get rid of them. I was trying to knock your head off!"

"I know, but that doesn't matter now. You didn't really mean it."

"But I did!" she argued. "I heard Stefan say you were married, and I just went crazy. I thought you'd been using me. Why in heaven's name didn't you tell me that you had a sister here in France and that she was posing as your wife?"

"The opportunity just never presented itself, my love. You see, I didn't know that she had left Paris before we did. The last time I'd seen her, she was still at our hotel, and I was worried as hell that Boland or his murderous cohorts had gotten hold of her. All I could think of was getting here to Cannes so that I could get her away from them in one piece." He suddenly frowned. "How do you know about Judith?"

"She's here!"

"Here?" he repeated disbelievingly. "In Cannes?"

"No, here in the villa." Charlotte glanced at the drawing room, where she knew Judith to be, then looked back at Jeremiah. She quickly turned to look at the doorway again when she realized that four people were standing there, gaping at her and Jeremiah.

"Judith!" Seeing his sister, Jeremiah released Charlotte with such haste that she almost fell back and hit her head on the marble tiles. Her elbow, hitting the floor with a thud, broke her fall, and she cried out softly.

"Roman!" Jeremiah remarked with surprise. "What the hell are the two of you doing here?" He got to his feet and started toward them but then remembered Charlotte and turned back to her. Reaching down, he roughly hauled her to her feet.

"We've been following you for days, Fox." Roman stepped forward and clasped Jeremiah's outstretched hand. "I must say, it's been quite an interesting trip."

"But how long have you been in France?" With one arm wrapped possessively around Charlotte's waist, Jeremiah approached his sister and dropped a kiss on her cheek, then addressed Roman again. "The last I heard from you, you were still back in Washington."

"I know," Roman nodded. "But you weren't sending me any reports, and I thought it would be a good idea to come over here and check up on your progress myself. You know I didn't want any rumors of this mission to leak out." He then proceeded to explain how he had arrived at the hotel where Jeremiah and Judith were staying, only to learn that his agent was long overdue in returning. Judith had been frantic, tearfully wringing her hands and worrying that her brother had met with some fatal calamity.

"I knew you could handle yourself in any tight situation that might arise," Roman continued, "but I couldn't convince your sister of that. She was determined to go out and find you herself. So, not knowing what else to do, I checked her out of the hotel, and we started looking for you. It was just a coincidence that we were crossing the Seine at the same moment Jean-Claude and Charlotte were fishing you out of it."

"Yes," Judith added. "If it hadn't been for all of that horrible traffic, we would have gotten to you sooner, too. But there were so many carriages blocking the streets, we couldn't turn around. It took us hours to get back to the river, once we'd crossed it."

"Well, not exactly hours," Roman disagreed indulgently. "But by the time we *did* get back to the river, there wasn't a sign of the boat that we had seen rescue you.

"Knowing what direction it had been headed

in, we had no other choice but to follow. We didn't get to the village until late the next morning. I started asking around. That must have been when this impetuous young fool here saw me." He glanced pointedly at Jean-Claude, who had the grace to lower his gaze in shame. "When no one seemed to know who I was talking about, we started to go on."

"That's when we saw the balloon," Judith explained. "I recognized you in an instant, Jeremiah, even at that distance. Whatever possessed you to get into that silly craft anyway?"

"I'll tell you all about it later," Jeremiah grinned, and squeezed Charlotte's waist.

"I had one devil of a time trying to hire a carriage in that village," Roman resumed with a shake of his head. "Our driver flatly refused to go any further, and the villagers seemed most reluctant to take us. So I ended up having to buy a farm wagon and two swaybacked nags.

"By the time we got back on the road and were following you again, your balloon had almost disappeared. The rest of our journey, I suppose, is self-explanatory. After all, here we are, and almost in one piece." He rubbed his back for emphasis.

"Yes," agreed Judith. She pulled her brother's head down to hers and kissed his mustache-framed mouth. "And thank God you're all right. I was so worried!" Her concerned expression cleared and was replaced with a smile. "And you're married!"

"No," Jeremiah chuckled. "Not yet, at least. But we—"

"Yes, we are." Charlotte gazed lovingly up into his face.

"Sweetheart, we're not Catholic," Jeremiah stressed.

"Well, according to Great-Aunt Marie, that doesn't matter."

"She's right, too," Roman agreed, a devilish gleam sparkling in his black eyes.

Jeremiah blinked in confusion at his superior, then turned to look down at Charlotte. "You mean that ceremony was—"

"The real thing," she nodded.

"Well I'll be damned!" Jeremiah could only shake his head, so thoroughly astounded was he by the notion. "I didn't even get to carry you over the threshold."

"That's all right, darling," Charlotte demurred. "I didn't get to wear white, either. Remember? I had to wear red!"

"You wore a *red* wedding dress?" Judith gasped, completely appalled at the thought.

"To gypsies white is the color of death," Francesca explained. "But now that I am no longer a gypsy, my wedding dress *will* be white."

Jean-Claude's head slowly turned toward the girl, his gray eyes narrowing into angry slits. "That is not all, either. From now on there will be no more dancing in the streets with strange men. If I catch you with one, I will—" He broke off as his gaze encountered her still-disarranged clothes. *"Mon Dieu*, look at you! Have you no shame? Cover yourself! No wife of mine . . . no Comtesse du Beauvais is going to look like some *fille de joie!" What am I saying?* he thought, thoroughly aghast at what he'd heard himself say. *My wife? I am thinking of this child as my wife?*

Francesca pulled her blouse up to cover her shoulders with a delighted giggle. "Whatever you say, Jean-Claude."

"Now if only I can get you to be that submissive," Jeremiah remarked, turning Charlotte in his arms and embracing her fully.

"You can try, my love," she beamed, and lifted her lips for his kiss.

"Oh look, Lafayette," purred Judith. "Aren't they the perfect couple? They were made for each other."

"Probably because no one else would have them," Roman chuckled, and turned to look over his shoulder at Great-Aunt Marie, who still sat on the settee in the drawing room. He gave her an audacious wink, and she, pleased with the outcome of this fiasco, slyly winked back.

"Ah, Zonya was so right," Francesca sighed, leaning her head against Jean-Claude's chest. "She told me that I would become a great lady and that a very important, dignified, forceful man would complete my destiny. You are that, Jean-Claude. You are that indeed!"

Zonya's prediction for Francesca wasn't the only one to come true. Her predictions for Judith and Charlotte came true as well.

Judith went back to her husband Albert and their two children, as she had planned to do all along once she was assured that her brother was safely in one piece and that the counterfeiters would no longer be of any threat to the United States. When she, Albert, and the children returned to Virginia, she had all but forgotten the strange little gypsy woman who had told her fortune—until one day, six months later, she woke up to find her husband standing on his own two feet. The wounds in his legs had healed sufficiently, just as Zonya had said they would, and Albert never had to use a wheelchair again, only a walking cane.

Charlotte's prediction took a bit more time to come true and was a lot more shocking.

She resigned her teaching post at the girls' school in Baton Rouge before she took Jeremiah home to meet his new in-laws in Waxahachie, Texas. Her mother and father, of course, were flabbergasted by their arrival, for they hadn't known that she was married. But they welcomed Jeremiah with open arms.

Charlotte's two older sisters were another matter altogether. They had always been envious of their younger sister's intelligence and wit and had taken every opportunity to use it against her as she grew up. It had made Charlotte feel dowdy and unimportant. But when they met Jeremiah, the two women were positively outraged. They could not understand how Charlotte, as plain as she was, could attract someone so handsome, so important, so rich!

Managing to ignore their cattiness, Charlotte secretly glowed inside. She knew she was loved and adored, and what her sisters thought or said now really didn't matter.

Nine months after their arrival back in the United States, Charlotte gave birth to their first child, a happy, healthy little boy who looked just like Jeremiah . . . except for the mustache, of course. And thirteen months after *his* birth, their daughter arrived.

They were living in Washington at the time, but Charlotte and Jeremiah decided that they and the children would be much happier living out of the city and in the country. They found a huge farmhouse in nearby Maryland, not far from Washington, and moved into it just before the birth of their first set of twins.

The second set of twins arrived a year after the first, and the third set a year after the second. Then they had another boy and a set of identical twin girls. It was only after Charlotte had delivered their last child, another girl, that she recalled the old gypsy woman's prediction from years before and started laughing.

Standing by their bedside was Jeremiah. He looked down at her as she lay there with their precious little girl in her arms, giggling like someone demented, and wondered for a moment what had happened to her.

"She was right," Charlotte chuckled.

"Who?" Jeremiah raked a confused hand through his now silver-streaked blond hair, momentarily exposing the gold earring he still had not been able to remove.

"Zonya."

"Who?"

"Oh, you must remember, darling."

"Zonya," he repeated thoughtfully, "Oh yes, Zonya! Good Lord, now I remember. But that was years ago, Charlotte. What about her?"

"Well, she once told me that my lie would become truth, and it has. We have twelve children."

307

Looking down into her glowing face, Jeremiah couldn't suppress the chuckle that rumbled out of his broad chest. "You never told me about that," he accused gently.

"To tell you the truth, I didn't remember it myself until just this moment."

He dropped down to the bed beside her and kissed her smooth cheek before letting his long finger stroke the tiny arm of their newest daughter. "What'll we name her?"

"How about Zonya?" Charlotte suggested with a giggle. "It seems rather appropriate, I think."

Jeremiah cast her a baleful look and shook his head. "No daughter of mine is going to be named after some old gypsy witch."

"Zonya wasn't a witch, darling. Not really. She just had the sight." Charlotte thought for a moment and then suggested, "How about Alexandra, then. We can call her Zandra for short. That's sort of close to Zonya."

Looking down at his wife's tiny replica, Jeremiah thought about the name for a moment, then nodded his head in agreement. He turned his gaze adoringly to Charlotte and murmured, "How is it possible that you're even more beautiful now than the day I first met you?"

"I've improved with age?" she offered flirtatiously.

"Either that, or motherhood is the cause." Outside, they could hear the sounds of their children playing in the warm summer sun. It was true, they had a houseful, but each child was loved with an equal amount of affection. "Whatever the case," he continued, letting his head descend toward Charlotte's, "just keep on improving, my precious love." Before his mouth closed over hers, he whispered, "But don't have any more babies. Please! We simply don't have the room!"

Charlotte welcomed his mouth with ease, knowing that her life, and her destiny, was at last complete.

Free At-Home Examination

Each month, we'll send you 2 new Tapestry novels—*as soon as they are published*—through our Tapestry Home Subscription Service. Look them over for 15 days, FREE. If not delighted, simply return them and owe nothing; but if you enjoy them as much as we think you will, pay the invoice enclosed.

There's never any additional charge for this convenient service—*we pay all postage and handling charges!*

Simply Fill Out The Coupon

To begin your subscription, fill out and return the coupon today. You're on your way to all the love, passion and adventure of times gone by!

HISTORICAL *Tapestry* ROMANCES
